WRONGED *and* *Respected*

THE GENTLEMAN'S VALIANT WIFE

BY
BREE WOLF

Cover Art by Victoria Cooper
Copyright © 2022 Bree Wolf

E-Book ISBN: 978-3-96482-116-4
Paperback ISBN: 978-3-96482-117-1
Hard Cover ISBN: 978-3-96482-118-8

www.breewolf.com

WRONGED
and
Respected

THE GENTLEMAN'S VALIANT WIFE

Prologue

La Roche-sur-Mer, France Summer 1812
Three months earlier

Darkness had long since fallen over the little house standing upon the edge of La Roche-sur-Mer, a small French village by the sea. It was a peaceful place with endless meadows and high cliffs, blue skies and invigorating winds, far from any bustling city. The people here knew one another and cared about one another. A neighbor was a friend, more often than not even family. It was a small community and a close one.

And once, Noèle Clément had been one of them.

By the light of a single candle, she gazed down at the small bundle sleeping peacefully in a makeshift crib she had fashioned out of a drawer. Her eyes drifted over the child's tuft of black hair on the top of her head, her eyes slightly slanted, their color a brilliant blue even now, only days after she had been born.

How many days had it been? Noèle could not recall. Each one seemed to blur into the next.

The baby stirred in her sleep, a soft, breathy sigh drifting from her lips. Her little hands clenched, her fingers curling into fists, as she began to wave them about, as though fighting an imaginary monster.

Noèle shuddered at the thought. *Oui*, she knew about monsters, had encountered one such creature...and it had left her scarred.

Again, her daughter stirred, the breathy little sigh changing, now containing a note of distress, of alarm.

Without thinking, Noèle reached out a hand and placed it upon her daughter's chest. "Hush, *ma petite Ophélie*. Hush."

The moment the words left Noèle's lips, she froze, shocked speechless by what she had just uttered without conscious thought. *Oui*, long ago, when Étienne had still been alive, they had spoken of children, of a little girl who might have Noèle's dark tresses and his warm brown eyes. They had spoken of naming her Ophélie, after Étienne's late mother.

Only this child, right here, whose little chest rose and fell with deep breaths beneath Noèle's hand, was not Étienne's daughter.

None of their dreams had come to pass.

Almost two years ago, Étienne had lost his life when a storm had come upon the *Voile Noire*. The privateer had been tossed about by fierce winds and rolling waves, bobbing upon the sea like a teacup. Henri Duret, its captain and Étienne's childhood friend, had done his utmost to maneuver the ship through the torrent of rain and wind... and he had.

Only he had been unable to prevent Étienne from being swept off the ship's deck by a powerful wave, reaching out like a monster from the bottom of the sea and swallowing him whole.

Noèle still remembered the day the *Voile Noire* had returned to La Roche-sur-Mer. She remembered the moment her eyes had fallen upon Henri's face.

One glimpse had been enough.

She had known instantly.

And her world had fallen apart.

Noèle flinched as the sound of hoofbeats echoed to her ears, and she looked up, her eyes narrowing as she gazed through the window at the dark world outside. The moon was barely a sliver in the night sky, casting no more than a few faint silvery beams across the village nearby. Nothing stirred, as far as Noèle could tell, and so she turned her attention back to her sleeping child.

To this day, no one in La Roche-sur-Mer even knew of Ophélie's existence. Noèle had hidden her pregnancy as best as she could, relieved when no one had pressed her to mingle, to accept dinner invitations or strolls along the seaside. Indeed, everyone had been most considerate, giving her the time and space she needed to mourn her husband.

Oui, Étienne's death had been a welcome excuse. Of course, Noèle had mourned him—still mourned him!—and yet his death had not been the reason for why she had retreated from the world.

A soft nicker drifted to Noèle's ears, and once again, she looked up, a cold chill crawling down her back. Was someone there? But who—?

An involuntary shudder gripped Noèle, and she felt her teeth cluck together painfully as her jaw tensed abruptly.

The last time someone had sought her out late at night—

Instantly, painful memories resurfaced, all but flinging Noèle backward. Staggering, she felt her breath catch in her throat when her back collided with the wall behind her, her gaze fixed upon the door. Were those footsteps? Was someone—?

A quick, hard knock echoed through the still night.

Noèle flinched, unable to move her muscles beyond that short involuntary response. Her gaze darted to the table, upon which her daughter still slept in her makeshift crib. She knew she needed to move. She needed to get the child and flee.

Only her legs would not move, her eyes once again fixed upon the door.

Again, that knock came, now more forceful.

Noèle pinched her eyes shut, and she felt her fingers dig into the flesh of her arms. "Go away," she whispered under her breath, her voice trembling. "Please, go away."

As though to defy her, the door suddenly burst open, a hard kick shattering the fragile lock, splintering the wood around it.

Noèle's eyes widened in shock as she stared at the monster from her nightmares, now returned to haunt her.

Capitaine Dubois.

3

A French privateer like Henri Duret.

Only Bastien Dubois possessed none of Henri's compassion and consideration. He knew neither respect nor mercy. His soul as black as the depth of the sea.

Like a shadow, he moved into her home, stepping across the threshold, as though he had every right to do so. But then again, he believed he did, did he not? In his mind, he had the right to do whatever he pleased.

In the dim light, his hard features appeared almost ghostly, as though he were not truly there. Yet the moment the blue of his eyes flickered as he stepped into the light of the candle, Noële knew that she was not dreaming. Indeed, his eyes shone in the same blue as Ophélie's.

Panting with fear, Noële pressed her back against the wall as she stared at him with wide eyes. Fear and panic crawled up and down her back, clawed at her heart and conjured more and more images from Dubois's last *visit*.

The moment his gaze fell on her, a slow smile curled up the corners of his mouth. "Ah, Madame Clément," he mused, closing the door behind him, as though he had come to join her for a cup of tea and a lively conversation. "It has been some time, *n'est-ce pas?*"

"Get out!" Noële snapped, surprising him as much as herself. Her breathing quickened, and she began to feel lightheaded.

At her words, Dubois's expression darkened. Something cruel and almost inhuman sparked in his eyes, and his lips thinned as he stalked toward her. "How dare you speak to me like this?"

Noële almost laughed. After everything he had done to her, he now took affront at a few impolite words?

"You forget your place," Dubois snarled as he watched her, a sneer of disgust upon his face. "I came here tonight to continue our conversation."

Conversation? Again, Noële felt a sense of almost hysterical laughter bubbling up. "We never—" she began, her voice ringing with fear and weakness. "You..."

A vicious smile teased his lips. "I did what?" he asked, clearly savoring the moment, enjoying the fear that undoubtedly played across her face at the memory of their last encounter.

"Get out!" Noèle repeated, only this time her words were no more than a whisper, a pleading, terrified sound.

Ignoring her, Dubois inhaled a deep breath. "Have you given my request any thought?" he inquired, a warning note in his voice.

Noèle swallowed, then lifted her chin despite the trembling that seemed to shake her entire body. "I will not marry your brother." She forced herself to hold his gaze. "Never."

Despite the lack of light, Noèle could see the look upon his face darken in a way that almost made her lose her nerve. Something feral rested in his eyes, soulless pools, that reflected no feeling upon seeing another's pain. "You do not deserve him," he snarled in a frighteningly calm voice, "and yet he desires you to be his wife. You should feel honored," he moved closer, "and cherish your good fortune."

Panic froze Noèle's limbs as she stared into his face, now barely an arm's length away.

"I urge you to reconsider," Dubois hissed before his gaze dropped from her eyes and swept lower, lingering upon the places of her body he had already known intimately, "or do you require further persuasion?"

For a second, Noèle felt as though she was about to lose consciousness, her mind still torn between disbelief and horror. Was this truly happening? Again? Was he truly—?

Her daughter's soft cry broke through her thoughts, and Noèle's eyes whipped around, beyond Dubois's shoulder to the small makeshift crib upon the table.

"What...?" A frown came to his face before he turned, taking note of the child. For a moment, he remained still, then Dubois once more looked at Noèle. His gaze held something contemplative as he read her expression, slowly adding up all the pieces until the image in front of his eyes shone as bright and clear as day.

He knows! A terrified voice in Noèle's head screamed, sending a fresh wave of panic through her.

A slow smile spread across Dubois's face, a triumphant gleam coming to his eyes. "Our encounter," he murmured in a sickeningly sweet voice, "appears to have been blessed." He raised a brow in question. "A boy?"

Unable to utter a single word, Noèle stared back and forth between the monster of her nightmares and her innocent daughter, her mind circling frantically over what to do.

Denied an answer, Dubois stepped away from her and toward the crib, a possessive gleam lighting up his face that finally shocked Noèle into movement.

Rushing past him, Noèle stepped in front of her child, blocking his path. "You cannot have her! She is mine!" she stated in a voice that no longer trembled. "Get out! Now!"

For a split second, Dubois appeared caught off guard, the expression in his eyes dumbfounded. Then, however, that familiar snarl returned and before Noèle knew what was happening, his fist collided with her jaw.

Her head felt as though it would explode as the force of his punch flung her sideways. Every inch of her screamed out in pain, and yet all she took note of was her daughter's piercing cry.

In the next instant, Dubois was upon her, his hands grasping her by the arms and hauling her upward. He shoved her against the wall, and her head collided painfully with a wooden beam. Her vision began to blur as he snarled into her face, rage radiating off him.

Again, he struck her, and Noèle was flung across the small room, colliding with some piece of furniture. Pain stole her breath and closed her eyes before she wrenched them back open. Panting, she lay on the floor, the dim outline of Dubois standing over her all she could see.

With her last bit of strength, Noèle tried to push to her feet, but a swift kick into her belly sent her sprawling across the floor. Curled into a tight ball, she lay on her side, trying to breath, as her mind fought to abandon its hold on reality. Noèle knew she could not take much more of this, and yet...she...knew...she...had...to...remain...conscious.

With Herculean effort, her eyes fluttered open once more. Yet the only thing she saw was the small flame of her candle as it rolled across the floor in front of her.

A moment later, everything went dark, the echo of her daughter's cries following her into the dark abyss.

Chapter One

SCARS

La Roche-sur-Mer, France Summer 1812
Three months later

Flexing her fingers, Noèle felt the tightness of her skin as it stretched across her knuckles. It no longer shone in a bright, angry red as it had after the night Dubois had paid her another visit. The night her house had burned down. The night her daughter had been taken.

"How are you today?"

At the sound of Alexandra's voice, Noèle turned from the window overlooking the sea. "Stronger," she told Henri's aunt. "Every day, I feel a little bit stronger." Holding Alexandra's gaze as the woman closed the door behind her, Noèle inhaled a deep breath, willing her words to be true.

"That's good," Alexandra replied with a kind smile as she moved toward Noèle.

Almost thirty years Noèle's senior, Alexandra was still a beautiful, vibrant woman. A woman who loved her life, her family. She had found love after all but giving up hope on her own happily-ever-after when Henri's uncle, Antoine, had stumbled upon a beach in Norfolk one night and had whisked her and her daughter away to France. *Oui*, Noèle had always loved their story. It whispered of Fate and belonging, of beating the odds and finding the one soul that completed one's own. To this day, Alexandra and Antoine were deliriously happy.

Noèle had always looked at them and prayed that she and Étienne would be equally fortunate.

Fate had had other plans.

"Do you need more of the salve?" Alexandra asked as her eyes swept over Noèle's burns. Most had faded or were fading while others would forever remind her of the night she had lost her child. Was Ophélie still alive?

As always, that thought brought tears to her eyes and caused a painful tightening in her chest. Fear and hope warred with longing and guilt, and Noèle knew not what to feel, what emotion to give dominance over the others. In truth, Noèle knew that only hope would serve her, and so she pushed all the others away, determined to cling to that small sliver of hope that one day...one day she would see her daughter again.

"I believe I have enough," Noèle answered Alexandra's question, gesturing to the jar upon the table in the corner. "I no longer need it as much as I did in the beginning."

"I'm glad to hear it," Alexandra replied, her watchful eyes sweeping over Noèle's face. "And how are you?"

Noèle could tell from the way Alexandra was looking at her, watching her, that she was not inquiring after Noèle's burns, after the injuries she had sustained at Dubois's hands. *Non*, as awful as these moments had been, their effects would fade.

Shrugging, Noèle turned back toward the window, her eyes gliding over the still sea, bright sunlight reflected here and there, making it sparkle like a sea of diamonds. "I cannot say," she finally whispered, feeling that ache in her heart grow more painful. "It does not matter, does it? It changes nothing that is." She looked at Alexandra as the woman moved to stand beside her. "All that matters now is finding my daughter."

Alexandra nodded. "Yes, as a mother, you think first and foremost of your child." She reached out and gently took Noèle's scarred hands into her own. "Yet you will never be the mother she needs if you do not see to healing yourself as well." She exhaled a slow breath, her kind eyes once more searching Noèle's face. "To this day," she continued gently, "you have not once spoken of what happened, of what was done to you."

Noèle closed her eyes as the ache in her heart grew and grew, threatening to overwhelm her. Bright spots began to dance in front of her eyes, and her head spun, as though she no longer stood steady upon her own two feet.

"I understand that you wish to flee from it." Alexandra gently squeezed her hands. "However, there are things we cannot run from, for they will follow us to the ends of the earth. Think on it. Please." Gentle fingers touched Noèle's face, and she opened her eyes. "If you do not wish to speak to me, then seek out another soul to confide in. Please, Noèle. All of us, we wish to see you happy once more."

After Alexandra left the room, Noèle sat down on the bed where she had spent the past few weeks, doing her best to recover. She knew she needed to be strong for her daughter and had given all she had to strengthen her body, to heal and reclaim her old self. Yet to this day, she shied away from the memories that lingered somewhere on the edge of her mind. Memories that sometimes ventured closer, demanding her attention, when she closed her eyes and lost herself to sleep. More than once, she had woken abruptly to the feel of rough hands upon her body or the touch of flames crawling across her skin.

Even now, even after all this time, a shudder went through her again, and Noèle closed her eyes, disappointed in herself and the weakness she felt within. *Non*, seeking out the past would change nothing, would help no one. It was better left buried, eyes firmly fixed upon the horizon, upon the task that needed to be accomplished.

Blinking open her eyes, Noèle swept her gaze across the room. Indeed, the house was not unfamiliar to her. It was the home of Henri Duret and his family. His grandparents had built it long ago, and it now housed, at least, four generations. She had been in this house countless times with Étienne, joining the Durets for supper or some sort of family celebration. That had been long ago. Now, she had been granted sanctuary here, a place for her to stay and recover.

Still, she was a guest, and now, the only home she had ever had was gone.

A knock sounded on her door, and Noële rose to her feet. Her hands wiped over her face, ensuring that no tears lingered before she called, "Enter."

After a moment of hesitation, Henri stepped across the threshold. As always, Noële found herself craning her neck, his tall stature forcing her to tilt her head back the closer he stepped. His black hair was tied in the back, and his green eyes, usually so full of mischief and amusement, were serious, guarded. He, too, felt guilt and regret over what had happened. Noële knew that he blamed himself. After all, she was his best friend's widow, and he felt responsible.

"How are you?" Henri asked, the look in his eyes hesitant, as though he could not bear to look at her.

Noële sighed, having come to hate this question, for she never knew how to answer it. "What brings you here?" she asked instead, aware of the strange tension in his shoulders, something that whispered of a subject not easily broached.

As expected, Henri's gaze fell from hers and he inhaled a deep breath. "I have to go after Juliette," he said without preamble before his gaze rose to meet hers once more. "I'm sorry. I know I promised to reunite you with your daughter, but −" He broke off, gritting his teeth before stepping forward, his hands settling upon her shoulders, his green eyes looking deep into hers. "Ian will find her."

For a moment, Noële felt caught off guard, confused by the name. "Ian?" The moment the name fell from her tongue, her mind conjured the image of Henri's first mate, a tall, taciturn Scotsman, a tame wolf always by his side. "Oh, *oui*. Mr. Stewart."

Henri nodded. "I have every confidence that he will find her. Otherwise, I would not..." His green eyes looked almost pleadingly into hers.

Noële sighed, understanding him perfectly.

Years ago, Henri had lost his heart to an English lady, but he was convinced that there could not ever be a future for them. He had all but run from her, run from the reminder of her, determined that time would change how he felt. However, love did not work like that. Noële knew it well. The heart could not be steered in one direction or another. It did as it pleased, and it seemed Henri had come to realize that as well.

Better late than never.

After losing consciousness the night of the fire, Noèle had woken up upon Dubois's ship. Exhaustion and the strain upon her body had kept her eyes closed most of the time, and yet she had been aware that there had been someone else in the cabin with her.

A young English lady.

Juliette.

At that point, Noèle had not known how Juliette had ended up upon Dubois's ship nor had she been aware who the young lady was. Still, the two of them had eventually bonded as they had tried to find a way to escape the devil's clutches. And then Henri had come.

He had come for Juliette...and had been shocked to find Noèle there as well.

After all, he had thought her dead.

Succumbed to the flames the night of the fire.

No one in La Roche-sur-Mer had known that Dubois had taken her back to his ship upon his brother's behest, who had begged him to save her life. Indeed, Benoit Dubois had always fancied Noèle, even before her husband's passing. He had always been kind, his shy eyes following her whenever their paths would cross. And then a year after Étienne's death, Benoit had come to her, offering her his heart and asking for her hand. Of course, Noèle had refused him...after all, her heart had not been free. Benoit had been disappointed...but he had left without a bad word leaving his lips.

His brother, however, had taken affront.

"Ian is readying the *Chevalier Noir* as we speak," Henri assured her. "We have given him command of my uncle's ship, and they will be leaving within the week."

Noèle remembered the night Henri had come for Juliette, the night they had both escaped Dubois and been taken upon Henri's ship, the *Voile Noire*. Ian Stewart had been the one to lift Noèle into his arms as she had been too weakened from her injuries to take even a single step. His arms had held her gently, and although Noèle had been barely conscious at the time, she remembered one short moment.

The moon had shone overhead, casting a silvery glow over the Scotsman's bright hair. His eyes had been hidden in shadows, and for a moment, she had been afraid upon finding herself in his arms. She had felt his gaze sweep over her, tracing the burns upon her face and down her neck, and had seen his jaw harden. His arms had tightened around her protectively, as though she meant something to him, as though someone he cared for had been hurt, and in that moment, she had felt safe with him.

"*Merci*," Noèle said, and Henri exhaled, the strain falling from him. "Thank you for all you did. Had you not come..." She swallowed, then willed a smile onto her face. "Go after her," she told him then, knowing Henri would never forgive himself if he allowed Juliette to vanish from his life for a second time. "You two are meant for each other, and I wish you all the happiness in the world." Her voice broke, and Henri pulled her into his arms, allowing her to hide her tears from his gaze.

There was still a chance for them to find happiness, for they were not separated by death.

By fear and stubbornness, *oui*.

But not by death.

Neither were Noèle and her daughter, and she knew she would do everything within her power to find her child. "I want to come," she whispered into Henri's ear.

At her words, he stilled, understanding her meaning perfectly. Then he stepped back and met her eyes. "It might be dangerous. Perhaps you—"

"I *need* to come," Noèle amended, holding his gaze. "When Dubois took Juliette, could you have stayed behind?"

At her challenge, Henri's expression hardened. He looked at her for a long time before releasing a deep breath. "*Bien sure*," he murmured with a slight nod of the head. "I'll inform Ian." Then he turned to go.

"Do you trust him?" Noèle blurted out when a sudden shiver gripped her.

Henri turned back to look at her. "I do," he said without a

moment's hesitation. Still, his green eyes remained upon her, looking deeper. "Do you have any reason to fear him?"

Noèle swallowed, for it had not escaped her that Henri had spoken of fear instead of trust. "No," Noèle replied in a small voice, for it was the truth. Still...

Two large strides carried Henri back to her. Gently, he cupped her face with his large hands, his eyes never leaving hers. "You will be safe with him. You have my word." For a second, something flickered in his eyes. "If need be, Ian will give his life to ensure Ophélie's safety as well as your own."

Noèle felt her breath lodge in her throat, caught off guard by Henri's words. Why would Mr. Stewart...? After all, they hardly knew one another, had barely spoken a word. Why would he risk his life for someone—?

Of course! This was not about her. It was about him! Mr. Stewart knew the meaning of loss just as she did. Was that not so? *Oui*, she had seen it in his eyes the night he had carried her off Dubois's ship.

The shadow of pain.

Had he lost a child?

Noèle wanted to ask, but did not dare.

Chapter Two

A NEW PURPOSE

S tanding upon the small docks of La Roche-sur-Mer, Ian
watched as the *Voile Noire* made way, leaving the harbor on her
way to England. Up on the quarterdeck, Henri looked back
over his shoulder and lifted a hand in farewell.

Ian inclined his head in return, aware that the man by his side,
Antoine Duret, Henri's uncle, shifted uneasily upon his feet. Of
course, there was a risk! After all, England and France were still at war.
However, from experience, Ian knew how capable Henri was. Over the
years, he had learned a lot from the at-times reckless Frenchman, and
he had no doubt that the *Voile Noire* would find her way to one particular spot along the English coast.

"How is everything going with the *Chevalier Noir*?" Antoine asked,
his gaze still fixed upon his nephew's ship.

"Well," Ian replied, his hands linked behind his back. His wolf lay
by his feet, head leisurely rested upon its front paws.

"I'm glad to hear it."

Ian glanced at the tall-masted ship that was now his to command. He
still felt a sense of disbelief to have been granted such a measure of trust.
After leaving his past behind, he had lived from day to day, never seeking

a closer connection with those around him. He had been content sailing the seas, his hands and mind occupied, his past banished for good. Yet somehow, he had not only become part of Henri's crew but also been taken in by his family. To this day, Ian could not say how it had happened.

He certainly had not sought it.

After all, entanglements of the heart were dangerous. They had once destroyed his life, and he did not care for that to happen again.

He was content, and he wanted no more and no less.

Still, he could not refuse the Durets' offer, their request, their call for aid. They counted on him, and he would not fail them.

His gaze swept over the *Chevalier Noir*, now being outfitted with black sails to match Henri's. Ian had requested it, for he wished to signal his loyalty to the Durets. It made him feel proud but, at the same time, sent a shiver of unease down his spine. Aye, life had been easier, simpler when it had only been him.

However, it had also been lonely.

"Have you spoken to your new crew?" Antoine asked, shifting his feet until Ian felt the man's gaze upon him.

Lifting his chin a fraction, Ian nodded. "I have."

"Good." For a moment, Antoine watched him before he glanced out toward the open sea once more, where Henri's ship was slowly being swallowed up by the horizon.

Ian felt his shoulders pull back as he watched the men upon the *Chevalier Noir*, preparing the vessel for the upcoming voyage. How did they feel about their new captain? Ian wondered yet again. After all, they had not known him for long nor did they know him well. No one did, for Ian rarely exchanged a word with those around him. He had always liked it this way.

Now, though, it might make things more difficult.

Would they trust him to lead them? Would Antoine's word, his command, be enough for them? On top of everything, Ian was a Scot. He was not even a fellow countryman, a fact they were reminded of every time he opened his mouth to bellow a command. Did they resent him for it? Or was he overthinking this? Seeing problems where there were none?

"What is your plan?" Antoine asked as his attention returned from his nephew's departure and once more settled upon Ian.

Ian moved to meet the man's gaze. "Head south to Monpont."

Antoine nodded in agreement.

Monpont had been Dubois's hometown, and considering their lack of information concerning the child's whereabouts, it was the best place to start.

While they knew that Dubois had taken the child the night of the fire, he had never disclosed the girl's location. And now, Dubois was dead, his body at the bottom of the ocean after a shoot-out on the high seas when the Durets had come together to save Juliette from that madman's clutches. But where was the child?

All Dubois had let slip was that the girl was being taken care of by someone named Duval. Unfortunately, they knew not who that person was nor how he or she was connected to Dubois. All Antoine had been able to find out in Paris—by sheer happenstance no less!—was that the name Duval was somehow connected to a traveling circus. Which traveling circus and where it might be at this moment was anyone's guess.

"I shall send word," Antoine said, a deep crease of concern between his brows, "should we unearth any more information." He took a step forward, his gaze fixed upon Ian's. "Is there anything else you require?"

Ian shook his head no.

Antoine nodded, the hint of a smile playing across his features at Ian's tight-lippedness. "Then I wish you good luck. Do what you can to bring the girl back alive."

Ian nodded solemnly, struggling in that moment to hold the memories of his own little girl at bay. Over the past years, he had done his utmost not to think of her or his son, and thus far, he had managed quite admirably. Now, however, things were different.

As Antoine returned to the village, Ian stepped onto the quarter-deck of the *Chevalier Noir*, his wolf following upon his heel. He watched his crew go about their tasks, their faces serious, their movements precise, and only a few glanced at the beast by Ian's side. They all knew what was at stake. They had all known Étienne Clément. They all knew his widow and would do all they could to see her child returned to her.

It was the way of the Durets.

Family above all.

And family was not made by blood alone.

"All is going well," Louis, Ian's new first mate, informed him as he came to stand next to Ian, both men overlooking the deck. "Provisions are being loaded, and all repairs will be finished by nightfall."

Ian nodded in acknowledgment. "*Bien*," he said in an attempt to converse with the man. Under normal circumstances, Ian would not have done so; however, he needed his crew to accept his command, to trust him. Only he did not quite know how to go about it. Never had he been able to converse easily with a wide variety of people, and he had been out of practice these past few years.

Out of the corner of his eye, Ian thought to see a bit of a grin come to Louis's face. How awful had Ian's attempt at companionship sounded to a native Frenchman? How badly had he mispronounced the word?

Louis, however, made no comment nor did he give any other indication that he disapproved. He merely grinned.

Ian suspected they were of similar age and of almost identical height. However, that was where their similarities ended. A bit of a burly man, Louis possessed a full beard the color of rust. Unlike Henri and Ian, he did not wear his hair long and tied in the nape. Instead, it was cut short, but long enough to stick up in all directions of the compass. It gave him a bit of a disheveled look, like a wild savage barely able to hold a civilized conversation. That assessment, however, would be wrong.

"The men are eager to get underway," Louis said, resting his arms leisurely upon the railing. "Most of them have little ones at home, and none can bear the thought of Noèle's daughter out there by herself." He looked at Ian from over his shoulder. "They will do what must be done."

Ian nodded. "Good," he replied, uncertain what else to say. Indeed, it had been a long time since he attempted to converse with others.

Again, Louis grinned, then straightened. "Henri Duret spoke highly of you, and there is not a man here who would doubt his word." He nodded to Ian. "Welcome aboard, *Capitaine* Stewart."

Ian did his utmost to return the man's smile. "*Merci.*" Another attempt at camaraderie.

Louis grinned, then grasped Ian's shoulder companionably before striding off to assist a young sailor.

Ian exhaled slowly, surprised by the relief he felt after such a simple exchange. He could only hope it would bear fruit.

The animal by his side whined softly, its ears perked as it looked up at Ian. Reaching out, Ian placed a comforting hand upon its head, his gaze darting to the wolf's ripped ear. How the creature had sustained this injury Ian did not know. It had happened before their paths had crossed.

Straightening, Ian's gaze moved to the hatch and the captain's quarters beyond. Now that Madame Clément was to accompany them, Ian would bunk with his crew. Perhaps it was a blessing in disguise. Of course, Ian preferred to remain apart from those around him. He had always liked solitude. However, being in close quarters with his crew might benefit him after all. And that was all that mattered, was it not? That they were successful in locating the child and returning her to her mother's arms.

Again, an unbidden image of his own daughter flashed through Ian's mind. He still remembered how small Blair had been the day she had been born. He remembered seeing her, her tiny fists and those softly slanted eyes, pinched shut against the sudden rush of sensations. He had stood and stared, unable to believe that such a small creature could exist, that she could be so utterly perfect.

Ian wondered if Madame Clément had felt the same upon her child's birth. He could not imagine it to be differently. Did not every parent feel like that?

He also remembered the night they had saved her and Lady Juliet from Dubois's ship. He remembered seeing her lying on the deck, unconscious, her dark hair hiding her face. He had crouched beside her, gently brushing back her hair, needing to know that she was breathing, when his gaze had fallen upon the burns snaking down the side of her face.

For a short, heart-stopping moment, Ian had been unable to move. The sight of such pain, of Dubois's cruelty had stunned him. In his life,

Ian had encountered awful deeds now and then; however, never before had he come across a man as dark and soulless as Dubois.

And even now, with the man safely removed from this world, people still suffered. A mother was parted from her child, uncertain if she would ever lay eyes upon her again. It was a thought that pained Ian, made his heart clench tighter and tighter in his chest until he felt he could no longer draw breath into his body. After all, he knew what it meant to be separated from one's child.

However, while Blair was lost to him—though safe and sound back in Scotland, but still lost to *him*!—Madame Clément's daughter could be reclaimed, could be returned to the parent who loved her more than life itself.

Lifting his gaze, Ian looked toward the far horizon, knowing that come tomorrow they would set sail and he would do everything within his power to reunite mother and child. He had a purpose again. After years of existing from one day to the next, Ian once again had something to focus his mind on, a reason for being here. Once again, he was needed. There were others relying on him, counting on him, and he would not fail them.

That thought brought him a small measure of contentment.

Chapter Three

INTO THE UNKNOWN

Upon Alexandra's arm, Noèle walked up the gangplank onto the *Chevalier Noir*. She lifted her face into the wind, savoring the cooling touch upon her skin, and her eyes fell upon the ship's black sails. Of course, they were still furled, but they were still unmistakably black.

A shiver snaked down Noèle's back, for the sight reminded her of Henri's ship, of Étienne and the many times she had watched her late husband sail away upon it.

"Are you all right?" Alexandra inquired, one brow raised doubtfully. "Shall we return to the house? You know, you don't have to—"

"*Oui*, I am," Noèle hastened to assure Henri's aunt. As a mother of five, Alexandra had a way of seeing with a single glance when someone was hurting. "I'm fine. I promise. It is just..." She heaved a deep sigh as her gaze swept over the tall-masted ship once more. "There are so many memories."

Alexandra nodded knowingly, then assisted Noèle onto the ship.

For a moment, Noèle felt her knees tremble, but she willed the tremor away, reminding herself that it was not her body that was still weak but her mind instead. Indeed, memories could be crippling! A body healed much faster than a soul, and she gritted her teeth, forcing herself onward. After all, she *had* gained strength these past few weeks. Of course, there were still limits that had not been there before. Scars had formed, and some of her skin was still tender to the touch. Yet her muscles finally remembered their duty.

Antoine smiled at her as they approached, the silent Scot standing at his side. "Welcome aboard," he greeted her, gently wrapping her hands within his own. "You shall have the captain's quarters, which will grant you privacy and a place to rest upon this long journey. *S'il te plait*, do not hesitate to ask for anything you might require."

Noèle felt tears prick the backs of her eyes at the way he looked at her, the way he reassuringly squeezed her hands. "*Merci*, Antoine."

Sweeping her gaze across the deck, Noèle saw that each and every member of Antoine's crew looked at her in that same utterly devoted way. She saw their compassion and their loyalty but also their anguish and their rage. Of course, they knew what had happened to her. How could they not? They knew what she had suffered at Dubois's hands, and they felt for her.

Noèle could not deny that a part of her had not expected it to be so. She knew them all to be good men, and yet they all had either watched her late husband grow up or grown up alongside him. Étienne had been one of them, a bond existed between them Noèle would never understand, having grown up far from La Roche-sur-Mer. Never would she have doubted their devotion to him, but to her? *Oui*, she was his widow, and yet Ophélie was not his child.

For a brief moment, Noèle closed her eyes, wishing for what seemed like the thousandth time that Ophélie had been her husband's child.

Again, Antoine squeezed her hands, jarring her back to the present. "May I introduce you to the *Chevalier Noir*'s new *capitaine*, Ian Stewart?"

Noèle swallowed and directed her gaze to the tall, stoic man next to Antoine. More than anything, she wanted to look into his eyes and feel reassured; after all, her life, her well-being, everything she was would be in his hands the moment they set sail. Could she trust him?

"*Madame Clément*," the Scotsman greeted her, his voice hard and detached. Not a flicker of emotion graced his features as he met her gaze, his own slightly narrowed, as though he did not wish to look upon her. Still, after the first wave of unease that briefly threatened to send her running from the ship, Noèle thought to glimpse something else below the man's hard shell.

Pain.

Again, she saw a flicker of pain.

As she had the night he had carried her off Dubois's ship.

It was an odd sense of recognition, and it calmed her fears a little.

"Bonjour, Capitaine Stewart," Noèle returned his greeting, doing her best to offer him a small smile. Perhaps, with time, they would feel more comfortable in each other's company. For now, however, this would have to do. After all, there was something more important at stake here than Noèle's peace of mind.

A soft whine suddenly drew Noèle's attention downward, and her eyes fell upon the Scotsman's wolf. Of course, she had seen the animal now and then in the village, always following upon the man's heel, always alert to his commands. Yet Noèle had only ever glimpsed him from afar. Never had she stood so close as to see the tear in his right ear or the brilliant yellow of his almond-shaped eyes.

Startled, she drew in a sharp breath, taking a step backward.

Instantly, *Capitaine* Stewart's left hand moved downward, giving a quick wave, and the wolf retreated a few steps, then sank down upon his belly, resting his head upon his paws. It was such a familiar behavior, one she had observed in dogs countless times, that Noèle had to smile.

"You have nothing to fear from the wolf," Antoine said soothingly, stepping forward and positioning himself between her and the animal. "He looks fearsome, but he is quite docile, is that not so?" Over his shoulder, he looked at the Scot.

Capitaine Stewart gave a quick nod but said nothing.

"Come," Alexandra called, drawing Noèle away. "I'll show you to your quarters. From experience, I can say that they are quite comfortable." She cast an affectionate smile at Antoine, no doubt remembering the time she and her husband had spent together upon the *Chevalier Noir.*

Following Alexandra, Noèle nodded.

As they moved toward the hatch, Noële saw Antoine step toward *Capitaine* Stewart, his head slightly lowered, as though he did not wish to be overheard. However, the wind carried his words to Noële's ears. "I'm entrusting her into your care." His voice sounded tense and imploring as he held the Scotsman's gaze.

Capitaine Stewart nodded, the expression upon his face as stoic as before. Yet as he spoke, his voice affected her deeply, sending a shiver down her back. "I shall guard her with my life."

Even though Henri had said something similar to her as well, Noële had not quite believed him. She had told herself that he had simply spoken so in order to ease her fears. Yet now, *Capitaine* Stewart had said the very same thing again. Did he truly mean it?

Indeed, one look into his stoic face told her that he did. Yet the tone in his voice as he had spoken made Noële wonder. It, too, had held pain. Had there been a moment in his life when such a vow had not been enough?

Following Alexandra down into the ship's belly, Noële felt a moment of panic well up inside of her. Perhaps she ought to have expected it. Perhaps she was a fool for thinking that she could do this. That she could spend days, weeks upon a ship, a ship like Dubois's, and not succumb to the memories it conjured.

"Are you all right?" Alexandra inquired as she opened the door to the captain's quarters. Reaching out, she took Noële's hand and pulled her across the threshold, then closed the door. "You can still change your mind," she counseled gently. "There is no shame in that."

Noële disagreed.

If she ran now, she would be running and hiding for the rest of her life. *Non*, she needed to go after her daughter, and in order to do that, she needed to, at least, face that part of her past that threatened to bring her to her knees. *Oui*, she needed to stand tall. She could not break down now.

Still, as her gaze swept over the cabin, Noële felt transported back onto Dubois's ship. She remembered what it felt like to be his prisoner, to be locked away in a small cabin, constantly afraid of the next time he would choose to visit her. Fortunately, at the time, Noële's injuries had prevented him from–

Closing her eyes, she cringed away from the thought. Yet she remembered well his presence, the way his eyes had always lingered upon her, reminding her of what he had done to her, of what he might do to her again. It had been this constant fear that had robbed her of every bit of strength, more so than any of the injuries she had sustained in the fire. It had crippled her, and it still did. For even though Dubois now lay dead, his memory still lived within her.

"What is it that worries you?" Alexandra inquired, stepping around Noèle and meeting her eyes. "Say it and it might lose some of its power."

Noèle nodded, and yet every fiber of her being cringed at the thought. "*Capitaine* Stewart," she said instead, "what do you know of him?"

Sighing, Alexandra shrugged. "Not much. You might've noticed that the man does not speak much." A teasing smile flashed across her face, one meant to lighten the mood. "As far as I've heard, he was fished out of the sea about three years ago. The wolf as well."

Noèle nodded, having heard that story from Étienne before.

"The fisherman's ship was then boarded by Henri and his crew, at which point Ian asked to join them." Alexandra moved around the cabin, straightening the blanket upon the small cot in the corner. "Of course, Henri severely tested him. You know how he can be. As reckless and hot-headed as he might often appear, he is a cautious man." Affection swung in her voice. "However, Ian did not only prove capable but also loyal." She stepped toward Noèle once more, reaching out to take her hands. "I assure you, you have nothing to fear from him. Henri as well as Antoine trust him completely or they would never have allowed you to go with him."

Noèle nodded, relieved to be assured of the Durets' trust in *Capitaine* Stewart. "Is there anything else you know about him? How did he end up in the sea? What of his family?"

Alexandra shook her head. "I doubt anyone knows." Gently, she brushed a stray curl behind Noèle's ear. "He, too, refuses to share his past with those around him." Her brows rose meaningfully. "Still, I believe there is pain in his past. You saw it as well, did you not?"

Noèle heaved a deep sigh, momentarily shaken by Alexandra's

suggestion that she and *Capitaine* Stewart had something in common, something that lay at the very core of their being. "I did," she finally said in a small voice.

"Are you certain you wish to do this?" Alexandra inquired, looking deep into Noèle's eyes.

Blinking back tears, Noèle shrugged. "It doesn't matter what I wish." She wiped a tear from her cheek. "I must."

Frowning, Alexandra pressed her hands, giving them a slight tug. "You must do nothing," she insisted. "Whether you are on board or not, Ian will go after Ophélie. He will find her, and he will return her to you."

Of course, Noèle knew this, and yet she could not shake the feeling that she had to be here. Was it simply a matter of duty? Did she simply feel responsible? Or guilty? *Non*, it was more than that. It went deeper. This was her child, and even though Ophélie was not Étienne's, she *was* Noèle's.

No doubt reading Noèle's determination upon her face, Alexandra nodded. "I pray that the two of you shall be reunited soon." She leaned forward and pressed a kiss to Noèle's forehead. "Be safe, and come back to us soon."

Noèle embraced Alexandra. "I shall." She could only hope that it would prove true.

Chapter Four

COMFORTABLE SILENCE

Bellowing orders, Ian watched as the sails were readied, released from their binds and allowed to catch the wind. Their black stood in stark contrast to the light blue sky and the snow-white clouds. The sight reminded Ian of his time upon the *Voile Noire*, Henri's ship. Indeed, Henri Duret had gained himself quite a reputation, his black sails announcing his arrival from afar, for they said more than the flag under which he sailed.

Slowly, the *Chevalier Noir* gained speed, lazily drifting out of the harbor of La Roche-sur-Mer and out onto the open seas. The men worked well together, years of experience visible in the way they moved, relied on one another, acted almost like a single organism. It had been Antoine's doing, and Ian wondered yet again whether he would live up to the Durets' expectations.

It had been a long time since someone had placed such faith in him.

Even though Ian had never been close to any in Henri's crew, he knew he had found a place among them. Now, he once more stood on the outside. He would have to get to know the men as a captain should, learning their abilities, their strengths, their weaknesses.

As they would learn his.

Ian could only hope they would not find him wanting.

Looking up and seeing the black sails, Ian thought back to his time upon the *Voile Noire*. He remembered Étienne, Noèle's late husband and Henri's oldest friend, a man with an easy smile and a kind heart. Of course, they had not known each other well, but...Étienne had tried. He had been one of those men, who sought to put others at ease, who saw pain and felt compelled to heal it. Ian had thought him a good man, and he remembered the shock he had felt upon watching him washed overboard. He remembered the feeling of helplessness as Étienne had disappeared beneath the waves. He remembered the look of shock upon Henri's face.

Henri had been ready to jump in after him; however, his crew had held him back, Ian included. By the time, they had tied a rope around Henri's waist, there had been no sign of Étienne.

As La Roche-sur-Mer fell behind, Ian inhaled a deep breath. Indeed, out here at sea, he breathed more easily. He had never known that about himself until he had joined Henri's crew.

The wolf resting by his feet stirred, and then its head rose from its front paws, its ears twitching, not in alarm but in awareness.

Moving from one foot onto the other, Ian glanced over his shoulder, knowing who was there even before his eyes fell on her. Somehow, he had known. Perhaps it had been the animal's reaction, alert and watchful but not tense. Its yellow eyes followed her movements as she made her way across the deck toward him.

Ian swallowed, feeling a sense of unease crawl down his back. Had she come to speak to him? Oddly enough, few things in life unsettled him; however, the sight of another intent upon holding some sort of conversation with him made his skin crawl. It was something he no longer knew how to do.

Madame Clément held herself upright, shoulders drawn back and her chin lifted, as though she was afraid to portray any sign of weakness no matter how small. Something cautious lurked in her blue eyes, as though she sensed danger, her body ready to fight at a moment's notice.

Yet there was none. Ian knew that with certainty. Still, the look upon Madame Clément's face remained.

Apprehensive.

Cautious.

Fearful.

Indeed, upon a closer look, it became clear that the strength she sought to portray was no more than an illusion. Exhaustion lay upon her features, and Ian saw the slight tremble that shook her delicate frame as she placed one foot in front of the other. Why was she here? He wondered. Why did she not simply remain in the cabin?

"*Capitaine* Stewart," Madame Clément greeted him as she finally reached his side, her hands grasping the wooden railing tightly. A deep breath rushed past her lips, and for a moment, Ian thought she might sink to her knees.

Ready to catch her if necessary, Ian watched her, uncertain what he ought to do or say. And so, he said nothing but simply stood there, waiting.

Closing her eyes, Madame Clément inhaled another deep breath, holding it in for a bit before exhaling slowly. Then she opened her eyes, and although she did not turn her head, her gaze shifted to him. "I'm fine. No need to worry."

Ian nodded, then moved to stand as he had before, his own hands settling upon the railing as they both looked out toward the horizon.

Silence stretched between them, and yet Ian could not rightly say that it was an uncomfortable silence. He knew that some people feared moments that were not filled by words. These moments unsettled them, and they tended to grasp for straws, saying anything simply to have something to say.

Ian was not such a man, and neither, it seemed, was Madame Clément such a woman.

The wind brushed her black curls out of her face, toyed with her hair as it billowed behind her like a dark cloud on a sunny day. Out of the corner of his eye, Ian caught sight of the last remnants of her burns. The skin upon her temple still had a tinge of red, which lazily trailed down the side of her face and proceeded along her neck.

At the sight, the night Ian had carried her off Dubois's ship resurfaced in his mind. At first, he had not even recognized her. Of course, they had never been well acquainted. He had only ever seen her face from afar, though not within the last year. His thoughts had not been on her when he had gently picked her up and her black hair had fallen from her face, revealing her features.

In that moment, they had meant nothing to Ian. All he had been able to see had been her injuries, those angry burns etched into her features as though carved from stone, and he had felt sickened.

"I came to thank you," Madame Clément said all of a sudden, and for a split second, her blue eyes darted to his face. However, she averted them quickly, a touch of wariness upon her face, and Ian wondered if she feared him.

His hands tensed on the railing as he considered how to reply, how to put her at ease. Was it possible that she looked at him and thought of Dubois? However, he was not even certain what it was she was thanking him for. After all, what had he done?

Nothing.

A few weeks past, Ian had carried her off Dubois's ship upon Henri's orders. Nothing more. He had taken her to François, the ship's surgeon. Again, upon Henri's orders. And now, he stood as captain upon the deck of the *Chevalier Noir*, granted this position by the Durets, determined to repay them for their trust in him by reuniting a mother and her child. Was there truly something he deserved gratitude for?

Ian did not think so.

"There is no need," he finally replied, casting a careful glance at her face, wanting to know how his words were received.

Madame Clément turned to look at him and their eyes met...and held, and for the first time in years, Ian felt as though someone was truly seeing him.

This was no simple exchange of words, which often entailed a shared look that signaled understanding or agreement. This meeting of the eyes had no function, no purpose beyond the need or wish to make out the other's character, to understand who that person was and whether one was justified in trusting them.

Ian wondered what she saw, what conclusion she would come to, and he realized that he wanted her to trust him. Not simply because it would make this voyage easier, but because...

...that meant that he was no longer the man he had once been.

The sea breeze tangled in her dark tresses, and a single curl danced sideways across her eyes, breaking the spell.

As though jarred out of her thoughts, Madame Clément dropped her gaze and drew another deep breath into her lungs, her eyes once more returning to the far horizon. "Where are we headed?" she asked, and this time, her words did sound like those one would say to fill an uncomfortable moment.

Clearing his throat, Ian shifted back from one foot onto the other. "Monpont." Beside him, he felt the wolf shift as well, as though it wished to keep her in sight.

"Monpont?" Madame Clément's brows drew down. "Why Monpont?" With her mind focused on her question, Ian saw her relax, her hands no longer grasping the railing so very tightly that her knuckles almost stood out white.

Reluctantly, Ian turned to face her, wishing someone else had already informed her of their destination as well as its meaning. "'Tis Dubois's hometown."

Madame Clément flinched, her blue eyes going wide as she stared at him, her breath lodged in her throat, and for a moment, he feared she might faint on the spot. However, the moment passed, and he watched as she forced her panic back down, slowly regaining control of her features. "I see."

The sight of her fear pained Ian, made his heart constrict painfully within his chest, for it conjured thoughts of all she had suffered at Dubois's hands. Rage surged through him, quickly replaced by a powerful desire to protect her, to reassure her, to alleviate her fears.

Without thinking, Ian moved toward her.

Instantly, Madame Clément drew back, her eyes widening as she retreated a step.

Ian snapped to a halt, then quickly retreated himself, hands raised in a reassuring gesture. "I apologize. I mean ye no harm."

Again, their eyes locked as stillness fell over them. Ian was barely aware of the activity around them as the *Chevalier Noir* picked up speed, cutting through the waves as though on wings. All he was aware of were those wide, blue eyes of hers as they looked into his, trying to see deeper, to determine the man he was.

Ian almost cringed at the thought of what she might find.

Finally, Madame Clément exhaled, and the tension vanished from her posture, relief marking her features. "I'm sorry," she mumbled then, a touch of red coming to her cheeks as she dropped her gaze. "I didn't mean... I..."

"Dubois is dead."

Her head snapped up, and Ian regretted having spoken so plainly. Yet it was the truth, and although her mind was familiar with it, her soul had yet to believe it.

"Ye're safe here," Ian insisted, holding her gaze, praying that she would not come to perceive him as a threat. "I willna let any harm come to ye. I swear it."

Her eyelids fluttered as she swallowed, the look upon her face an odd mixture of relief and puzzlement. "*Merci, Capitaine* Stewart, for all you're doing." She nodded her head up and down. "*Merci.*"

Ian inclined his head in acknowledgment before he once more turned to face the sea, both hands grasping the railing.

After a moment of hesitation, Madame Clément did the same, and for a long time, they simply stood there, side by side as the seagulls screeched overhead.

"I wonder if I'll even recognize her," Madame Clément said then, her voice barely audible over the rush of the wind. Still, Ian could hear the sorrow and fear in those few words all the same.

An image of Blair and Niall rose in his mind, the way they had been when he had last seen them over three years ago. What did they look like today? Was it possible that he would pass them on a crowded street and not even recognize them? Of course, the odds of their paths crossing were nonexistent. However, if...

Ian closed his eyes, remembering the blue of Blair's eyes, as sparkling and deep as the sea and shining with a wisdom beyond her years. And Niall with his wild red hair and cautious green eyes, always watchful, always looking out for others.

The ghost of a smile teased Ian's lips. No, he *would* recognize them. Always. There was not a single doubt in his mind.

31

Glancing at Madame Clément, her head slightly bowed and her eyes downcast, Ian cleared his throat, then said, "Ye will."

For a moment, she stilled, then moved to look at him.

Holding her gaze, Ian nodded. "Ye will."

Tears misted her eyes, and yet the soft twitch that came to her lips might have been a smile.

Chapter Five
A NEW WORLD

Blinking her eyes open, Noèle paused. Her body stilled completely, her muscles tense as she stared up at the wooden ceiling. For a moment, she could not recall where she was, while the sight before her eyes conjured images of her past, almost making her believe that she had never escaped it. But this was not Dubois's ship, was it?

Closing her eyes, Noèle breathed in deeply before opening them once more. Then she pushed upright and swung her legs off the side of the cot. Her gaze swept over the cabin, the captain's quarters, and she noted with relief the marked differences to Dubois's. *Oui*, this was the *Chevalier Noir*, currently under the command of *Capitaine* Stewart...

...a man quite unlike Dubois.

Running her hands over her face, Noèle leaned back against the wall, then pulled up her knees and hugged her arms around them. As much as she wished, she could not ignore the tremble that never quite seemed to leave her. It lingered in her muscles, even in her bones, and made her feel tense and fearful. It brought tears to her eyes even when she willed them away, and it conjured images...of Ophélie.

Closing her eyes, Noèle rested her forehead upon her bent knees, giving in to that sharp tug upon her heart. She did her best to recall her daughter's little face, the slight slant of her eyes, the tuft of black hair atop her head, the way she would sometimes smile in her sleep. Yet the image was no longer clear. With time, it had become blurred, unfocused, and Noèle feared that one day it would completely slip from her grasp.

Yet, so much time had already passed, so much time in which they had been separated, that Noèle wondered what Ophélie even looked like today. Were her eyes still blue? Did her hair still shimmer in the same midnight black as her own? Would Noèle even recognize her daughter if someone were to place Ophélie in her arms right now?

Ye will.

Noèle flinched, for *Capitaine* Stewart's words echoed through her mind in that moment so loud and clear, as though he were sitting beside her. He had spoken with such conviction, as though not a single doubt lived in his mind. How could he know when even she did not?

Ye will.

No more than strangers, acquaintances perhaps, his words still gave Noèle hope. They warmed her heart and eased that cold shiver that refused to release her.

Perhaps she was not wrong to hope.

Knowing that lingering thoughts of her daughter more often than not reduced her to a weeping lump, Noèle pushed to her feet, determined to seize the day, to go above deck, to breathe in the fresh sea air and know that with each push of the waves and wind, she was getting a little closer to reclaiming her child.

Friendly faces met her as Noèle slowly made her way across deck until she came to stand at the stern. Her hands grasped the railing once more, giving her a feeling of being tied to this moment, here, now. Too often, her mind felt carried away by a fleeting memory, all painful, all filled with regret. At least, for now, Noèle wished to remain where she was.

Of course, life was far from perfect! However, it was easy enough to bear...if she did not think about it too much.

"Madame Clément," Louis greeted her with a tip of his head as he walked by, a wide smile somewhere beneath his unruly beard.

Noèle managed a smile, then turned and rested her back against the rail, her gaze moving up the tall masts, glimpsing sailors high up in the rigging. What did it feel like to be up so high? To see the world so small below one's feet? Was that the feeling sailors often referred to as *freedom*? Was that why they sailed the seas?

Noèle remembered how Étienne had once tried to explain how he felt every time he set foot on board such a vessel. To her, his words had been almost meaningless, and yet, even now, she recalled the awed glow that had come to his gaze.

Tears pricked her eyes at the memory, at the sudden longing that sprang to life, and once more, Noèle turned away. She did not wish for the crew to see her tears nor did she wish to feel them.

Oh, Étienne! Why had he been taken from her? If only—

Noèle closed her eyes, recognizing the futility of these thoughts. She knew them well, and she knew that they led nowhere and changed nothing. She knew so from experience.

A cry of alarm shattered the tranquility of the day, and Noèle whipped around, eyes wide as they flew over the deck.

For a moment, the world seemed to still, no one and nothing moved, before suddenly all hell broke loose. With their eyes raised to the sky, sailors rushed forward to the second mast, the one closest to Noèle, tension marking their features. Looking up, following their line of sight, Noèle drew in a sharp breath.

A young sailor had lost his footing and was now all but dangling like a fish on a hook, his foot caught in the rigging. His face was a dark shade of red as he flailed his arms in panic, unable to grab a hold of anything.

And then, *Capitaine* Stewart shot up the rigging.

Where he had come from, Noèle did not know. However, he moved with such speed that for a moment she wondered if her mind had conjured him.

His face was set in determination, his hands reaching higher, pulling him upward as his feet followed. The wind tugged upon his light hair, swirling strands around his head, as he climbed the rigging, his gaze fixed on the flailing sailor.

The young man—Guillaume, Noèle believed, was his name—called out in terror as his foot almost slipped free of the rigging. He seemed to drop downward—if only for a split second—before his foot managed to catch a hold again. Still, his situation was even more precarious than before.

On deck, the men had fallen silent, except for a few shouting up instructions and encouragements to Guillaume while *Capitaine* Stewart climbed ever closer.

No more than two meters separated him from Guillaume.

Then one.

And then Guillaume's foot slipped free...and he fell.

Noèle drew in a sharp breath, her hands flying to her lips, covering her mouth as she stared in shock.

Only Guillaume did not fall far.

Fortunately, *Capitaine* Stewart had managed to grab the young sailor's arm and yank him backward, slamming his back against the rigging. Guillaume's arms were still flailing until a sharp bark from his captain calmed him, and he reached around to grab a hold of the ropes running from the ship's deck to the top of the mast.

Collectively, the crew of the *Chevalier Noir* exhaled.

Closing her eyes, Noèle sank to the deck, her knees shaking, as though she had been the one to lose her footing, to fall from such a height. She hugged her legs to her chest and rested her forehead upon her bent knees, breathing in and out slowly, listening to the hammering beat of her heart.

And then something brushed her arm, and Noèle lifted her head, her eyes widening as...

...she found herself face to face with the wolf!

His yellow eyes were fixed upon her face as he sat on his hind legs, his tail curled across his front paws, his torn ear twitching.

For a moment, Noèle felt tempted to scream as panic shot through her. It was an instinct upon finding herself in such close proximity to a wild beast.

Only it was not a wild beast, was it?

Indeed, something...almost human rested in his eyes, as though the animal understood the terror in her heart and had hastened to her side in order to offer comfort. Was that possible? Could a wolf exhibit such empathy?

Breathing out slowly, Noèle righted herself, her eyes trained upon the creature in front of her. "*Salut*," she whispered a careful greeting, still uncertain of why the wolf had sought her out.

Again, his torn ear twitched, and Noèle wondered how he had sustained the injury. Had the animal suffered other wounds? If so, Noèle could not spot them, his thick gray coat hiding them from her view. And then she wondered how the wolf and *Capitaine* Stewart had found one another. Clearly, some sort of bond connected them, but how had that come to be?

A shadow fell over her and, looking up, Noèle caught the eye of *Capitaine* Stewart.

"Are ye all right?" he asked in that deeply accented voice of his. "It willna harm ye. Ye needna be afraid." He brushed an affectionate hand over the wolf's head, his chest still rising and falling with slightly accelerated breaths after his rapid climb up the rigging.

"I'm not," Noèle replied, surprised to hear these words ring true. Her eyes narrowed as she looked at the captain's face, trying to see...*him*. Indeed, for a moment, she could have sworn she glimpsed an almost tender, deeply devoted side of him. A side he did not share with anyone but the wolf.

"Are you married?" Noèle blurted out. "Do you have children?" The moment she saw his face darken, tense, Noèle knew her questions to have been a mistake. Still, something deep within her had wanted to know.

Had needed to know.

Still did.

Grumbling something rather unintelligible under his breath, *Capitaine* Stewart stepped back, his hand slipping from the animal's head. The wolf looked up, and their eyes met as the captain gave some kind of hand signal. Then he turned and, without another word, strode away.

Noèle exhaled, confused, her gaze moving back and forth between *Capitaine* Stewart's receding back and the canine now lying comfortably at her feet. Had the captain told the wolf to stay? Here with her? She met the creature's gaze and thought to see concern there, as though the wolf, too, worried for the man.

Once again, Noèle wondered about the events that had shaped *Capitaine* Stewart's life. How had he become the man he was today? Had he always been this taciturn? Was he perhaps so devoted to finding her daughter...because he had lost his own?

Noèle wished she knew.

Chapter Six

NIGHTMARES

Darkness would have engulfed the entire ship if it were not for the moon high in the sky, its silver rays casting an ethereal glow over the world. Ian stood up on deck, the wolf by his side, his gaze moving from the man at the helm, Laurent, over the calm sea. Only a mild breeze stirred, and the *Chevalier Noir* drifted along like a phantom, shrouded in a faint mist.

Countless times, Ian had spent up on deck on a night like this. He had always enjoyed the serenity, the soothing calm that spread through him upon finding himself...alone and at peace. Indeed, over the past few years, he had become Ian Stewart, a man with no past, a man who lived in the moment, a man who cared for no one and nothing.

Aye, Ian MacDrummond had died the day he had gone over the cliff. He had left behind all he knew...and all he loved.

His emotions had become dulled, his thoughts firmly fixed upon the present moment. He rarely experienced any sort of upheaval, good or bad.

Lately, however, something had changed.

Ian could feel it.

He felt it in every fiber of his being, like a soft tug or a hum. He felt it in the way his heart sometimes seemed to pause in his chest, as though suddenly remembering something he had thought lost for good. He felt it at night when he closed his eyes...and saw the faces of his children.

For the longest time, Ian had pushed all thoughts of them to the edge of his being, and day by day, their hold on him had lessened. Sometimes weeks had passed at a time without him thinking of them even once.

And now, he had begun to dream of them again. Why? What did this mean?

Even though Ian stared with all his might at the brilliant moon far above him, he could almost make out his daughter's face. It hovered there, in front of his eyes, her daring spirit reflected in the way her lips curled into a smile. Her blue eyes shone with knowledge, in that way she had always possessed even as a babe, and Ian felt the ache in his heart reawaken.

"Blair." Her name slipped from his lips in a whisper, carried away by the wind, back to Scotland.

A greeting from afar. Could she feel it? Ian wondered. Somehow, he thought she might.

Perhaps a part of him even wished for it.

He knew he should not. It would only make it harder for him to stay away, to leave that part of his life behind. Yet his treacherous heart did not care.

Perhaps it had been Madame Clément's presence. Ian had wondered about that before. Perhaps it was the look in her eyes when she thought of her lost child. He had seen it more than once, the way the blue of her eyes deepened, darkened, overshadowed by sorrow and longing alike. It felt like an echo of something Ian had known himself... and now remembered.

Each time he looked at her, he felt an odd tug upon his heart, a faint echo, reminding him of his old self, of his children, of his wife, of the life he had once had.

Indeed, perhaps it had been unwise to accept this mission. Yet, at the same time, Ian knew he could never have turned it down. Not simply because the Durets counted on him, trusted him, but also because Ian knew he would never forgive himself if something happened to Madame Clément's little daughter and he had not done all he could to prevent it.

Aye, when he thought of that little girl, in his mind's eye, he saw Blair.

With a heavy heart, Ian stepped below deck, barely aware of his four-legged companion. His thoughts were rebellious, urging him in a direction he knew he ought to shy away from. He cursed below his breath, uncertain what to do with himself, how to regain control. He knew he had to stop thinking of his children, and yet the longing he felt reawaken would not allow him. His teeth ground together, and his muscles tensed to the point of breaking. It felt like a war waging within himself, tugging him back and forth. He all but stumbled onward down the narrow, dark gangway until he reached the door to the captain's quarters.

There, he paused, blinking his eyes rapidly in order to clear his head. Why had he come here? Aye, he was the *Chevalier Noir*'s captain now, but he bunked with the crew. Indeed, his presence here proved how distracting these thoughts were, how they messed with his mind... and his heart. Could he even still trust himself? Could his crew?

Rubbing his hands over his face, Ian breathed in deeply, trying to calm himself. He needed to regain his balance, organize his thoughts and banish emotions that would serve no purpose. He needed to bury Ian MacDrummond for good and become Ian Stewart now and forever.

Ian was about to turn away from the door when a sound drifted to his ears. At first, he thought it might have been only the wind. However, when it came again, he felt that odd tug upon his heart.

It whispered of something familiar.

Something painful.

Ian stilled instantly, his gaze returning to the closed door, unseeing in the dark. He listened and waited, felt the wolf brush against him, and then flinched when the sound came again.

A whimper.

A cry for help, for that was what it was, was it not?

Hanging his head, Ian looked down at the wolf beside him, its yellow eyes glowing in the dark like a beacon guiding him to the present moment. He knew he could not simply turn away. He did not wish to move any closer, to get himself involved, and yet—

The whimper came again.

Tensing his jaw, Ian lifted his hand and gave a quick knock on the door. Then he paused and listened, waiting for any sign from inside, any movement.

Yet nothing came.

And then another whimper drifted to his ears.

Slowly, Ian opened the door. He felt like a trespasser, every fiber of his being urging him to turn back. Yet his heart would not allow him, for he knew the meaning of pain and sorrow and regret, being trapped in the past, wishing and never once believing or hoping. He knew what it was to be alone.

The large windows in the stern of the ship allowed for the glistening moonlight to reach inside and faintly illuminate the cabin. It was sparsely furnished and kept neat. A table with two chairs in its center. A chest on the far side and another in the corner by the door. The cot was on the starboard side, a shapeless figure upon it, tossing and turning.

After allowing the wolf to step over the threshold behind him, Ian then closed the door, not wanting the crew to see him here. Who knew what they would think? Then he slowly made his way across the wooden boards, feeling them creaked beneath his boots, and stepped closer to the cot.

No doubt due to the lingering warmth of early autumn, Madame Clément slept only in her shift, a thin linen sheet draped over her for a blanket. Indeed, the air felt a bit stuffy down here, a far cry from the refreshing balm above deck.

Ian wished he could simply turn and leave.

Instead, he inched closer, feeling compelled to avert his eyes, but knowing that he could not. He saw her turn onto her back, then back onto her side, her eyes pinched shut and her hands curled tightly into the linen sheet. Whimpered sounds left her lips as she seemed to cringe away from something.

What nightmare had sunk its talons into her? Ian wondered, thinking of her loss, of Étienne and her daughter. Yet the look upon Madame Clément's face seemed dominated by fear...and disgust.

A sickening feeling settled in Ian's stomach. After all, somehow everyone knew who had fathered her daughter...and how that had come to pass.

"Madame Clément!" Ian called quietly, knowing that he needed to wake her as soon as possible. If she was truly reliving— "Madame Clément!"

Her eyelids fluttered, but instead of waking, she once more rolled onto her back, her head pushed sideways into the mattress, her eyes pinched shut as she seemed to be holding her breath.

Beside Ian, the wolf whined quietly, no doubt sensing Madame Clément's emotional state.

Determined, Ian stepped up to the cot and placed his right hand upon her shoulder. He gave her a slight shake, then a stronger one and called her name again and again. At first, nothing he did seemed to have any effect, and for a horrifying moment, Ian feared his touch might only serve to terrify her more.

Then, however, her eyes suddenly flew open.

Ian flinched, not having expected that. He swallowed and gazed down, meeting her eyes, dark pools in the dim light of the cabin. "Madame Clément, are ye all right?"

For a moment, she lay completely still, her eyes holding his, as though it were the most natural thing in the world.

And then understanding dawned.

Ian could see it in the way her eyes widened, her breath suddenly lodged in her throat. Instinctively, she shrank back, pressing her back to the wall, her eyes fixing him with a panicked expression.

Ian knew the feeling of a woman looking at him with regret. He had spent years of his life like that. Yet no woman had ever looked at him with fear.

Except...

"Ye're safe," he assured her, backing away with his hands raised. "Ye had a nightmare. I heard ye cry out in yer sleep, and so I came to wake ye." He held her gaze. "Nothing more. I swear it."

Slowly, her breath evened, and she brushed damp hair from her forehead. Her eyes swept over the cabin, and he could see her recalling where she was. "*Merci*," she finally said, her voice no more than a breezy whisper. "I thank you." She drew in a deep breath and released it slowly, tears still clinging to the corners of her eyes.

Then suddenly, her jaw tensed abruptly, her teeth clicking together almost violently. She began to shiver, her body shaking, as silent tears trailed down her cheeks.

Aye, she was in desperate need of comfort, and yet Ian knew he could not step any closer. Indeed, his presence would not bring her comfort. It would unsettle her, send terror through her heart. He glanced down as the wolf by his feet whined softly. The creature looked up with pleading eyes, and Ian gave a quick nod.

As though freed from a leash, the animal moved forward, determined steps carrying it to the cot. "Dunna be afraid," Ian said softly. "It only seeks to give ye comfort." He nodded to Madame Clément reassuringly as her eyes went back and forth between him and the approaching wolf.

For a second, Ian thought she would shrink back, and he questioned his judgment in giving the animal free rein. Then, however, her features relaxed as she watched the wolf climb onto the cot, then lie down with its front paws and head in her lap. For a split second, her eyes widened and she looked up at Ian, as though asking for instructions or perhaps reassurance, before her arms quite naturally settled around the wolf's neck. Her fingers began to stroke its fur as she hugged the animal to her chest, exhaling a long breath.

Settling himself on one of the chairs, Ian waited, not wishing to intrude. Should he leave? Or would she be frightened to find herself alone with the wolf?

"What's his name?" Madame Clément asked as she brushed a hand over its head, then scratched behind its ears.

Ian shrugged. "It doesna have one."

Her hand paused briefly, then continued scratching the wolf, which tilted its head quite purposefully so she could reach the place it favored. "Why not?"

"I never thought of naming it."

A slight frown line appeared between her brows, the look upon her face no longer tortured now that her thoughts were directed else-where. "How...did you...meet him?"

Ian inhaled a deep breath as the day up on the cliffs resurfaced in his mind. "We tried to kill each other." He omitted the part where the wolf had gone after his daughter.

Blair, his heart whispered, and he closed his eyes.

Chapter Seven

IN THE DARK OF NIGHT

At *Capitaine* Stewart's words, Noèle felt her eyes go wide. Her hand stilled, still settled in the creature's luscious fur, and she looked down at the large beast in her lap. "Then...how...?" Had she understood him correctly?

Capitaine Stewart shrugged. "'Twas no ill will," he assured her, a hint of regret upon his face, as though he were cursing himself for saying too much, for revealing what he had meant to keep hidden. She knew that he sought to ease her fears, not introduce new ones. "'Twas hunger, nothing more. It saw easy prey, and it went for it."

Noèle nodded and continued her stroking. Of course, it made sense. Every carnivore hunted for prey in order to sustain itself. Still, as her eyes swept over the animal, Noèle could not imagine this gentle, caring creature as a snarling beast. It seemed impossible!

Indeed, in its presence, Noèle felt...safe, comforted even. Her nightmare had once again left her feeling cold and shivering, the memory of Dubois as real as the damp linen clutched in her hands. And now?

Oui, she breathed easier, that pressure upon her heart all but gone.

Looking up, Noèle met *Capitaine* Stewart's gaze. He looked uncomfortable; if possible, even more than her. She could see that he had not wanted to involve himself in her personal life like this, and yet he had. "*Merci*," she said once again, wanting him to know how much he had done for her. "These dreams come and go as they please," she whispered quietly, forcing herself to speak, knowing that not giving them a voice made them stronger. "I always feel so helpless and frightened and..." She swallowed, hugging the wolf tighter. "Holding him helps." A grateful smile teased her lips.

Capitaine Stewart nodded. "Aye, it may not understand, but..." He paused, and Noèle could see that he was reluctant to go on.

"But?" she urged, curious about the man beneath this rigid exterior.

He swallowed, and his eyes fell from hers. "No soul can forever exist on its own."

Noèle stilled, watching the man seated across from her as he ran a hand through his hair, that look of regret once more upon his face. "You do not converse much with others, do you?"

His gaze snapped up and met hers. For a second, he looked startled, caught off guard by her directness.

"Why?"

He shrugged.

"But you speak to him, do you not?" Noèle asked as her gaze darted from the man to the wolf and back. "He may not understand, but he listens."

Pushing to his feet, *Capitaine* Stewart stepped over to the window, the need to flee visible in his rigid posture. And yet, he did not. Perhaps a part of him buried somewhere deep still longed for closeness, to have someone listen who *would* understand.

Despite the comforting presence of the animal in her arms as well as the man across the cabin, Noèle still felt a few lingering effects of her nightmare, of the memories that had sparked it. *Oui*, she felt safe again, safe in the knowledge that Dubois was dead and could no longer harm her. Still, memories had a way to make one doubt the truth, doubt what one knew to be true.

Most nights when Noèle woke from her nightmares, she *felt* certain that Dubois was nearby. The fear that lived in her heart was not simply the echo of a memory but a living thing.

Here and now.

It sent icy shivers across her skin and tensed her muscles, readying them to fight or flee—if possible. She *knew* him to be gone, and yet her fear cared little for that knowledge, dismissing it as though it held no meaning.

Indeed, knowing something to be true with one's head was something utterly different from feeling that truth in one's heart.

Lifting her gaze to the tall, silent man staring out the windows at the quiet sea, Noèle wondered what demons lived in his past. He knew the meaning of nightmares too well, for it to be simply an observation. *Non*, he possessed personal knowledge. He knew their power, the way they twisted one's mind, made one uncertain of anything. What was *Capitaine* Stewart running from?

Noèle brushed her hand over the wolf's head and felt his soft fur run through her fingers. She smiled when the creature lifted his head and looked at her, the soft yellow glow of his eyes almost sorrowful. "You worry about him, do you not?" she whispered to the wolf.

As though in answer, a low whine escaped him, and he turned his head to look at *Capitaine* Stewart.

Noèle heaved a deep breath. It had been a long time since she had felt compelled to reach out to another, to offer comfort and counsel. Lately, she had only been on the receiving end, and...it had made her feel weak and thrown off balance.

"What loss did you suffer?" Noèle asked into the stillness of the cabin, and although *Capitaine* Stewart did not answer—not that she had expected him to—nor react in any way beyond a barely noticeable jolt briefly offsetting his rigid posture, she thought that, at least, a small part of him appreciated her asking.

After all, he did not spin upon his heel and flee her presence.

Long moments passed in silence. "Not looking at a wound will leave it open and raw," Noèle said gently, drawing strength from the wolf's warmth, "and unable to heal." She swallowed hard, feeling the shiver return, bringing with it that ice-cold sensation. Involuntarily, her arms tightened around the wolf, and she sighed when he snuggled closer, happy to oblige her.

"My memories still torment me," Noèle went on after her pulse had calmed a little, "and I hate when they catch me unawares. Nightmares are the worst because they strip me of every bit of control. They make me feel as though I'm right back in *that* moment." Tears pricked her eyes. "The moment the *Voile Noire* returned and I saw Henri's face. The moment I knew Étienne..." Her eyes closed, and she swallowed, feeling tears run down her cheeks. "The moment Dubois forced his way into my home. The moment he attacked me." Pain sliced through her at the memory, and yet she knew there to be strength in her for facing it. "The moment I knew Ophélie to be gone." The weight of her emotions was crippling, and she felt the overwhelming desire to give in, to lie down and allow them to bury her under them.

But she would not.

Lifting her chin, Noèle blinked the tears from her eyes...and her gaze met *Capitaine* Stewart's. Why she had spoken to him in this manner, Noèle did not know. After all, he was a stranger. And yet she did not regret it, for the look in his eyes told her that he had truly heard her.

He still seemed uncertain, judging from the way his gaze dropped from hers before returning almost hesitantly. Yet Noèle could see that the rigid barrier he had hidden behind was no longer as formidable. Gaping holes now showed in its structure, allowing her words to reach him.

"Who did you lose?" Noèle asked carefully, sensing his need to confide in her. Yet, she also knew there to be a great curiosity within her. She truly wished to know, not only for his sake, but for her own.

Closing his eyes, *Capitaine* Stewart shook his head. "I lost no one," he finally said, meeting her eyes, self-reproach within his own. "Ye went through hell—more than once—while I...I..." He scoffed, then shook his head. "My wife simply couldna love me." He shrugged his shoulders, as though to shrug off the pain of his words as insignificant. "Dunna worry for me, Madame Clément. See to yerself." He nodded to her and then strode across the cabin to the door.

"Noèle," Noèle called out the moment his hand grasped the door handle. "Please, call me Noèle. After the way we've spoken to one another, it feels...odd to address each other so formally, *n'est-ce pas?*"

Capitaine Stewart stilled, and for a moment, Noèle thought he would refuse her. Was he worried that the use of first names would make him too vulnerable? Was he desperately trying to rebuild that barrier around himself?

His head turned sideways, and he looked at her. "Verra well. I'm Ian." A touch of shock sparked in his eyes, as though he could not believe he had agreed.

"Ian." She smiled at him, feeling something deep inside her sigh with...relief, perhaps, to have formed this connection to someone who understood...and she could not bear to see him go. "The wounds that hurt the most are not the ones etched into my flesh." She glanced down at her arm, the skin there puckered, bearing the memory of the fire.

Ian inhaled visibly, his shoulders rising and falling, before he turned and leaned back against the door.

"Losing my husband nearly killed me," Noèle forced herself to continue, a hitch in her voice. "As did losing my daughter." Tears once more ran down her cheeks, and she let them fall. "What...What Dubois did to me was...," she swallowed, willing herself not to hide, "horrible, but it was not the worst I've ever suffered." She held his gaze and wondered if she was only imagining the shimmer of tears she saw in his eyes. "To have one's heart broken—in whatever way—is not nothing...Ian."

Ian's face fell. The hard edges softened, and the unyielding, rock-solid mask he always wore evaporated, leaving behind a broken man.

"Tell me what happened," Noèle urged him, wondering how any woman could resist loving him—a thought that momentarily startled her! Where had it come from?

For a long time, Ian simply looked at her, his eyes lingering, contemplating. Then he sighed. "I loved her the moment I saw her," he finally said, his voice rough, as though he had not used it in a long time. "I was young and a fool." He scoffed.

"You can only be a fool for something that was your own choice," Noèle counseled, trying to meet his eyes. "It was never my choice to love my husband. Neither could I have chosen *not* to love him."

Doubt lingered in Ian's gaze. "She already loved another, an Englishman. And when she learned that in her absence he had married, I thought I could win her heart, and so I asked for her hand." He shook his head. "I *was* a fool. I doomed us both." Anger swung in his voice, and that rigid mask slipped onto his face once more.

Squaring his shoulders, Ian cleared his throat. "If ye wish, I'll send the wolf to ye every night to keep ye company." He nodded toward the animal.

Noèle smiled at him, grateful. "Will you not miss him?"

Ian did not answer, his face immobile.

"Will he not miss you?"

A slight frown drew down his brows, as though such a suggestion was nonsense. "He willna mind. 'Tis easy to see that he cares for ye."

Noèle held his gaze. "He cares for you as well."

Clearly uncomfortable, Ian shifted from one foot onto the other. "Dunna concern yerself with me, Madame Cl—"

"Noèle!"

He paused, then nodded. "Noèle." Her name left his tongue only hesitantly. "Good night." He inclined his head to her and then stepped from the cabin, his footsteps echoing down the gangway.

Scratching behind the wolf's torn right ear, Noèle looked down at him. "Does he truly believe no one could ever love him?" The wolf whined mournfully. "*Oui*, it pains me as well." Her hand moved to scratch down along the animal's throat. "But you and I will prove him wrong, *n'est-ce pas?*"

A delighted yip escaped the wolf, and Noèle smiled.

Chapter Eight

A LONG WALK

Not knowing where the loyalties of the people of Monpont lay, Ian decided on a cautious approach. Even with Dubois out of the picture, he did not want to risk alienating the villagers by sailing into port on a ship clearly belonging to the Durets —Dubois's sworn enemy. He glanced up at the black sails, watching his crew as they lowered them down and then dropped the anchor around an outcropping along the coast. The upside was that they lay hidden from curious eyes. The downside, however, was that they, in turn, had no view of the village.

Not only Dubois himself but also his brother had perished in the sea battle between the two families. However, as far as Antoine had shared with Ian before their departure, Dubois's parents—though elderly—were still alive, and there had been a sister once. No one quite knew what had happened to her, for she seemed to have disappeared one day. Ian could not help but wonder if perhaps Dubois had somehow felt betrayed by something she had done and...

Ian shook his head. Indeed, the man had committed countless atrocities, and there was not a doubt in Ian's mind, that Dubois would have acted against his own family if he thought himself *provoked*.

Also, Dubois had been married. What kind of a woman would

marry a man like that? Ian wondered. Perhaps one without choice? Or one unaware of his true character? Or one with a soul as black as Dubois'?

Indeed, it was advisable to act with caution.

Seagulls circled overhead, and the smell of vegetation mingled with the familiar scent of sea air. His crew expertly brought down the sails and bound them, their eyes sweeping the countryside as well. Ian could see the tension that stood upon all their faces.

"This is it?"

At the sound of Noèle's voice—oh, he ought not to have agreed to first names!—Ian tensed, his hands tightening upon the wooden railing, his gaze remaining focused out at the land before them.

"Monpont?" Noèle inquired as she came to stand beside him, her dainty hands grasping the wooden rail as well.

Beside Ian, the wolf perked up its ears, a sound of affection leaving its throat before it padded over and bumped its head against her leg.

Smiling, Noèle brushed a hand over its head and then scratched behind its ears. Then she exhaled deeply and turned her attention back toward Monpont, hidden from them by a large rock outcropping reaching far out to sea. Her smile slowly faded, and a tense silence settled over them.

Ian had all but forgotten the words she had spoken, the questions she had asked—after all, they did not truly require an answer, for she already knew. He could see it upon her face...even out of the corner of his eye.

Exhaling slowly, Ian cursed himself. Indeed, he ought never have agreed to first names! More than that, he ought never have spoken to her of his wife! He ought never have spoken to her at all! What had possessed him?

After all these years, Ian knew how to keep to himself, and he liked it that way. He liked solitude, the quiet peace that settled in one's soul when there were only strangers around. Only she was no longer a stranger, was she? Now, she *knew* things about him. Had no doubt read them upon his face. And she had been inquisitive, curious to learn more.

Aye, he had been a fool.

Again.

"What will we do now?" Noèle asked and turned to look at him.

Ian could all but feel her gaze trailing over his features, trying to see inside him. Was he merely imagining this? He wondered. Because of the way she had looked at him the other night?

Oh, there was a very good reason why Ian preferred solitude! Why he disliked close relationships with those around him! Why he never allowed more than a passing association!

He loathed these entanglements! These questions that assailed him now! This sense of uncertainty!

"Ian."

Ian blinked, the sound of his name upon her lips like a slap to his face. He cleared his throat and tightened his grip upon the railing before he dared meet her eyes. "Accompanied by a handful of sailors, I will go ashore. We shall attempt to find out more about Dubois's dealings and perhaps unearth who goes by the name *Duval*." He glanced down at the wolf sitting by their feet, its yellow eyes going back and forth between the two of them, as though it were following their conversation intently. "I'll leave the wolf here with ye. Be assured that ye'll be safe."

"I want to come!"

Ian's head snapped up.

Seeing his expression, Noèle nodded. "I want to come," she repeated a little less forcefully but with the same determination.

"I canna allow that."

Her jaw hardened, and she crossed her arms defiantly. "I'm not asking for your permission."

Ian's eyes narrowed. "'Twouldna be safe."

Noèle swallowed, and in that moment, Ian could see how terrified she was. "I have to," she whispered, blinking back tears as her fingers dug into the flesh of her arms. "I have to go. She is my daughter."

Ian stilled, for that one word triggered an armada of memories, thoughts, feelings, hopes and wishes...but also fears.

Pressing her lips into a tight line, Noèle inhaled deeply through her nose. Then she took a hesitant step toward him, her blue eyes never leaving his. "Do you have children?" she whispered, quiet enough so none of the sailors working around them would hear.

Ian remained as still as a rock, his muscles so tense that he was certain he could not have moved. Still, a look of understanding came to Noèle's features, as though she had received her answer.

"A daughter?"

Ian's eyes closed. He could not help it. He did not wish to answer her. He did not want her to know. Yet an image of Blair's face drifted into his mind, and he could not bear to have it disappear. He could not bear the longing that surged to life with full force.

Even through the rough fabric of his shirt, Ian felt the soft touch of her fingertips upon his arm, and his eyes flew open.

"Could you stay behind?" Noèle asked, tentatively retrieving her hand and folding her arm over her chest once more. "If it were her, could you stay behind?"

A long silence followed as two opposing sides warred within him... before he finally surrendered. "Verra well," Ian agreed, knowing that nothing he said would dissuade her. After all, if it had been Blair or Niall, nothing would have dissuaded him, either. It was the way of parents, was it not?

A relieved smile came to her face, and she nodded, a hint of tears glistening in the corners of her eyes. "*Merci. Merci beaucoup.*"

Ian stilled suddenly at a thought...

What if Blair needed him? Or Niall? What if they already had?

Ian closed his eyes. He would not even be aware of it! He would not know! He would not come, not go after them, not be there if they needed him! It was a chilling, crippling thought!

"Are you all right?" came Noèle's voice, and her fingertips once more touched his arm.

Light as a feather.

Fleeting.

Gone the moment Ian opened his eyes.

Noèle's blue gaze still lingered upon his, something soft and gentle there that touched Ian, that touched Ian as much as the way she had reached out to him only a moment earlier. Aye, it had been a long time since anyone—other than the Durets—had cared enough to look at him beyond a fleeting glance. Since anyone had reached out to him, offered comfort. And she had done so twice now.

Ian wished she had not, and yet a part of him wished she would do it again.

The feeling of regret warring with longing was overwhelming, and Ian felt far removed from the man he had become over the course of the past three years.

"Where is she?" Noèle asked then, completely out of the blue, her tentative words upending Ian's world.

Ian jerked back, his heart suddenly pounding in his chest. His mouth opened of its own accord, and for a moment, he feared he might answer her. Then, fortunately, common sense returned, and he cleared his throat, able to push all thoughts of his children away. "Prepare the dinghy!" he called to the sailors. "Louis, ye take over command." The burly man with the rust-colored beard nodded. "Jean, François, ye're coming with us."

All but ignoring Noèle, pretending, at least, for the moment that she was not there, Ian strode across deck and bellowed a few last instructions before they all piled into the dinghy. Jean and François went first. Then Ian coaxed the wolf in, who greatly objected to the swaying boat as it hung from the ropes, suspended in midair. After that task was accomplished, Ian reluctantly turned to Noèle, offering her his hand.

Regret shone in her blue eyes as she looked at him. "I'm sorry," she whispered as she stepped closer and then slid her hand into his. "I did not mean..." Her voice trailed off.

Ian's fingers closed around hers, her skin warm and smooth against his own. It had been so long since he had felt a gentle touch such as hers, and for a moment, he was loathe to release her. Even more so when her small hand pressed his in answer. What was happening here? Ian thought frantically before calling himself to reason once more.

Seeing Noèle seated, her arms wrapped around the wolf's neck, Ian followed and then gestured to his crew to lower the dinghy. Once set down upon the water's surface, Jean and François began rowing them toward shore. Ian wished he could have traded places with one of them, for it would have given him a purpose, something to do, to focus his thoughts.

Away from her.

Intently looking past Noèle at the land beyond, Ian let his eyes sweep over the outcropping until it lay behind them and he caught his first glimpse of Monpont. Of course, he had been here before, the night they had gone after Lady Juliet.

The night Henri had asked him to carry an unconscious woman off Dubois's ship.

Noèle.

Ian cursed under his breath as he realized that his thoughts had once again circled back to her.

Noèle flinched at his muttered words. "Is something wrong?" Her eyes widened, and she swung her head from side to side, as though trying to spy an attacker.

Jean and François lifted questioning brows.

Ian shook his head. "Nothing." He narrowed his eyes, focusing them on the coast. It went in a slight curve, the land sloping upward, rock giving way to grassland. "Over there," he called, gesturing toward a smooth stretch of pebbled beach, easily accessible from the country-side above.

After securing the small boat in an unobtrusive spot—after all, they could hardly row into Monpont in a dinghy—Ian turned to Jean and François. "Circle the long way around and approach from the South," he instructed as the two young men nodded along eagerly, faces determined. "The tavern might be a good spot to find loosened tongues." Again, the two men nodded, then turned and strode away.

"Where will *we* go?" Noèle asked beside him as they walked up the small slope to a path cutting across the meadow, the wolf occasionally running ahead before returning to their side.

"The direct route that leads into the village," Ian replied, careful not to look at her. All of a sudden, he felt rather unsteady whenever he found her looking at him. Why was that? Was it simply the memories she conjured within him? After all, looking at her made him think of her daughter, which inevitably made him think of his own two children.

For a long while, they walked in silence, the soft sound of the waves rolling onto the beach below drifting to their ears. Neither of them spoke, and yet Ian could sense that words rested on the very tip of her tongue. Why was she hesitating? Out of fear? Or to spare him? Was it possible that she knew how deeply her questions unsettled him?

Torn between ending this unbearable silence and escaping her curious questions, Ian lengthened his strides. Truth be told, he did not even realize he had done so until her panting gasps reached his ears. He looked over his shoulder and saw her red cheeks, exhaustion lingering upon her features, as her chest rose and fell with each rapid breath.

Ian cursed silently, angry with himself for putting her through this. What he said, however, held no such admission. "Ye oughta have stayed aboard."

"I'm sorry I'm slowing you down." She quickened her steps, attempting to catch up with him. Even though autumn was already beginning to turn the leaves red and orange and golden, the sun beat down mercilessly, and for a moment, Ian thought to see her sway on her feet.

Pulling to a halt, Ian turned and offered her his arm.

For a moment, Noèle looked doubtful, her eyes lingering upon his face, as though looking for clues to his intention. "*Merci*," she finally said and slipped her arm through the crook of his. Her hand came to rest upon his lower arm, the soft pressure of her fingers feeling far too intimate.

Ian knew not what to think. Only a few months ago, Madame Clément had been no more than a mere acquaintance. He had seen her face in La-Roche-sur-Mer every now and then, perhaps offered her a greeting once, but other than that they had lived in separate worlds. And now?

Now, she was Noèle, and Ian felt as though he knew her. Worse! He felt as though *she* knew *him*. Had those few honest words the other night truly connected them in such a profound way? Or was he losing his mind, imagining things that weren't there?

"You need not walk slower for my benefit," Noèle stated with a sideways glance, her breathing still elevated. "I can keep up."

Ian kept his gaze firmly fixed upon the small village up ahead. "There's no rush," he assured her despite his better judgment.

"*Oui*, there is," Noële insisted before a tentative smile graced her features. "But it is kind of you to pretend."

Ian did not want to be kind. He—

"Will you not tell me her name?"

Jarring to a halt, Ian stared down at her, his feet suddenly standing on shaking ground. Again, he felt Ian Stewart slip away and Ian MacDrummond resurface. It was an odd feeling, overwhelming and yet surreal, as though he was trapped in a dream, one moment aware of it and then completely oblivious the next.

Tears glistened in Noële's eyes as she looked up at him. "My daughter's name is—"

"Ophélie," Ian finished for her without thinking.

Noële nodded, and the ghost of a smile danced across her face. "*Oui*. And yours?"

Ian closed his eyes. "Blair," he heard himself say, unable to resist the temptation of speaking her name out loud. How long had it been? When was the last time he had done so in the presence of another? "And Niall."

"A daughter and a son?" Noële whispered, a touch of surprise in her voice, as the pressure of her hand upon his arm increased. "Where are they? What hap—?" She broke off, a sense of foreboding in her voice. "Are they...?"

Ian felt no longer capable of speech as the lock to his past sprang open and Ian MacDrummond charged forward, shoving aside the man Ian had become—or pretended to be—these past few years.

All detachment fell from him. All distance evaporated. All peace slipped through his fingers.

Pain and longing gripped him mercilessly, mingling with a deep-seated sense of guilt that he had abandoned his children. He had simply left.

What kind of a man did that make him?

That question nearly brought Ian to his knees.

And then he felt a soft hand cup his cheek. He tensed instantly, yet he did not have the strength to stop her. He simply remained still, immobile, and savored the feel of her touch, gentle and comforting, as her hand reached higher, moved to the back of his neck and...

...urged him closer.

Ian knew he ought to stop this before it went any further. He would not be able to meet her eyes as it was. Still, he had little strength left, and to his great shame, he wanted what she was offering.

As though they had known each other for years, as though they were the dearest of friends, Noèle pulled him into her arms, pushing herself onto her toes to wrap her arms around his shoulders.

And Ian let her.

He sank into her embrace, burying his face in the crook of her neck, and slung his arms around her, pulling her close.

Oh, this was a bad idea!

A dangerous idea!

But Ian did not care.

For the first time in years, he threw caution to the wind.

Chapter Nine

INTO THE LION'S DEN

For a split second, Noèle thought she was dreaming. Indeed, she had fully expected Ian to push her away, to offer some half-hearted excuse, to fly into a rage even. He was a proud man. She had always known him to be. It was something one could tell with a single glance.

For him to surrender to this moment in such a profound way meant that he was severely wounded. It was a wound not unlike her own, and Noèle felt an odd sense of comfort, knowing that she was not alone in her heartache.

Even more than that, Noèle reveled in the fact that she was the one *offering* comfort. It made her feel strong after spending weeks, months even, weakened and dependent upon others. Of course, they had always meant well, but being forced to rely on them had made Noèle feel weak even beyond her body's current lack of strength.

With a sigh, Noèle tightened her embrace, her toes almost lifting off the ground when he did the same. Like two people drowning, they clung to one another, offering what little strength they had left. She felt his warm breath against the side of her neck and wondered how this moment would change things between them.

Rather unexpectedly, Noèle realized that it felt good to be in Ian's arms. As wary as she had been of him before, considering his hard stare and taciturn and rather gruff manner, now she felt utterly safe with him. She did not feel a touch of apprehension, sensed no shadow nearby only waiting for her to drop her guard. *Non*, the last time she had felt this comfortable in a man's presence had been...

...with Étienne.

Noèle pinched her eyes shut as a wave of guilt washed over her. She knew the feeling well, for it found her every time she longed for her child.

For a child that was not Étienne's.

While Noèle's mind argued that she had done nothing wrong, that this feeling of guilt was not deserved, her heart believed otherwise. No matter how she argued with it, it would not yield.

A soft yip ripped Noèle out of her thoughts a moment before she felt the wolf brush past them, then turn and brush past them again, as though to gain their attention.

In the next instant, Noèle's feet touched upon the dirt path once more as Ian loosened his hold, setting her back down and taking a step back. His blue eyes met hers, his jaw clenched painfully, and Noèle knew that he regretted the moment they had just shared.

The comfort they had given one another.

Clearing his throat, Ian turned back down the path. "We should continue on," he all but growled, ready to stride away. Then, however, he stopped, drew in a deep breath and held out his arm to her in a half-hearted offer.

Noèle accepted, wishing he would share his sorrow with her. After all, did *he* not know everything that had happened to *her*? Was that not why they were here, in this very spot, together?

Glancing at the stoic man at her side, Noèle sighed and concentrated on placing one foot in front of the other and breathing in calmly. Of course, he was right, though! There was something more important to think of now.

Ophélie!

Upon reaching the village, Ian slowly pulled her closer against him, his other hand coming to lie protectively upon hers. She sensed his alertness in the tight muscles beneath her hand as they walked along the pier, watching cargo being unloaded and ships repaired. A few stalls were set up, selling not only fish and crabs but also a few imported goods.

Across the small harbor, Noële glimpsed Jean and François as they mingled with other sailors headed to the local tavern. It would seem she and Ian had, indeed, wasted a good bit of time upon their comparatively short walk to the village.

"What now?" Noële whispered as her eyes swept over the houses and shops, from face to face, half expecting to see Dubois among them. The thought sent a shiver down her spine!

Instantly, Ian's hand tightened upon hers and he turned to look down into her eyes. "Dunna worry! I'll not let any harm come to ye."

Noële nodded, reassured by his presence. "I know." Again, she glanced around. "What now though?"

"We'll ask where the Duboises live," Ian replied, keeping a watchful eye on her, as though worried she might faint.

Noële had to remind herself that he was not speaking of Dubois himself but of the man's family. "There," she gestured to a stall selling fresh fish. "Let's ask there."

Ian nodded in agreement. Holding her close, he strode forward, nodding to passersby now and then, the wolf following upon their heels. When Ian was about to address the woman behind the stall, Noële placed her other hand on his arm to stop him.

With a frown, Ian turned to look at her.

"Perhaps," she whispered, leaning closer, "I should ask. Your accent will immediately give you away as a stranger to these parts."

"Verra well."

Stepping forward, Noële offered the woman a smile and a compliment, asked for the biggest fish on display and then casually inquired about the residence of the Dubois family.

"Oh, it's not far," the woman replied kindly, wrapping their purchase. "It is the big house over there." She pointed over her shoulder.

Noële thanked her kindly, and they were about to turn away when the woman drew in a sharp breath, her eyes going wide as she stared at their companion.

Noèle laughed. "I know what you're thinking," she told the woman, reaching down to scratch the wolf behind his ears. "He looks like a wolf, *n'est-ce pas*? My brother gave him to us as a gift after our first year of marriage." She smiled up at Ian, who looked rather uncomfortable. "I admit my brother has an odd sense of humor." Noèle chuckled and rolled her eyes at her imaginary brother. "When we were young, he would always frighten me with horror stories about a huge beast with sharp teeth. Well, he might be huge," she brushed an affectionate hand over the wolf's head, "but he is not a beast."

The woman still looked a bit doubtful, but she tried to smile. "My brother used to tease me with frogs in my bed," she offered, clearly relieved that it had been frogs and not a wolf.

Noèle laughed, offered a kind farewell and then they were on their way a moment later.

"Well done," Ian remarked with a sideways glance at her as they strolled leisurely across the market square.

Noèle smiled up at him, and for a moment, they looked at one another, as though they did not have a care in the world, as though the shadows of their past did not exist. It was a beautiful day. The sun was shining, and a soft breeze blew in from the sea. The scent of wildflowers lingered in the air, mingling with the savory aroma of food being prepared nearby.

If only it could be the truth. If only they were part of this village, lived here with their family and friends. If only they had a place here and could be happy. If only nothing bad had ever happened to change who they were.

For a moment—one short, fleeting moment—it seemed that anything was possible. And then that moment passed, reality returned, and once more they looked at one another remembering everything that had happened, everything that had brought them to this moment in time.

Ian cleared his throat and then tugged her along. He kept his gaze focused ahead, as though not daring to even glance at her. Noèle could all but sense his discomfort and wondered what specifically had brought it on. Was it the things he had revealed to her? Or perhaps the vulnerability he had shown? Or something she could not even name?

Feeling the strain of their long walk, Noèle drew in a deep breath, willing her muscles not to falter now. Her gaze swept from side to side, touched upon picturesque little houses of various colors and styles with flowers decorating windowsills and children running in and out, laughing in a way that made Noèle's heart ache.

If only Ophélie could live like this! If only they could have had such a family, she and Étienne!

Then they stepped around a row of stalls, and a towering house with whitewashed walls and a tall fence surrounding it came into view. Noèle inhaled a sharp breath, and her feet drew to a halt. Her eyes moved up, from window to window, and she felt a shiver dance down her spine.

Ian's hand squeezed hers, and she could feel him turning concerned eyes to her. "Do ye wish to remain here?"

With her gaze still fixed upon the house, Noèle shook her head. "*Non*, I do not." Still, deep down, she was not certain if that was the truth. *Oui*, she felt compelled to join him, to go along and make inquiries. Yet the thought of entering this house made her feel dizzy, even fearful. It was illogical, but it was the truth, nonetheless.

With her hand resting on Ian's arm, Noèle managed to place one foot in front of the other. Slowly, they approached the house, then stepped through the gate. Ian signaled for the wolf to wait for them here before they walked up the few steps to the front door. It was a massive door, as though to keep those inside from escaping. Noèle did not know where this thought came from, but she could not seem to shake it. Was this a happy place? Had it been during Dubois's lifetime?

Ian's arm beneath her hand tensed before he lifted the other one to use the knocker upon the door. The sound echoed to their ears like gunshots, and Noèle flinched. Her muscles contracted almost painfully as they stood and waited, eyes fixed upon the piece of wood barring their way, as though somehow they could will it to open.

And then it did, and an elderly man appeared in its frame. His glassy eyes swept over them, and a mild frown drew down his brows. "May I help you?"

Ian kindly inclined his head to the Dubois's servant, and Noèle saw his lips part...before he suddenly paused, sealing them once more. He turned to look at her, eyes widening meaningfully.

Noèle understood, her fingers now almost digging into Ian's flesh as she lifted her chin and greeted the servant. "*Bonjour*, is the lady of the house present? There is something rather important we wish to discuss with her."

The elderly man paused thoughtfully, considering them through slightly narrowed eyes. "And what matter would that be?"

Noèle tried her best to offer him a kind and reassuring smile. "I'm afraid it is of a most sensitive nature. Something I am only allowed to divulge to the lady herself." Yet again Noèle found herself wondering how much Dubois's widow truly knew about her late husband. Would she be able to shed any light upon Ophélie's whereabouts? Or would anything Noèle and Ian had to say shock her witless?

Fortunately, the servant then stepped back, gesturing for them to step inside. He closed the door and led them onward into a lovingly furnished salon. "I shall inform Mme. Dubois of your presence, Mme....?"

"Clément," Noèle replied, then turned to smile at Ian in a way that implied a far deeper relationship than they truthfully possessed. "Our name is Clément."

After the servant had closed the door behind himself, Noèle sank down onto a settee, her knees no longer able to hold her upright. Her breath came fast, and she briefly closed her eyes.

And then Ian was suddenly beside her. "Are ye all right?" Gentle hands touched her shoulders, her face, brushing the hair back from her temples. "Ye shouldna have come."

Meeting his gaze, Noèle felt her inner turmoil wane. It was rather unexpected, and for a moment, she thought she might be imagining it. Yet there was something in the blue depth of his eyes that instantly calmed her. Noèle did not know what it was, but she clung to it, feeling her breathing even out, her heartbeat settling into a more normal rhythm.

Suddenly becoming aware of their proximity, of the way he was touching her, Ian dropped his gaze, his hands falling from her face. He rose to his feet and moved a few steps across the room toward the windows. There, he inhaled deeply, his shoulders moving up and down as he kept his back turned to her.

Noèle wondered about what to say, how to break that odd tension between them, when footsteps echoed closer. She turned toward the door a moment before it opened, revealing a tall, slender woman, perhaps ten years Noèle's senior. Her pale brown hair was braided back and then curled into a chignon at the back of her head. Her green eyes swept over Noèle and then moved to Ian, narrowing slightly as she considered them, no doubt aware that they had no connection to her. Something shrewd lay in her gaze, calculating and cautious. Still, Noèle breathed a sigh of relief to see none of the cold, heartless demeanor that had dominated Dubois's character in this woman.

"Mme. Dubois?" Noèle inquired as she rose to her feet. "I apologize for intruding upon your day so unexpectedly. However, there is something we need to discuss with you." Again, an image of Ophélie flashed through her mind, and Noèle clasped her hands together, fighting to remain in control.

The other woman stepped farther into the room, her eyes once more traveling to Ian, who watched the scene with a stoic face. "I'm afraid I do not know what you speak of nor who you are. The name Clément does not sound familiar." Her brows rose meaningfully, demanding an explanation.

Noèle licked her lips, uncertain how to begin, how to explain. "Does the name Duval mean anything to you?"

Again, Mme. Dubois's eyes narrowed, something suspicious in her gaze now. "Why do you ask? Who are you?"

Noèle felt her heart almost beat out of her chest. She knew the name! She knew *something*, at least! "I... We..." Noèle felt her fingernails dig into her own flesh as she stepped toward Mme. Dubois. "I am looking for my daughter." She swallowed, fighting to remain calm. "I was...I was told she was being taken care of by someone named Duval."

The other woman's shoulders pulled back as her chin rose haughtily. "If that is the case, then why are you here? Why would you ask me?"

Before Noèle could answer, Ian suddenly stepped forward, his eyes flashing with outrage and his hands balled into fists at his sides.

"Because 'twas yer husband who took her!" he snarled, his chest heaving with barely contained anger. "He stole Madame Clément's daughter!"

Mme. Dubois's eyes widened, shock marking her features. Noële could not tell if it was the accusation itself, Ian's obvious outrage or perhaps the revelation of his accent. Yet Noële saw quite clearly that whatever compassion or decency might have inspired her to reveal whatever she knew now no longer existed. Every chance for cooperation had now evaporated into thin air.

"Leave!" Mme. Dubois insisted in a hard voice. "Leave my house this instant!" Her right arm shot out, and she pointed at the door, stepping back, as though unable to bear their presence a moment longer. "Now!"

A touch of guilt flashed across Ian's face as he realized what his words had done. Yet he stormed toward the woman, such an enraged look upon his face that Noële felt taken aback. Never had she seen him like this before. "We shall not leave!" Ian snarled into the woman's face. "Not without answers." Glaring at her, he shook his head, his lips curling in disgust. "Do ye even know what kind of man yer husband was? Or perhaps ye even condoned his actions?" His right brow rose in angry accusation. "Ye–"

"Ian, stop!" Noële exclaimed, shooting forward. She grasped his arm and tried to pull him back, but he would not budge. Indeed, she did not possess the strength to move him, to pull him away from their only lead. And so instead, Noële stepped in between the two of them, her hands grasping his face.

Ian flinched, as though she had struck him. His eyes dropped to hers, and he stilled, as though he had stopped breathing.

"I need you to give us a moment alone," Noële implored him, her hands still cupping his cheeks, feeling the slight stubble against her skin. "I need you to leave and wait for me outside."

For a moment, he did not say a word. He did not react in any way. Then, he slowly shook his head. "I canna." His gaze darted past her to Mme. Dubois. "It wouldna be safe. I canna–"

"But I insist!" Noële said, steeling her voice. "Leave now!"

Ian's eyes narrowed, and Noèle saw a touch of betrayal upon his face. Something painful. Something he had felt before.

Noèle instantly felt her heart go out to him, and yet she knew she could not relent. "This is about Ophélie," she whispered, imploring him to understand. "This is about my daughter. Do not make me say it again!"

Before her eyes, Ian deflated. All anger vanished, replaced by a mixture of the guilt and regret she had seen in his eyes before. He bowed his head, and then nodded. "Verra well. I shall be right outside." He took a step back, and slowly, her hands slid from his face. "I shall not be far." Then he stepped around her, and after glaring at Mme. Dubois yet again, slipped from the room.

Noèle felt tears prick her eyes, and she fought to discourage them before she turned to face Mme. Dubois. "I apologize–"

Holding up a hand, Madame Dubois shook her head. "You need to leave," she insisted, looking over her shoulder at the door Ian had left open upon his retreat. "You cannot be here." Another glance swept out the door, and she dropped her voice. "I cannot help you...for I know nothing of the name Duval. It is utterly unfamiliar to me." She pulled her shoulders back and lifted her chin. "I'm afraid you're wasting your time."

Despite Mme. Dubois's dismissive words and cold demeanor, Noèle thought to see compassion in her green eyes.

But also...fear?

Noèle could not suppress the shiver that slowly crawled down her back. She felt as though something was lying in wait for her, watching her approach. Something she knew nothing about. Every instinct told Noèle to follow Ian and leave this house, and yet...she could not.

Ophélie.

Stepping toward Mme. Dubois, Noèle looked at her with pleading eyes. "Please, I have not seen my daughter in months." Tears welled up in her eyes, and her voice broke. "I do not know where she is, and I'm afraid I shall never see her again. Please, if you know anything..." Tears rolled down her cheeks. "Please, help me."

Rather unexpectedly, Mme. Dubois surged forward, grasping Noèle's hands. "You must leave!" she whispered, urgency in her voice.

Again, she glanced over her shoulder, then quickly urged Noèle toward the door. "Please, heed my words. Leave now...before it is too late." Open warning now lay in the woman's eyes, and Noèle all but felt the ground drop out from under her.

"Why?" It was the only word she managed to utter, staring at Mme. Dubois as something ice-cold slithered down her back.

In the next instant, an all too familiar voice reached her ears. "Madame Clément, how good of you to grace us with your presence."

Noèle froze, her eyes widening as she stared straight ahead at Mme. Dubois. The other woman's eyes, in turn, closed in resignation, and she bowed her head, her hands falling from Noèle's. Then she stepped to the side, out of Noèle's line of view, revealing none other than her late husband.

Dubois.

Alive after all.

Chapter Ten

RISEN FROM THE DEAD

Rubbing his hands over his face, Ian sank down onto the steps
leading up to the Dubois's front door. He wanted to kick
himself for losing control like that. How had that happened?
Reason had completely fled his mind, and he had acted upon the
outrage boiling in his veins. He had quite possibly ruined everything.
What if Noële could not convince Mme. Dubois to assist them? What
would they do then?

Ian felt something furry poke the side of his head and looked up,
his eyes meeting the wolf's. The creature looked at him, as though it
understood the turmoil within him, as though it wanted to offer
comfort.

Reaching out a hand, Ian scratched the wolf behind its ears and
down its neck. He looked into its yellow eyes and felt himself breathe
more easily. Aye, the creature did care for him, did it not?

Somehow, Ian had always known that; and yet he had never quite
allowed that thought, allowed himself to believe that another being
could truly care for him.

A fleeting smile passed over his features. Indeed, Noële had seen it
right away, had she not?

Ian groaned. And now he had ruined everything! "What am I to do?" he asked the wolf, wishing it could advise him, wishing anyone could.

The animal ducked its head and slipped it under Ian's arm, snuggling closer, a soft whine emanating from its throat. Indeed, it could sense Ian's distress. Perhaps it even understood the importance of this moment. "Thank ye for everything," Ian murmured to the wolf. "Thank ye for being such a loyal friend these past few years. I–"

All of a sudden, the wolf tensed. Its muscles became rigid, and for a second, it simply froze, as though time had stopped. Then its head snapped up, eyes and ears turned toward the front door, and a low growl ripped from its throat.

Ian felt his breath lodge in his own. Aye, he had seen this expression upon the wolf's features before, this reaction. Danger lurked nearby!

Instantly, Ian shot to his feet. His hand went to the dagger on his belt as his eyes swept over his surroundings. Yet he spied nothing but neighbors going about their day, children laughing and playing. He saw nothing threatening...

...and then the wolf growled again.

"Noèle." Her name left his lips in a whisper. To Ian, though, it felt like a scream. He shot up the few steps to the front door, and he reached for the door handle without thinking. But it was locked! Why was it locked? His fists banged on the wood as he bellowed orders to anyone who might hear to open the door and allow him in.

Unfortunately, nothing happened. No one came. The door remained closed. His fists had no effect.

Gritting his teeth, Ian willed his mind to focus. Panic served no one. Rash actions served no one. He needed to focus his mind and consider this moment and its implications from all perspectives. What could he do?

Slowly, he took a few steps back from the door, his eyes sweeping to his right and left along the front of the house, taking in the bushes and flowers adorning the garden. A narrow path led through the greenery and around the corner of the house to the back.

Before Ian had even formed another conscious thought, he had already reached the corner of the house. Long strides carried him onward, the wolf as always faithfully by his side. It, too, moved swiftly, alert to its surroundings, that sense of imminent danger still visible in the way it held itself.

Ian turned toward the corner of the house that harbored the salon where Noèle and Mme. Dubois were at present. Faster and faster, his legs carried him forward, past window after window. Ian tried to glance inside but saw nothing. What had happened? Was Noèle truly in danger? How?

The garden toward the back of the house was expansive and lush, the furniture on the terrace set up, as though visitors were expected sometime soon.

Crouched low, Ian moved closer, gesturing to the wolf to stay back and not rush ahead. They could not know what was going on, and he was determined not to act rashly once again. With his gaze fixed upon the large windows to the salon, Ian snuck closer and closer. Dimly, he heard the sound of voices.

Noèle.

But who was she speaking to? Ian wondered. The voice did not sound like Mme. Dubois's. In fact, it did not sound like the voice of a woman at all. Had someone else entered the room? Was it the old servant?

Creeping closer, Ian saw that one of the windows on the far side of the salon had been left ajar. It would be a way in; yet was there any need? Was he simply overreacting?

Slowly lifting his head, Ian peeked over the rim of the windowsill. He saw the familiar outline of the salon, spotted furniture he had seen, before his eyes fell upon Noèle.

Instantly, Ian froze.

Aye, he knew nothing of what had happened, of what was going on at present; however, he knew without the shadow of a doubt that something was very wrong. Noèle's face was as white as a sheet, her eyes wide and fearful as he had never seen them before. She held her hands clutched to her chest, her posture signaling the wish to flee. "How?" Noèle gasped, the sound so faint that Ian could barely make it out. "How is this possible?" Shaking her head, she backed away.

Suddenly, Mme. Dubois stepped forward, in front of Noèle, her back to her. Her face, too, had lost all color, the pulse in her neck racing. She lifted her hands, as though in appeasement, and her lips parted before she spoke with a calm Ian knew she did not feel. "Perhaps it would be best if she simply left," Mme. Dubois suggested to someone Ian could not see, someone on the other side of the room. "There is no reason for her to be here. I was about to ask her to leave when—"

"Leave us! Now!"

Although Ian had only ever heard his voice upon a few rare occasions, the moment it drifted to his ears he knew it to be Dubois's. He knew it with every fiber of his being, and his heart slammed hard against his rib cage, as though wishing to break free. How was this possible? Was he hallucinating? The man was dead...wasn't he?

No, the look upon Noèle's face told him loud and clear that whatever was happening was real.

Beside Ian, the wolf growled, a low sound deep in its throat. It, too, lifted its head, peeking in through the window, the need to act only too visible in its trembling body.

Ian placed a calming hand upon its back, uncertain about what to do. Where was Dubois? How far away was he?

"Bastien, please, be reasonable," Mme. Dubois pleaded, retreating a step closer toward Noèle. Her hands began to tremble as she backed away from her husband.

One step, and then another...

...and then Ian saw Dubois.

Advancing upon the two women, the man looked disgustingly pleased with himself. His eyes were as cold as Ian remembered them, and that twisted snarl upon his face betrayed the lack of a heart. Had he truly never possessed one? Dressed in rather simple clothing, Dubois still carried himself as a king might, no doubt believing himself the superior of others, believing he had every right to do as he pleased with no regard for others. "Sandrine, leave us!" Dubois snarled at his wife. His gaze, however, remained fixed upon Noèle. "And not a word to anyone!"

Mme. Dubois looked over her shoulder at Noèle, then back at her husband. "Please, she will leave and not say—"

"Out!" Dubois bellowed in a tone so harsh and demeaning that Ian flinched. Truly, this man possessed no soul, no mercy, no decency. Never in his life had Ian met such a creature!

Beside Ian, the wolf crouched low, its paws trembling, and another low growl rumbled in its throat.

Taking in the scene, Ian knew that no matter how fast he moved, Dubois would reach Noèle before him. He inhaled a deep breath, yet again contemplating what to do. His gaze moved to his companion, and seeing the almost pleading look in the wolf's eyes...

...Ian nodded.

In the blink of an eye, the wolf shot forward.

Chapter Eleven

THE DEVIL INCARNATE

Noèle felt close to fainting. Every fiber of her being wanted to surrender, wanted to lie down and accept whatever Fate would bestow upon her.

Oui, upon first seeing Dubois, Noèle had felt a surge of energy shoot through her, strengthening her muscles and urging her to run.

To flee.

However, with that option outside of her grasp, Noèle's body had remembered that it was nowhere near strong enough to do as she wished. The surge of energy had quickly dissipated, bit by bit, with each moment that passed in Dubois's presence. She had remembered how insignificant, how vulnerable, how defeated Noèle had always felt when she was near him. A single look into his eyes had always been enough to make her knees tremble, to send fear through her, to make her wish she could simply lie down and die. He had that effect on people.

On her.

For a moment, Noèle was grateful for Mme. Dubois's efforts to interfere. *Oui*, the woman possessed a kind heart, had somehow held on to it, trapped in a marriage to a monster. Yet at the same time,

Noèle knew that nothing Mme. Dubois said or did would make any difference. Dubois would do as he pleased.

It had always been thus.

And then, something unexpected happened.

Noèle could not say what it was that first drew her attention. Was it perhaps the sound of the window banging open? Or the startled gasp torn from Mme. Dubois's lips? Perhaps the flash of movement Noèle noticed out of the corner of her eye?

Yet when her eyes fell on the wolf, snarling, his hackles raised, as he landed inside the salon, Noèle could have wept with joy. Instantly, the animal moved to her side, his eyes fixed upon Dubois, his body tense, ready to fight.

Shocked by the sight, Mme. Dubois spun around, a scream ripping from her throat, and she stumbled backwards. Unfortunately, her steps carried her in the wrong direction and into her husband's arms.

Instantly, Dubois grasped her, pulled her in front of him like a shield, a blade gleaming in his other hand as he stared at the wolf.

And then Ian was there.

Crouched upon the windowsill, he surveyed the scene, his eyes dark and thunderous as he glared at Dubois. Yet he did not rush forward. He moved slowly, something calculated and deliberate in every flex of muscle as he lowered himself to the ground.

Silence settled over the room as the two men eyed one another. Noèle could hear the blood rushing in her ears as she reached out to touch the wolf's head, reassured by the feel of his soft fur. As though in answer, the animal moved closer, brushing against her leg, another threatening growl rising from his throat.

"Where is the child?" Ian demanded in a voice as cold as ice, his eyes fixed upon Dubois as he slowly unsheathed his own blade.

Having recovered from his initial shock, Dubois laughed. It was a maniacal sound, one that reverberated in Noèle's bones and made her skin crawl. "Is this why you're here?" He looked from Ian to her. "You want the girl?"

"Of course," Noèle heard herself gasp, wondering how Dubois could not know the bond that connected mother and child. Had he truly never known it? Not even as a boy?

Dubois scoffed, and his hand upon his wife's arm tightened, making her yelp. "And I see you've enlisted the help of the Durets." He all but spat their name as he glared at Ian. "Where are Henri and Antoine?" He looked from her to Ian and then out the windows. "Are they outside? Waiting for a signal?" Another maniacal laugh left his lips.

Noële shuddered, completely overwhelmed as memories of past encounters with Dubois resurfaced. Fortunately, Ian was here. As incensed as he had seemed earlier, now he possessed a calm Noële envied. With a steady voice, he took control of the situation, meeting Dubois's hateful glare with a matching one of his own. "Yer only chance out of here alive is for ye to reveal the girl's location," he stated matter-of-factly as he moved closer to Noële's position. "Ye know as well as I do that ye will never live as a free man in France ever again. Ye betrayed yer country, yer people." A vicious smile drew up the corners of Ian's mouth. "Ye're wanted for treason. Surely, ye know that."

Dubois's teeth ground together, and his eyes narrowed into furious slits. "I'll make you all pay for what you did!" he hissed, and his knife pressed deeper into his wife's side, making her yelp. "You accuse me of treason when it was you who collaborated with the English, who—"

"I dunna care for what ye have to say," Ian interrupted, shrugging his shoulders in dismissal. "Ye may twist the truth into something that suits ye, but it willna change that ye're out of options." He took a step toward Dubois. "Ye're wanted for treason. Yer allies are growing thin." His brows rose questioningly. "I doubt anyone outside this household even knows that ye're here. Is that not so? Ye know they would turn ye in."

Dubois's face turned a dark shade of red. Anger rose like steam out of his ears, and Noële could see that more than anything he loathed being at another's mercy. Yet he had never possessed any scruples when he had been the one in control. "You do not know me!" he snarled. "I always survive!" He laughed, pride illuminating his face. "I'm a man who prepares for every eventuality. Otherwise, I would not be here now." His shoulders drew back as he spoke, his words reminding him of the power he held. "Did you not think me dead?" Triumph now showed upon his features.

Noële could not suppress the sob that rose in her throat. "Please, where is my daughter? We want nothing else from you. Tell me where she is and—"

"Ha!" Dubois exclaimed as he moved backward, closer to the door, pulling his wife along. "Do you truly think, madame, I would give up this prize?" His eyes gleamed with madness as he laughed. "The Durets will never forgive themselves if something happens to her!" His jaw hardened. "And they don't deserve to after what they've done! After what they've taken from me!"

"But she is innocent!" Noële called as her knees buckled and she sank to the floor, tears streaming from her eyes. "Please, tell us where she is!"

Moving in front of her, Ian faced Dubois. "What good will holding on to her do if ye're arrested, awaiting execution?" He took a threatening step closer, leisurely twirling his own blade in his hand. "Would ye not rather survive and make a life for yerself elsewhere?" Ian's brows rose in question as he swept his hand outward, the tip of his blade gleaming in the soft light filtering in through the windows. "Ye willna leave here without my permission, and I willna grant it unless ye give up the girl."

Noële held her breath at Ian's bluff. *Oui*, the *Chevalier Noir* was nearby, but still too far away to make a difference. Even though Jean and François were in the village, they could not be certain where the two sailors were at this very moment. Had they already returned to the dinghy?

Again, that evil laugh fell from Dubois's lips, a sound that would haunt Noële until the end of her days. "You do not understand!" he snapped. "I do not care what happens to me! All I care about is paying back those that wronged me!" He glared at Noële, his lips curled in disgust, as though *she* had been the one to wrong *him*. "You will never see her again! Never!" Then he spun his wife around in his arms, pressed a kiss to her lips and stabbed the knife into her belly.

Noële screamed as Ian jumped forward, his own blade drawn in attack. However, Dubois pushed his wife's limp body at him, and Ian caught her on instinct, preventing her from hitting the hard floor.

When they looked up, Dubois was gone.

Chapter Twelve

LOSS

Gently, Ian eased Mme. Dubois to the floor. Her face was twisted in pain and shock, and her hands clawed at his arms, her fingers digging into his flesh. Her body felt tense, and yet Ian could already sense her strength waning.

As he settled her on the floor, her eyes closed and then opened in a way that whispered of darkness encroaching. Blood seeped from the wound in her belly, running down onto the floor boards and pooling around her. Ian quickly loosened the bandanna tied around his neck and pressed it to the wound; yet he knew even then that there was no hope. A deep wound to the belly was always tricky business, and with no one around to treat it immediately, Mme. Dubois's chances were slim to none.

"Oh, *mon dieu!*" Noële exclaimed as she fell to her knees beside them. Her eyes were wide with shock as they flew from Mme. Dubois's face to the bleeding wound in her belly. "What do we do?" She looked up, turning pleading eyes to Ian. "What do we do?"

Ian sighed and then almost imperceptibly shook his head.

Noële's face fell as she understood his meaning.

"Madame Clément," came Mme. Dubois's weak voice, interspersed with panting gasps. Her eyes still closed and then opened, as though it took a lot of strength for her to remain conscious.

Noèle grasped the woman's hands, holding them tightly within her own. "Do not worry," she tried to assure her in a trembling voice. "We shall see to you. All will be well."

Ian felt the bandanna beneath his hands soaking through with the woman's blood, her skin already frighteningly pale.

Mme. Dubois tried to swallow, her throat working hard to accomplish the task. "North," she whispered in a barely audible voice. "Go north." Again, her eyes closed.

Noèle leaned closer, her eyes slightly squinted as she tried to understand the words. Ian heard no more than a faint echo of them, something familiar though. The name of a town perhaps an hour land inward from a harbor the Durets sometimes frequented. Everything else was too faint for him to make out; yet he could see the look upon Noèle's face change.

All of a sudden, there was hope there.

And gratitude.

And then stillness.

As Mme. Dubois breathed her last, Noèle held her hands, held them tightly, whispering words of comfort, ensuring that the woman's last moments were filled with something other than disregard, apathy and fear. Ian could not imagine what her life must have been like, married to a man like Dubois. Was there perhaps even a part of her that felt relief that this life had come to an end?

Ian watched Noèle close her eyes, tears running down her cheeks, as she bowed her head. "*Merci*," she whispered to the woman's spirit. "*Merci beaucoup*."

Stepping back, Ian wiped his bloodstained hands on his breeches, relieved that the dark fabric all but hid the stains. Then he gently touched Noèle's shoulder. "We need to leave," he murmured softly, knowing that they had to hurry. If Mme. Dubois had truly informed Noèle of her daughter's whereabouts, there was no time to lose. After all, Dubois had fled. But where to? Indeed, the man seemed to care very little for his own family nor his life, his thoughts dominated by triumph and revenge. Was he at this very moment going after the girl?

Heaving a deep sigh, Noèle nodded, then gently folded the woman's hands on her belly. Swaying slightly, she rose to her feet, her eyes still filled with tears as she looked up at Ian. "Part of me cannot believe he truly did this," she sobbed quietly. "She was his wife." Disbelief shone in her eyes as she stared at Ian, slowly shaking her head. "His wife."

For a moment, they simply looked at one another before Noèle suddenly reached out her hands toward him, as though wishing...to embrace him?

Ian all but flinched, and she immediately withdrew her hands, a slight shudder going through her. "I'm sorry." She bowed her head, then turned away when her eyes fell upon Mme. Dubois's body. Her teeth dug into her lower lip as she almost frantically looked around for something on which to focus her thoughts.

Without thinking, Ian stepped forward and drew her into his arms. To his surprise, it felt completely natural, the way her head settled against his shoulder and her arms slunk around his middle. "Did she tell you where to find Ophélie?" Ian whispered against her temple, feeling her soft breath against the side of his neck.

"*Oui*," Noèle whispered, and he felt her arms tighten around him. A part of him wondered if she was pressing her eyes shut against the memory of Mme. Dubois's death. He could easily imagine it to be so.

Indeed, Noèle had been through a lot in her life. She had faced great sadness and tragedy, fear and terror. She had known her fair share of pain...and more, and she still remained standing. Ian felt a deep sense of pride swell in his chest at the thought. Yet at the same time, he knew her to be a sweet and gentle woman, kindhearted and compassionate, someone who suffered with another, even a stranger.

"We needa go," Ian said once more, hardening his voice to convey urgency. He grasped her shoulders and held her at arm's length, his eyes seeking hers. "We needa return to the *Chevalier Noir* now." However, he omitted the second half of that sentence: *so Dubois willna reach Ophélie first.*

Blinking back tears, Noèle nodded. Then her gaze reluctantly dropped and moved back to Mme. Dubois. "What about her? Can we simply leave her here like this?"

Ian nodded, his gaze sweeping over the salon and out the door into the hall. He could make out no sounds, no footsteps or voices. Yet he was certain that servants lingered within the house. In all likelihood, they were hiding, afraid of what might happen to them should they get in Dubois's way. Yet once they knew that not only Dubois but also the strangers who had arrived today had left, they would return and see to Mme. Dubois. No doubt, throughout her life, she had been kind to them.

With his hands upon Noèle's shoulders, Ian steered her to the door. He almost stepped on her heels when she suddenly paused and turned to look back at the salon. "Where's the wolf?" she asked, her eyes flying over their surroundings.

Ian blinked, realizing the animal was nowhere around. "I dunna know," he replied, unwilling to reveal how puzzled he felt by the creature's unusual behavior. "Perhaps...it's waiting for us outside...or it has already returned to the dinghy."

Doubt rested to Noèle's eyes. "Would he truly leave without us?" She shook her head. "I do not believe he would."

Ian tried to smile at her. "He wasna injured," he replied, dimly aware that he had switched from thinking of the wolf as *it* to *he*. "He is well. Perhaps something caught his attention. Whatever it was, we canna wait here."

Sadness lingered upon her face at the thought of leaving the wolf behind, and Ian realized that his own heart felt heavy as well. The beast had become a loyal companion, and the thought that he would now just abandon him pained Ian in a way he would never have expected. Still, there was nothing to be done. They simply could not wait here for the wolf's return.

With his arm still wrapped around her shoulders, Ian steered Noèle back the way they had come. They kept to the sides, avoiding the small crowds that were gathering in the marketplace. Out of the corner of his eye, Ian glimpsed the woman who had pointed them toward the Dubois's mansion. Fortunately, her attention was focused on a young woman perusing her wares.

Soon, the harbor lay behind them and they found themselves back on the dirt path leading away from the village and toward the place where they had left the dinghy. Yet with each step, Noèle seemed to grow smaller, her shoulders sagging and her steps slowing. Yet, her lips pressed together, determined to continue on. Nevertheless, exhaustion stood upon her features.

Ian stopped and grasped her arm, pulling her to a halt. Her gaze was distant, and it took a moment for her to meet his eyes. "Are you all right?" he asked, searching her face, concerned with the resigned look in her eyes.

Noèle's lips parted, and yet no sound came out. Her eyes held his, something almost pleading in them, mingling with confusion and pain. And then they closed, and it took a moment for them to open once more.

Gritting his teeth, Ian made a choice.

Without asking permission, without saying anything, he simply swept her into his arms, held her tightly against his chest and then strode onward. She felt as light as a feather, her delicate hands coming to rest against his chest as she once more settled her head upon his shoulder. A deep sigh left her lips, and he felt her body relax, her muscles giving in, no longer determined to appear strong, to continue onward. She was simply too exhausted, and...

...and a distant, generally suppressed part of Ian's mind thought—hoped—that she simply felt safe in his arms.

When the dinghy finally came in sight, Ian was relieved to see Jean and François already there. Concern narrowed their eyes when they saw Noèle in his arms, but they said not a word. Simply readied the dinghy.

The wolf was nowhere to be seen.

This time, as Jean and François rowed them back to the *Chevalier Noir*, Ian continued to hold Noèle in his arms. He feared that should he release her, she would simply fall over, unable to hold herself upright, all the tension in her body gone.

And then they were back on board the *Chevalier Noir*.

Informing Louis of their destination, Ian quickly related all that had happened in a few brisk words. "Send word to Antoine. There's no time to lose," he told his first mate with an imploring look. "See to everything and alert me the second land is in sight."

With a grim look upon his face, Louis nodded. "Aye, Captain." Then he turned to the crew and bellowed orders, sending them rushing to their posts. The sails were hoisted and the anchor pulled up as Ian guided Noèle below deck to the captain's quarters.

There, Ian quickly washed the remaining blood stains off his hands before turning back to her. She stood facing the back windows with her back to him, her eyes looking at the sea as they were slowly making way. The sky remained blue, and the sun shone brilliantly, glittering like diamonds upon the water's surface.

"Ye should rest," Ian said carefully, feeling unease creep up his spine, for he knew not what to say. He wished he could put her at ease but knew it would be a futile attempt. How could a mother ever be at ease with her child in danger? Was there anything he could possibly say to ease her mind?

"He will kill her, will he not?" Noèle suddenly whispered, her voice so quiet and fleeting that it took Ian a moment to understand what she had said.

He swallowed hard. "No," he replied with vehemence. "No, he willna."

Slowly, Noèle turned to look at him, her eyes filled with tears, and such anguish upon her face that it almost brought Ian to his knees. "You cannot know that," she whispered as tears ran down her face. "You only hope it to be true. But–"

Ian took an abrupt step toward her. "Ye heard what he said. He wants revenge for imagined wrongs done to him."

Noèle's vision blurred, and she nodded her head up and down. "Precisely."

Ian reached out and took her hands in his. They were so small and soft and trembling so fiercely. "He willna kill her. He will keep her from ye, from the Durets, delighted by the thought that ye will spend the rest of yer lives searching for her. That is what he wants."

An anguished sound escaped Noèle's lips, and she almost sagged into his arms. "I shall never see her again," she wept as her hands clutched his. "I shall never see her again."

Ian cursed himself. He had been so focused on assuring her that her daughter's life was not in danger, that he had failed to realize what his words would mean to her. "Aye, ye will." He grasped her chin, gently tilting her head upward until her eyes met his. "Ye will."

She shook her head. "You cannot kn—"

"Aye, I do know, for I willna rest," he vowed, his gaze holding hers imploringly, "until she's back in yer arms. Ye have my word on that, lass. I swear. I will do whatever necessary to return her to ye."

A shuddering breath left Noèle's lips, her blue eyes fixed upon his, disbelief shining in their depths. "Why could she never love you?" she whispered breathlessly, then she reached out a hand to cup his face. "You're so easy to love."

If the Kraken had risen from the depth of the sea in that moment and devoured the *Chevalier Noir* whole, Ian would have been less astonished!

For the second time that day, he acted against his better judgment.

Dipping his head, Ian kissed her.

Chapter Thirteen

IN THE ARMS OF ANOTHER

N oèle had never meant to speak those words. They had simply come. Without thought. Without motive. They were no more than a simple expression of what she felt. Of what she knew to be true.

He was easy to love because...

...because...

All thoughts fled Noèle's mind when Ian suddenly lowered his head and kissed her.

It felt like a lightning strike, surging with awareness, while at the same time, she felt wrapped in a comforting cocoon, safe and treasured. And although her body had become all but unaccustomed to this wave of sensation that swept through her, Noèle felt neither guilt nor revulsion at Ian's touch. Of course, an image of Étienne flashed through her mind in that moment! How could it not? Yet he was smiling at her, relieved to see her safe and cared for.

Surprised, Noèle felt no inclination to stop Ian, to break their kiss. For a moment, she expected herself to, fearing the memories Dubois had forced on her. Yet, they did not resurface, did not taint this moment. She felt safe with Ian. *Oui*, it felt wonderful to be held like this again, to be in someone's arms. Someone she trusted and cared for. Someone who knew her. Someone she could count on.

Someone like Ian.

All of a sudden, Ian stilled, then he stepped back, his expression hard. "I'm sorry. I shouldna have—"

"I'm not," Noèle replied without hesitation, without doubt. Her arms rose and snaked around his neck, pulling her back into his arms. Her eyes held his, and she saw surprise and disbelief spark there. "I'm not." Then she closed her eyes and returned his kiss.

Ian's resistance melted quickly, and his arms wrapped around her once more, holding her gently as they both sank into this kiss.

This moment.

Dimly, Noèle felt the ship make way, heard shouts and the sound of footsteps from above deck. They were on their way...toward an uncertain future, and for one short moment, she did not want to think about it.

For one moment, Noèle wanted to forget everything that had happened. All the pain and sorrow. All the heartache and loss. She wanted to forget everything looming upon the horizon and only live in the moment.

In this beautiful moment.

Ian's gentle touch surprised Noèle, for he seemed to cradle her in his arms, as though he feared she might break. He had always seemed so hard, his rough hands strong and unyielding and made of steel. He never smiled, his features rigid, stone-like, like a marble column without a heart. But he was not a man like Dubois!

Belatedly, Noèle realized that, at first, she had feared to discover that Ian was a man without compassion, without feeling. A man like Dubois. Only the hardness in Ian's gaze had come from a different source. Oh, he did possess a heart! One that had been bruised and broken and now feared to be hurt yet again...as hers did as well.

And he had smiled, had he not?

He had smiled at her.

It had not been the kind of smile that lit up the world, but rather the ghost of one; however, from a man like Ian, it meant everything.

Tenderness lingered in every touch as he held her, kissed her; and yet Noèle sensed in Ian an almost desperate need to feel something. *Oui*, he was cautious, afraid to allow this moment to mean more than a short reprieve from a life that had never treated him kindly. Only he, too, wished to be close to another soul again. It had been too long. For the both of them. They had lived too long on their own, separate from all those around them, suffering in silence, pretending the pain was not there.

But it was.

Loneliness.

Oui, Noèle had felt lonely these past two years, unable to confide in another, or receive the comfort of a simple embrace or a kind word. People had tried, certainly! The Durets had tried. But they had not known the truth, and she had been unable to speak the words.

Ian, though, knew. He knew what it meant to be alone. To sense that wall between himself and those around him, separating them even though they stood so close.

And here, now, in this moment, Noèle and Ian spoke to one another without words. They saw one another for who they truly were. They saw each other's past, all that had made them the people they were today.

Almost dazed, Ian gazed down at her, clearly overwhelmed that she had reached out to him. Noèle could see that a part of him still believed this to be some kind of mirage. *Oui*, his marriage had made him doubt his own worth. He now believed himself unworthy of love, thinking of himself as deficient.

Sighing, Noèle wondered what kind of man Ian had once been, what kind of man he could have been. Somehow, she thought he had been someone naturally cheerful once. Someone who spoke with ease. Someone who held nothing back. Someone who always saw the best in people. Could he be that man again? Would he ever again smile a smile that lit up the world?

Gently, Ian skimmed a finger down her temple, tracing a scar from the fire. It usually lay concealed under a curl of her hair, but now Noèle had no desire to hide it.

Not from him.

Tears ran freely down her cheeks, and Noèle did not feel the slightest inclination to bow her head or avert her gaze. Instead, she looked up into his eyes, knowing that he understood, for his own eyes shimmered with tears as well. His heart beat strong beneath her hand, and the look upon his face made her reach for him once more.

Their kiss felt wonderful, soothing and healing in a way nothing else ever had before.

"Ye have my word," Ian whispered against her lips. "I shall return her to ye." He bowed his head, but he did not release her, and Noèle realized that he believed he needed to earn her affection. Did he truly think the only reason she was in his arms right now was the vow he had made?

Of course, she wanted her daughter back! She longed for her child more than anything in the world. Yet Ian's promise to retrieve Ophélie was not the reason why her heart beat for him. It beat for him because of his kindness, his compassion, because of who he was, because of the part of him that had made him give her that promise.

Somehow, she would have to find a way to prove to him that her words had been the truth. That he *was* easy to love. That she...in fact... had come to...care...for him.

Deeply.

Resting her head against his shoulder, Noèle clung to him, her emotions suddenly in an upheaval. Had she truly come to care for him in such a profound way? Within a day? Or a matter of days, perhaps? When had it happened?

"I swear it," Ian whispered, wrapping his arms tightly around her, the tips of his fingers brushing a curl behind her ear.

Noèle closed her eyes, for even though the odds were against them, she believed him...and her heart felt lighter. Sinking into his arms, she clung to him, savoring the moment, unwilling to release it just yet.

It had been too long.

Chapter Fourteen

WHAT IT IS TO LOVE

S eated upon the cot in the captain's quarters, his back against the wall, Ian gazed down at the sleeping woman in his arms. Her head lay on his chest, her left hand linked with his. Gently, he continued to run his fingers through her hair, detecting fading scars upon her temple and down the line of her neck. The sight made him angry, and his body tensed with the need to move, to exact revenge, to kill Dubois for all he had done to her.

Exhaustion had closed Noèle's eyes, her body still too weak to undertake such a taxing journey. Not to mention, the emotional turmoil she had been through. Anyone would have crumbled under the weight, and yet she refused to surrender.

The thought of her determination made Ian smile. Aye, she was breathtaking—fierce and yet gentle.

And kind.

And...

He closed his eyes as the memory of their embrace resurfaced. He had kissed her, the feel of her lips upon his forever imprinted upon his mind. Had she truly not minded? Ian wondered, anguish twisting his heart.

Maggie.

An image of his wife rose in his mind, her fiery-red hair curled around her face, her green eyes lively and compelling.

So utterly compelling.

Ian had loved her from the first. How could he have not? She had been like a siren to him, and he had lost his heart to her.

He had lost his mind as well.

Otherwise, he might have acted with more caution and guarded his heart. After all, he had known that she loved another. That her heart had been broken when that *Englishman* had jilted her. That it would be unwise to ask for her hand.

Oh, he had been young and naive.

And he had paid for it.

They all had.

Aye, their kisses had never quite felt like...

Ian swallowed, and his gaze once more strayed to the sleeping woman in his arms. Kissing Noële had felt different. In that moment, he had almost believed that her embrace had been fueled by more than gratitude.

Gritting his teeth, Ian suppressed a groan. Was he making the same mistake all over again?

It would seem so. After all, Noële's heart belonged to Étienne and always would. Love did not die, did it? No, it lived on, whether it was returned or not did not matter.

A part of Ian still longed for his wife. Longed to see her smile at him, her green eyes lit up with joy and love.

And yet...

He paused, examining the feeling thudding within his chest. Somehow, it suddenly felt different. Not as all-consuming as before. Not as crippling.

For years, Ian had done all he could to win his wife's heart. Then, when he had finally realized that he was fighting a losing battle, he had done his utmost to rid himself of these unrequited emotions.

These efforts, however, had been equally ineffective.

These past three years, Ian had still loved her, longed for her whenever his wayward thoughts had strayed in the direction of home. Only now...

Frowning, Ian traced the curve of Noèle's closed eye, the soft sweep of her lips and the graceful line of her neck, and suddenly something stirred inside his chest, like a tug or a flutter.

It was utterly unexpected, and it stole the air from Ian's lungs. Oh, no! He *was* making the same mistake all over again, wasn't he? He was losing his heart to a woman who would never return his affections.

Despite pressing his lips into a tight line, Ian could not hold back the anguished groan that managed to slip through. Promptly, Noèle's eyelids began to flutter.

Ian held his breath as he watched her.

A soft yawn opened her mouth, and she breathed in deeply before blinking her eyes open, her nose slightly crinkled against the bright sunlight shining in through the window. And then her eyes met his, and she bolted upright. "Oh!" Her hand slipped from his, and a faint rosy tinge graced her cheeks as she looked down at the spot where she had just lain.

Ian cleared his throat and sat up. "Are ye all right?"

For a moment, Noèle hesitated, a somewhat distant, thoughtful look upon her face, before she lifted her eyes to his. "*Oui.*" A shy smile teased the corners of her lips, and yet Ian saw no regret in her eyes.

A small mercy!

Rising to his feet, Ian moved across the cabin, then seated himself in one of the chairs. "May I ask," he began, "what else did Mme. Dubois tell ye?"

The soft glow upon Noèle's face vanished, and she swallowed hard, swinging her legs over the edge of the cot, her hands folded in her lap. "I'm certain she mentioned a traveling circus by the name of *Arturo*."

Leaning forward, Ian rested his elbows upon his legs. "*Arturo?*" he mused. "The name sounds familiar." He shook his head, then asked, "Did she mention the name Duval?"

Noèle shook her head. "She did not. But it must be connected to the circus, do you not think? It must be what made her think of it." She paused, her hands trembling. "Or do you think she knew from the beginning where my daughter is? Even without the name?"

Ian shrugged. "That, I canna say." He sighed and then rose, stalking toward the door, not knowing what else to say.

"She begged me," Noèle suddenly said into the stillness of the cabin, "to stop him."

Ian pulled to a halt. Then he turned and met her eyes.

"What do you think she meant?" Noèle asked, her inner turmoil written clearly upon her features. "What did she want us to...?"

Ian swallowed. "She knew the man he was, and she couldna do anything about it." He held her gaze. "If given the chance, I will ensure he willna hurt another soul ever again."

Noèle drew in a slow breath, the look in her eyes revealing that she understood his meaning. "I think it would be for the best," she replied, clasping her hands together tightly. "He's hurt so many people." A tear rolled down her cheek. "And now her!" She shook her head in disbelief. "His own wife! He truly feels nothing, does he?"

"I doubt it," Ian replied before turning back toward the door. And yet again Noèle spoke, once more keeping him in place.

"What of the wolf?" she whispered, anguish in her voice, as though she were speaking of her child. "We cannot simply leave him."

"Once we have Ophélie, I shall go back and look for him," Ian replied, doing his utmost to appear hopeful. Yet in his heart, he doubted that he would see his four-legged companion ever again. After all, if the wolf was alive, would he not have met them at the beach where they had left the dinghy? Would he not have found them?

To Ian's surprise, losing the wolf brought on a pain he had not expected. All these years, Ian had never dared to think of the creature as more than simply another being brought to the same place and time as him by sheer coincidence. He had not dared think of the wolf as a friend. Only he had been, had he not?

Feeling Noèle's watchful eyes upon him, Ian looked up. He felt compelled to speak, to say something. Anything. Yet his mind was suddenly empty, his heart overflowing with regret and sorrow. Only that was something he did not dare express, so he once more turned toward the door, his hand upon the handle when suddenly a call echoed down from above deck.

"Land ho!"

At the sound, they both flinched. Then their eyes met, and Ian saw reflected upon Noèle's face the same thoughts that surged through his own mind.

"We have arrived," she whispered, quickly pushing to her feet, her steps unsteady as she all but stumbled toward him.

On instinct, Ian held out his hand, grasping hers the moment she staggered within reach. He pulled her against him, their eyes locked and–

"Land ho!"

Again, they both flinched...and yet he knew that it was for a completely different reason. As though burned, they both flew apart, suddenly unable to meet the other's eyes.

"I will head up on deck, and—"

"I'm coming as well!" Noèle insisted, rushing up behind him as he threw open the door and stepped out into the gangway.

Ian merely nodded, knowing there was no point in trying to dissuade her. Aye, she needed rest, and yet she could not stay back so long as she knew her child to be in danger.

Stepping out onto the deck, Ian momentarily squinted his eyes against the bright sunlight. He saw Louis standing on the quarterdeck, spyglass in his hands as he surveyed the coast. "Anything?"

Scratching his beard, Louis shook his head. "Nothing out of the ordinary, Captain," he reported, casting a concerned glance at Noèle, who stumbled toward the railing, her hands grasping the wood as though it were a lifeline. "Is everything all right?" he asked Ian, one brow cocked, indicating Noèle.

Ian nodded, well aware there was nothing any of them could do for her—except return her child. "Make berth in the harbor," Ian instructed, "and then immediately send men to inquire about a traveling circus by the name of *Arturo*. I suppose we shall also be needing horses."

Louis nodded and then marched off, bellowing orders.

Ian walked up to Noèle, careful not to step too close. "You should lie down," he said gently but insistently, not at all surprised when she eyed him with a doubtful look. "At least until we make berth."

Heaving a deep breath, Noèle nodded and then followed him below deck. Once in the cabin, she laid down upon the cot, doing her best to ease her breathing, to calm herself and allow her body to rest for at least a few more moments.

Meanwhile, Ian turned to a heavy wooden chest in the corner. Throwing open the lid, he gathered as many weapons as he could carry upon his body, sliding another dagger into his boot while attaching a pistol to the strap across his chest. He also reached for a small purse of gold coins.

"Dubois cannot be bought or persuaded with money," Noèle threw out from the cot, her blue eyes guarded as she looked at him. "You know that, do you not?"

Ian nodded.

Sighing, she closed her eyes. "He will always choose revenge, for he likes to inflict pain, to punish those who he believes have wronged him."

Ian wondered why she felt compelled to speak these words. They both knew them to be true. Perhaps she said them to prepare herself, to keep her own hopes from soaring too high. After all, life rarely turned out as one hoped. Tragedies happened every day. That, too, they both knew to be true. Did Noèle perhaps deep in her heart not believe that she would ever see her child again?

"Please," Ian began as he took a step toward her, meeting her eyes when she opened them, "stay here. Stay here, and I promise ye I will return yer daughter to ye."

For a moment, Noèle simply looked at him, her face almost blank, free of any emotion that might tell him what she was thinking, how she would respond. Then she slowly shook her head. "I cannot."

Although Ian had not truly expected a different response, he felt himself tense nonetheless. "Do ye not trust me?" he ground out, wondering in that very moment when her opinion of him or belief in him had come to mean so much to him.

Despite his harsh tone, her features softened. "You know that I do," she said with such conviction, as though it were a truth universally known. "I do trust you, Ian. Only I am a mother," she shrugged help-lessly, "and I cannot help it. It is not a choice for me to make, as you well know. Do fathers not feel the same?"

Sighing deeply, Ian nodded. "Aye, I suppose they do."

Chapter Fifteen

CIRQUE ARTURO

Fear tightened Noèle's muscles as she walked down the gangway and off the ship, her eyes sweeping over the small harbor. Like many others, the village mainly flourished upon the fishing trade. Still, two larger merchant vessels were moored at the docks, and sailors were running to and fro, loading and unloading cargo, tending to small repairs while others—their work accomplished —vanished in the local tavern.

Noèle felt her muscles begin to ache even now, the strain she put on them too much. She knew she needed to relax, at least a little, but that was easier said than done. She could not help it. She craned her neck from side to side, hoping and fearing to spot Dubois somewhere among the people crowding the docks. Was he nearby? Was her daughter?

Dimly, she heard Ian speak to Louis, giving instructions should something go wrong. He lowered his voice, and yet Noèle knew what he was saying, what eventuality he was planning for. She turned to look at him, at his face, set in determination, his blue eyes flashing in a way that boded ill for Dubois should their paths cross.

Looking at him now reminded Noèle of her first day on board the *Chevalier Noir*. She remembered how she had followed Alexandra up the gangway and onto the deck, how she had seen Antoine speak to Ian. She remembered what Ian had said in reply.

I shall guard her with my life.

Had he meant it? Knowing Ian, as she had come to know him, Noèle knew that he had. He never said anything he did not mean. Was he truly willing to give his life in order to save hers? Her daughter's?

At the thought, tears shot to her eyes, and she remembered the way he had looked at her not too long ago in the captain's quarters. *Oui*, something had changed between them. She had seen it in his eyes, in the way he had looked at her. She also felt it in her heart and knew that she, too, had come to look at him in a different way. Indeed, the thought of losing Ian pained her greatly. It was a pain that reminded her of the day she had lost Étienne.

Oui, it did seem far-fetched, almost impossible, yet Noèle remembered it had taken her no more than a few hours to lose her heart to Étienne. Was it possible to love again? To love one man with all her heart and do so again after losing him? Was it right?

That, however, was an entirely different question, was it not? Something could be possible and still be wrong. So, in fact, those were two questions. Two questions, Noèle did not dare dwell upon, for they frightened her, and she could not afford to be frightened.

Not today.

Not right now.

Fighting to regain her composure, Noèle accepted Ian's arm as he led her onward. Jean and François had procured horses and were waiting for them nearby. "Can ye ride?"

Meeting his gaze for no more than a second, Noèle nodded. "I shall be fine." Then she allowed him to assist her into the saddle. "Where are we headed?"

Ian urged his horse away from the docks. "The tavern owner said the *Cirque Arturo* set up camp roughly an hour down the road." He held her gaze. "Are ye ready?"

Noèle did not know how to answer that question. Was she ready? Ready for what? To come face to face with Dubois once more? Definitely not! To hold her daughter again? *Oui!* To see her ripped from her life forever? The thought alone almost reduced Noèle to a whimpering, shivering mess.

"Noèle," Ian said gently, guiding his horse closer to her. His hand reached out and brushed hers, a fleeting touch, no more, and yet Noèle felt it everywhere. What did that mean?

Gritting her teeth, Noèle nodded. "*Oui*, I'm ready."

Ian held her gaze for a moment longer before he finally nodded. Then they pulled their horses around and rode out of the village. It took a little time for Noèle to reacquaint herself with riding on horseback. However, before long she managed with ease, no longer needing to concentrate upon what she was doing. She lifted her gaze, eyeing the countryside, wondering when she might catch her first glimpse of the traveling circus.

Duval?

Who carried that name? And what connection existed to Dubois? It had to be someone Dubois trusted, and yet what did that mean for Ophélie? What kind of a person would Dubois trust? Someone like him?

Noèle shuddered at the thought.

"There!" François called, one arm pointing off the road and toward a small meadow. Clusters of trees grew nearby, almost hiding the tents set up there. No longer lost in her thoughts, Noèle could now hear the sound of people mingling, children laughing and calling to one another. It was like a small village, one not fixed to a specific location, but a village nonetheless. Something cheerful and vibrant lingered in the air, and if it were not for their purpose here, Noèle would have felt perfectly at ease.

"Keep your eyes out for Dubois," Ian instructed the two sailors as he turned toward the camp. "He may already be here." For a split second, he met Noèle's eyes, and she could see that he had not wanted to say these words, that he knew what they did to her.

Entering the camp, the first person they met was a young man in an acrobat's costume, its vibrant colors matching the broad smile upon his face. However, it did wane a little when he spotted the strangers entering the village. Ian signaled to François, and the sailor dismounted and approached the man, inquiring after someone by the name Duval.

The acrobat hesitated, asked a few questions, but apparently François managed to answer them to the man's satisfaction. Indeed, the young sailor smiled cheerfully and possessed such easy manners that the acrobat soon relaxed. He pointed over his shoulder at a tent at the southern end of the camp. François thanked him effusively, and then they were on their way.

"Exercise extreme caution," Ian warned as they quietly slid out of their saddles, then tied their horses to a pole by the tent. "We dunna know who awaits us inside."

François and Jean both nodded solemnly.

Then Ian stepped up to Noèle, gently taking her by the arm and pulling her aside. "Let us go in first," he said imploringly, the look in his eyes begging her to listen to him, to heed his words.

Noèle could barely contain the trembling that had seized her, but she nodded, wrapping her arms around herself. She watched as Ian stealthily neared the entrance of the tent, closely followed by François and Jean. All three men had their hands on the daggers at their belts, their faces alert.

And then they vanished inside, and Noèle felt as though she would sag to the ground at any moment. Her knees trembled so fiercely that she had to grab the pole they had tied the horses to in order to keep herself from sinking to the ground.

Were they too late?

"Ophélie," Noèle sobbed, her gaze fixed upon the flap in the tent, tears running down her cheeks.

Chapter Sixteen
AN UNEXPECTED RETURN

Ian blinked, for his eyes needed a second to adjust to the light inside the tent. Fortunately, though, the bright spots vanished quickly, and his gaze fell upon a young woman seated upon the ground, crying over an injured man, his head in her lap. Two small children were tugging on her sleeves, their faces white with fear and their cheeks tear-stained.

Upon the entrance of the three men, the woman's head snapped up, her eyes widening with renewed fear. Her mouth dropped open, but before she could scream, Ian lifted his hands in appeasement. "Please, we havena come to harm ye. Ye have my word." He signaled for François and Jean to stay back.

The woman stilled, a frown drawing down her brows. "Who are you?" Her gaze moved from Ian to the other two men and then back. "Why are you here?"

Ian turned to François. "Fetch Noèle," he instructed, and the other man vanished outside.

A moment later, Noèle came rushing into the tent, her eyes wide as she looked at Ian and then at the woman upon the ground. "Is she here? Is my daughter here?"

The woman on the ground paused, and her eyes met Noèle's. "You're her mother? My brother took her from *you*?"

At the woman's words, Noèle reeled back in shock. "B-Brother?" she stammered, and Ian moved to grasp her shoulders lest she crumble to the ground.

"Are ye saying that Bastien Dubois is your brother?" Ian asked the woman to clarify.

The woman nodded, turning to look down at the man in her lap as a low groan slipped from his lips. Mumbling a few words, she brushed a gentle hand over his forehead before lifting her eyes once more. "I am Coralie Duval," she said quietly, as though afraid someone might overhear. "This is my husband Claude, and our sons Jean and Maurice." Clinging to their mother, the two little boys watched the scene with wide eyes.

"Where is my daughter?" Noèle exclaimed, her shoulders trembling so hard that Ian wrapped his arms around her, enveloping her in his embrace.

Mme. Duval's gaze fell. "I'm sorry, but she is no longer here." Tears misted her eyes as she forced them back up and met Noèle's. "He came for her."

A sob tore from Noèle's throat, and her knees buckled.

Tightening his hold on her, Ian eased Noèle down gently, still holding her tightly, her hands like claws upon his arms. "Dubois took the child?"

Mme. Duval nodded. "My brother has always been...unpredictable. He came and took the girl without another word, the same way he dropped her off with us a few months ago." Tears ran down her cheeks as she looked at Noèle. "I did not want to let her go." She swallowed hard. "But...But he became angry, and...and...when he is angry..." Her gaze dropped to the man she cradled in her lap.

Noèle nodded, then bowed her head, and Ian felt her tears dripping onto his arm.

"Do ye know where he took the girl?" Ian asked, feeling his own heart constrict with fear—for the child as well as her mother.

The woman shook her head. "*Non*, I'm afraid I do not."

"How long ago did he leave? Did he say anything? Anything about where he was headed or what he planned to do next?"

Again, the woman shook her head.

Heavy sobs now shook Noële's delicate frame, and Ian felt a wave of rage well up at the sight of her misery. Never in his life had he felt so helpless! Why now? Now that another's life depended upon him! Was this truly it? Would Dubois take Ophélie God knew where and they would never see her again? Never knowing if she was even still alive?

"I'm sorry," Mme. Duval said with a choked voice. "I wish I could help y—"

In the next instant, the flap of the tent moved and a ball of gray fur shot inside. For a moment, Ian was too stunned to catch a clear thought. He saw Mme. Duval's eyes widen in fear as she shrank back, her arms wrapped protectively around her sons. He saw Noële's gaze fly up, a look of utter disbelief upon her face.

And then the wolf stood before Ian, his yellow eyes holding such depths as Ian had never seen before. A small yelp left his throat as he all but danced on the spot, clearly eager to be off.

"Where have you been?" Noële exclaimed, reaching out her hands to the wolf. Tears still clung to her lashes, and yet her mind seemed relieved to focus on something other than her own heart-breaking misery. "We were so worried about you."

One of Mme. Duval's sons giggled, then pointed at the wolf and said, "*Gros chien.*"

Noële offered the boy a weak smile. "*Oui,* it's a big dog, is it not?" She hugged the beast to her chest as fresh tears flowed from her eyes.

Ian kneeled down by the wolf's side, watching him carefully. "Where did ye go?" he asked, as though the creature could answer him.

Yet the wolf instantly sat up, alert. He moved to the tent's flap and then back, all but beckoning him to follow.

"Did ye follow him?" Ian asked amazed, staring at his companion. "Do ye know where he went?" All of a sudden, everything made perfect sense.

Before, when Henri had gone after Dubois to retrieve Lady Juliet, Ian had taught the wolf to wait and watch, to follow quietly and out of sight. Had he done so again? Had he gone after Dubois?

"What?" Noèle exclaimed, grasping Ian's hand. Her gaze moved back and forth between him and the wolf, the fear to hope only too visible in them.

Still dancing on the spot, the wolf disappeared out the tent flap only to return a moment later, his eager limbs saying more than a thousand words.

"To the horses!" Ian shouted as he helped Noèle to her feet. They staggered out of the tent, and he heard Mme. Duval call after them, "Please, find her!"

And then they were back in their saddles, charging after the wolf as he raced ahead. Ian cast worried glances at Noèle, her cheeks still pale and exhaustion clouding her features. Still, she clung to her horse's mane, sheer willpower keeping her upright and in the saddle.

"The beast is headed back to the harbor!" François shouted over the thundering echo of their horses' hooves.

"Perhaps Dubois has a ship there!" Ian replied, remembering the two merchant vessels he had seen moored there. Was it possible that Dubois knew one of the captains? Or had he simply bought passage? If he had done so...

"Jean!" Ian called as they rounded a bend, then charged onward. "Tell Louis to ready the ship immediately upon our arrival!" Who knew how much time they would have!

Chapter Seventeen
OPHÉLIE, AT LAST

Noèle teetered between fatigue and tension, as though her body did not quite know what need to respond to first. She was in desperate need of rest, and yet the energy shooting through her limbs urged her onward, responding to the need to find her child.

With her hands curled into her horse's mane, Noèle managed to hold herself in the saddle as their horses suddenly drew to a halt upon arriving on the docks. A number of people looked up, slight frowns upon their faces, before they returned to their tasks.

A dark growl slipped from Ian's throat, and Noèle's head whipped around. "One of the merchant ships is gone," he hissed, nodding toward an empty spot along the docks.

Noèle's heart all but paused in her chest, and she looked around frantically, hoping against hope to spot—

"Jean, hurry!" Ian instructed as he slid off his horse. The wolf seemed agitated, pacing near them, his muzzle on the ground. "François, speak to the captain of the other vessel!" And then Ian was beside her, his hands gently pulling Noèle out of the saddle.

Blinking, Noèle felt herself sway upon her feet before she bit down hard upon her tongue to chase away this dreaded fatigue that continued to linger.

"Ye need to return to the *Chevalier Noir*," Ian insisted as he grasped her chin and his eyes met hers. "Ye're in no state—"

"*Non!*" Pressing her lips into a tight line, Noèle shook her head. "There's no time. Don't concern yourself with me. Go and—" Her voice broke off when something beyond Ian's left shoulder caught her attention.

A man broke away from the small crowd, hurried steps carrying him toward the remaining merchant vessel, an alarmed expression upon his face as he looked over his shoulder. Noèle could not rightfully say that she knew him; however, his face looked familiar. She had seen him before...somewhere. If only she could remember...

Her heart slammed to a halt!

Upon Dubois's ship!

And then she spotted the wolf, drawing closer and closer to the merchant vessel, his muzzle on the ground sniffing and searching.

"What is it?" Ian's hands grasped her shoulders, his blue eyes narrowed in concern. "Are ye all right? Do ye need to—?"

"I...I know him," Noèle stammered breathlessly as she kept staring at the man, who swiftly made his way up the gangplank and onto the merchant vessel...closely followed by the wolf.

Ian turned, his gaze following her own. "How?"

"Dubois," was all Noèle could manage in that moment before her feet were suddenly moving, energy shooting up and down her limbs and carrying her forward. She was dimly aware of Ian by her side, grasping her hand and pulling her along as his large strides propelled him past her and toward the ship.

Noèle's gaze remained fixed upon the man, and she saw him call out...although his words did not reach her ears. Was it a warning? If so, did that mean Dubois was on that ship? And her daughter?

Pushing past the last remaining people between them and the ship, Ian shot up the gangplank. Noèle almost stumbled and fell as she tried her utmost to keep up. Only his tight grip upon her hand prevented her from losing balance. And then they were on deck and François stepped up to them, confusion marking his features. Yet one glance at

Ian's grim expression was enough. Spinning upon his heel, he fell into step beside his captain, eyes alert.

"He's here," Ian growled to François. "Go and fetch the crew!" Without a moment of hesitation, the young sailor darted away.

And then—even above the cacophony of voices on the docks and ship alike, the call of seabirds overhead, the sound of waves rolling in from the sea—Noèle suddenly heard the faint whimpering of a child.

"Ophélie!" her heart screamed, and yet her daughter's name fell from her lips in no more than a whisper.

The moment they stepped around a cluster of barrels currently sitting atop deck, Noèle felt her world begin to spin, for right there in front of them was Dubois. The man they had just pursued stood by his side, her daughter cradled in one arm while the other held a knife, its blade gleaming in the sun.

Ian drew to a sudden halt, his arm coming around her middle, holding her back as her feet continued to propel her onward. In that moment, Noèle saw only her child, her sweet, precious daughter.

Almost five months had passed since Noèle had last lain eyes upon Ophélie, and with a heavy heart, she saw that her infant daughter had disappeared. Indeed, she had grown, was now barely a babe, but instead possessed the wide-open gaze of a young soul, now turning her gaze outward and exploring the world. She looked well, her face round and her movements forceful as she scrunched up her face and shook her little fists in a displeased gesture. Instantly, Noèle felt that tug again, pulling her forward and to her child.

Ian, though, held her back.

A low growl came from the wolf standing between her and Dubois, his ears flattened and his hackles raised, as he watched the man who held her little daughter. Noèle wondered how the wolf could possibly understand any of what was going on, of what had happened. But perhaps he did not need to. Perhaps it was enough for him to know Dubois was the enemy.

For once lacking that triumphant gleam in his eyes, Dubois glared at them. Still, a hint of disbelief lurked beneath the merciless expression upon his face, as though he could not for the life of him understand how they had found him here.

Noèle whispered a quiet thank you to Mme. Dubois as well as the wolf. Now, if only—

"So, you've found me again," Dubois snarled, "but it will not do you any good." He glanced at Ophélie, and a vicious smile curled up the corners of his mouth. "I suggest you leave or I will be forced to..." His voice trailed off, leaving his threat dangling in the air to be completed by their imagination.

Noèle bit down hard, trying her best to soothe the trembling in her limbs. What was to be done? There had to be something she could do! She would not leave her child here with that man!

"I thought ye valued family," Ian remarked with a hint of chiding surprise, trying to appeal to the man's honor. If only Dubois possessed any! "The girl is family to ye, is she not?"

At his words, a cold shiver crawled down Noèle's back. Ian's jaw, too, was clenched, a nerve there ticking furiously as he fought to appear calm. *Oui*, the reminder that Ophélie was Dubois's kin pained them both!

A devious chuckle left Dubois's lips. "*Oui*, that she is." Then he shrugged, as though the matter deserved no further thought. "However, what good will a child do—a girl no less. *Oui*, she serves a purpose." He grinned at Noèle. "For you, though, she is more than that, *n'est-ce pas?*"

Of course, she was! Noèle thought as tears gathered in her eyes. "Please, let me have her back," she begged, pushing away Ian's hand as he tried to keep her from stepping forward. "You cannot make your escape with a child as young as she." A lump settled in her throat, but she pushed past it. "She will die on whatever voyage you hope to undertake, and then your advantage will be lost." Her heart twisted painfully at the thought of her daughter as nothing more than a bargaining chip. Her life worthless beyond the pain her abduction could bring others. Ophélie deserved more than that!

Dubois glared at her. "You want her back?" he asked with a menacing snarl before his gaze snapped to Ian. "Well, you should have thought of that before you took everything from me." Outrage now burned in his eyes, and his right hand tightened upon the handle of the dagger attached to his belt. "The Durets came after me for no reason at all. I did nothing!" he yelled, his face flushing a dark shade of red. "I served my country, boarded enemy ships and secured the spoils of war. Why should I not receive a fair share?" He yanked the dagger free, brandishing it in front of him. "The Durets had no right to come after me, to take what was mine." He glanced at Ophélie, madness contorting his features. "And they will pay for that."

Around them, silence had fallen. It felt as though the entire village was holding its breath, waiting to see how this would play out. Noële sensed Ian behind her, saw the wolf crouch into a charging position, knew all those around them to be staring back with shock or confusion. Only a handful of sailors appeared unsurprised, their eyes focused and alert, undoubtedly waiting for a command from Dubois. One even stood whispering to the merchant vessel's captain. The middle-aged man appeared a bit agitated by the current developments; however, a small leather pouch slipped into his hand seemed to dispel all his concerns.

"If you want your daughter to live," Dubois hissed at her, casting a sideways glance at Ian, "you will leave this ship. Now! And you will not pursue us, *comprendez?*"

Noële felt the air yanked from her lungs at the thought of watching her daughter sail away, uncertain if she would ever lay eyes on her again. *Non*, this could not be happening! She could not allow this to happen!

As though to agree with her, Ophélie opened her little mouth in that moment, expelling a heartbreaking wail. Her little hands were clenched into fists as she shook them, her eyes pinched shut.

Feeling her fingernails dig into the palms of her hands, Noële took a step forward, toward her daughter, ignoring the annoyed look upon Dubois's face as he glanced down at the screaming child. She did not even dare look over her shoulder at Ian, but focused her thoughts, her attention on what she hoped to accomplish. "Take me in her stead," Noële offered, bargaining for her daughter's life with the only thing she had to offer.

At her words, Dubois's eyes lit up with a sickening gleam.

Chapter Eighteen
ANOTHER WAY

Pain shot through Ian's entire being at Noèle's offer, and for a moment, he thought he had strayed into a dream...or rather a nightmare. Had Noèle truly just offered to—?

Lunging forward, Ian grasped her shoulders, spinning her around. Her blue eyes were wide as they found his. "No! Ye canna! I canna let ye—"

"*Oui*, you can and you will," Noèle whispered, gently touching her hand to his face. Tears stood in her eyes, and she looked at him almost pleadingly. "I need to do this. It is the only way. Please!" Her eyes looked imploringly into his. "Protect her as you would your own. Please!"

Ian tried to swallow around the lump that had settled in his throat. All of a sudden, the world had turned upside down. Nothing made sense, and yet he understood what Noèle was doing. He knew that she did not have a choice. She was a mother as he was a father, and he knew that he, too, would have done the same. Had he not already? Had he not been willing to give his own life to protect Blair from the wolf? He had. How then could he stand in her way?

And yet his hands tightened on her shoulders, unwilling to release her, to allow her to sacrifice herself, for the thought that she might be lost to him nearly brought him to his knees.

A dark chuckle drifted to their ears. "Oh, how touching!" Dubois sneered, the look upon his face almost triumphant as his gaze moved back and forth between them. The smile upon his face slowly grew, and Ian felt the need to charge across the deck and drive his dagger through the man's heart.

Noèle's hand fell from his face, and she moved to push him back, removing his hands from her shoulders. Her eyes held his for a moment longer as she stepped back. Then she turned to look at Dubois. "My offer stands," Noèle said, hiding her trembling hands behind her back. "I suggest you consider it. After all, taking care of an infant is not an easy task. Have you even thought of how you will feed her on board?" She swallowed hard, her gaze straying to her daughter again and again. "I, on the other hand, will be a simpler...prisoner by far, and taking me in her stead will accomplish the same. I, too, will grant you revenge upon the Durets."

Ian felt his chest rise and fall with panting breaths as he watched her. Every fiber of his being told him to intervene, and yet one look at Ophélie's little face stayed his hand. He knew he could not allow this, but at the same time he knew he could not interfere.

If it had been Blair or Niall, he would have done the same. Was this it then? Was this simply a question of whom to sacrifice? Was there no path that would lead to saving them both?

Trembling with rage, Ian felt Dubois's gaze move to him. He could see the way the other man was assessing him, taking in the hostile glare in his eyes, the tension in his shoulders, the desire to move, to act, to interfere written upon his face. Ian needed no mirror to know that it was so. He knew what Dubois saw when he looked at him.

Indeed, Ian's reaction to Noèle's offer served as proof that it would incense the Durets. Knowing her to be in Dubois's hands would bring them pain, which was precisely what Dubois wanted. For a split second, Ian considered offering himself. Yet he did not possess the same worth, and he knew that Dubois would never accept it.

With a pleased smile upon his face Dubois took a step toward Noèle, his gaze drifting over her appreciatively. "An intriguing suggestion indeed," he murmured as his gaze trailed over her, lingering here and there, setting Ian's blood on fire. "I suppose you'd be by far better company, my dear."

Ian felt sickened, seeing the look upon Dubois's face. Rage surged through him, and once again he felt his entire being tremble with the effort to remain where he was. Still, this could not be it! He had to do something! He had to save them both!

Holding her head high, Noële did not flinch under Dubois's gaze. Yet Ian could see how terrified she was and how desperate. Indeed, being in Dubois's hands once again was her worst nightmare...only surpassed by the thought of losing her child.

"Very well," Dubois nodded. "We have an agreement, *madame*."

A touch of relief marked Noële's features. She inhaled deeply and then placed one foot in front of the other, slowly approaching Dubois and the man who held her child.

With one hand on his pistol, Ian watched helplessly as the distance between them grew. The wolf whined sorrowfully, moving from one paw onto the other, his gaze swinging around to meet Ian's. He did not like what was going on. Ian knew how that felt.

Yet they were both forced to simply stand by and let it happen.

Only an arm's length away from Dubois, Noële chanced a look at the man. She inhaled deeply and lifted her chin another notch. Then she stepped past the man at whose hands she had suffered countless atrocities and held out her hands to receive her child.

For a short moment, Ian saw no fear or sorrow upon her face. Aye, she seemed to be glowing, wonderment lighting up her eyes as she gazed down upon her precious child. Gentle fingers touched Ophélie's cheeks and forehead, brushing away a tuft of black hair. A sob of relief and joy slipped past Noële's lips, and then she swept her daughter into her arms.

It was a perfect moment, one long-awaited, and it broke Ian's heart.

"Be quick about it," Dubois snarled, shattering that look of utter bliss upon Noële's face as he pulled out a pistol and trained it upon her.

Ian flinched, drawing his own, aiming it at Dubois.

Dubois laughed manically. "Not to worry," he said with a quick glance in Ian's direction. "I only wish to protect my interests." Then, he met Noèle's eyes. "Hand the child to whomever you wish, but one wrong move and I will not hesitate to kill you both. Is that understood?"

Swallowing hard, Noèle nodded, cradling her daughter deeper into her embrace. "*Oui*," was all she said before she turned and stepped away from Dubois, the man's pistol aimed at her back.

Watching Dubois out of the corner of his eye, Ian kept his focus upon Noèle. With her blue eyes upon the child in her arms—as though she wished to commit these few last moments with Ophélie to memory—Noèle approached him.

Ian knew without a doubt what would happen now.

Noèle would hand him her daughter, make him promise to see her safe and then send him off the ship, forcing him to watch her sail away with Dubois.

Everything within Ian screamed out against it. *No!* There had to be another way. If only his crew were here! But what could they do? He could even see them approaching, hastening down the docks toward the merchant vessel. However, they would not make it in time to interfere; and even if they did, Dubois would not hesitate to shoot Noèle if anyone so much as took a step too close.

No, there had to be another way!

A low growl rose from the wolf's throat before his head suddenly perked up and he moved toward Noèle. He sniffed the child and bumped his head against Noèle's side. "This is Ophélie, Wolf," Noèle whispered, her gaze never leaving her daughter's face. "You will take good care of her, will you not?"

As though in answer, the wolf yipped, something playful now in his demeanor.

Aye, Ian thought, the wolf would protect them. He already viewed Noèle as part of his pack and...

Ian glanced at Dubois. Although the man frowned at the wolf, he did not move to interfere or demand Ian remove the beast. While Dubois would not allow anyone else closer to Noèle and the child, he clearly did not see the wolf as a threat to his plans.

Making a show of looking over his shoulder and out over the docks, Ian moved sideways and closer to the railing.

Dubois chuckled deviously as he followed Ian's gaze. "There is no use," he sneered triumphantly. "Tell your men to stay back or she will pay for your mistake."

Ian gritted his teeth, showing Dubois a face contorted with anger and powerlessness. Then he made a show of halting his men's steps, signaling them to draw to a halt before even reaching the gangplank. At the same time, he quietly clicked his tongue...

...and the wolf's ears perked up, all playfulness gone.

Rocking her daughter in her arms, Noèle hummed a soft melody, her natural presence slowly calming the child. With wide eyes, Ophélie stared up at Noèle...and then her little hand closed over one of Noèle's fingers.

Ian saw the breath lodge in her throat, and the tears that had collected in her eyes now spilled over. Overwhelmed, Noèle wrapped her arms around her child and met Ian's gaze.

The anguish he saw in Noèle's gaze felt like a punch to the stomach, and Ian almost groaned at the pain of it.

"Promise me," Noèle sobbed, hugging Ophélie to her body. "Promise me that you will protect her. Please!"

Swallowing, Ian nodded. "Aye, I promise," he whispered before briefly glancing over the railing at the gap of water between ship and dock.

At the look of distraction upon his face, a furrow stole between Noèle's brows. Her gaze held his, a question there before she shook her head, fear coming to her eyes.

"Dunna worry," Ian said softly as he stepped closer, holding out his hands as though to take the child. "Do you trust me?" he whispered as he placed his hands upon hers, ensuring that Ophélie lay securely in her mother's arms.

Fear and hope mingled in Noèle's eyes, but she nodded. "*Oui,* I do."

"Ready the ship!" Dubois bellowed at the captain. "We'll be leaving immediately!" Instantly, the man barked orders to his crew and the deck erupted in activity. "Get on with it!" Dubois snarled at Noèle, large steps carrying him closer, quickly eating up the distance between them.

Swiftly, Ian leaned closer, as though to take the child, and whispered, "Hold on to her. Now!" Then he swept Noèle and Ophélie into his arms, spinning at the same time so that his body was now shielding them from Dubois.

Instantly, a low curse flew from Dubois's lips, but Ian did not hesitate. He lifted mother and child over the railing and—

—felt a searing pain cut into his shoulder as a shot rang out!

His arms slackened as the bullet dug into his flesh, and he dropped Noèle and Ophélie over the edge of the ship. "After them!" he ground out as he sank to his knees.

The wolf charged instantly, nothing more than a gray blur to Ian's eyes, as he shot past him and leapt over the railing and into the water.

Shouts from his crew down on the docks drifted to Ian's ears as stars exploded in his vision. His head spun, and the pain in his shoulder dulled his senses to such a degree that everything suddenly seemed far away. He struggled to his feet and turned around the moment Dubois reached him.

The man's face was contorted into an outraged snarl, and his fist instantly connected with Ian's jaw.

Flung backwards, Ian hit the deck hard, his vision once again unfocused as he looked up at Dubois standing over him.

"You'll pay for this!" Dubois snarled, his pistol trained on Ian, his finger twitching...when his head suddenly snapped up.

Loud shouts echoed closer, and although Ian could not make out what they were saying, he recognized some of the voices. His crew! Louis! François! J—

"Pull up the gangplank!" Dubois shouted, rushing past Ian. "Make way immediately!"

Resting his head back against the wooden boards, Ian closed his eyes and breathed in deeply, trying his best to stay conscious. Around him, the deck was awash in noise. The sound of running boots and urgent shouts mingling with the screeching of seagulls and the unfurling of sails overhead.

And then Ian felt the ship move beneath him, and he knew that once again Dubois would get away. Still, it did not matter. All that mattered were Noèle and Ophélie. Surely, they were fine. Shocked and wet, but fine. They had to be!

Ian exhaled slowly as the world darkened around him, swallowing him whole and pulling him under. Dimly, he wondered if this was how Étienne had felt the day the sea had taken him.

And then Ian wondered no more.

Chapter Nineteen

WITH HIS LIFE

P anic seized Noèle's heart the moment Ian's arms around her suddenly vanished and she felt herself falling. Instinctively, her arms tightened upon her daughter, clutching her to her chest as she pinched her eyes shut.

And then, she felt the cold water envelope her, stealing the breath from her lungs and sending a chill over her skin. For a split second, Noèle all but froze in shock before her legs started kicking against the water, seeking to propel her back upward.

Only a moment later, her head broke the surface and she drew in a deep breath, shifting her daughter in her arms so her head was above the water as well. Although Noèle expected Ophélie to cry and scream, her daughter merely expelled a soft whimpering sound, filled with annoyance, her little hands tangled in Noèle's hair. Relieved, Noèle continued to move her legs, and yet her skirts, now heavy with water, began to drag her back down.

Again, panic spread through Noèle's being, her head turning frantically from side to side, taking in her surroundings. *Oui,* she was not far from the docks. Alone, it would have been no problem for her to swim the distance. Yet with her infant daughter in her arms, Noèle feared she would not be able to do it.

And then she felt something move beside her in the water. She spun around, kicking her legs frantically, eyes wide as they searched the surface. Was there something in the water with her? Some kind of creature that–?

A deep sigh rushed from Noële's lungs, when her gaze fell upon the wolf, paddling toward her. He moved swiftly, eagerness in his gaze, and reached her side in no time. As though the creature had communicated his plan to her in some way, Noële knew precisely why he had come, why he was here.

Deep in her heart a voice whispered, *Had Ian sent him after them?*

Curling one hand into the fur at his neck, Noële held on tightly, allowing the wolf to pull them through the water and toward the docks. She felt the ship beside her pull away, its sails now unfurled, catching the wind as it slowly drifted out of the harbor. Shouting drifted to her ears from above, and she tried to crane her neck to see. Yet the deck was too high.

Noële felt her heart grow heavy. Only she knew she could not focus on Ian right now. She needed to take her daughter to safety. He would want that. She was certain of it. After all, had he not just sacrificed himself to save them both? Had he not just done precisely what he had promised Antoine? *Oui*, he had risked his life to see them safe. Had he also...given his life?

Closing her eyes, Noële felt that question circle in her mind, its paralyzing effect slowly drifting through her body. Suppressing a sob, Noële pressed her lips shut and opened her eyes, reminding herself that she could not fall apart now. And so, she blinked away the water that clung to her eyelashes and looked up, relief sweeping through her as she spotted Ian's crew heading toward her. They were rushing down the dock toward her, and then François jumped in not far from where she clung to the wolf, his head bobbing up quickly. "Hand me the babe," he said, holding out his arms.

Noële could not help the reluctance that swept through her. Still, she slowly released her grip upon her daughter and entrusted her to François. The young sailor took her gently and then held her up to Louis. Ian's first mate eased Ophélie into his arms, murmuring comforting sounds under his breath as he gently rocked her from side to side with practiced ease, which made Noèle wonder if he, too, was a father.

"You're next," came François's voice as he reached for Noèle's arm. He pushed her up as two sailors reached down to grasp her hands, pulling her upward and out of the water.

"Does he need help, too?" Noèle heard François's voice behind her, and she turned to see him eyeing the wolf reluctantly.

Noèle hesitated, uncertain. Then, however, she shook her head when she saw the wolf paddle along the dock swiftly toward a spot where the shore sloped gently upward, offering him sufficient footing to pull himself out of the water. "He'll be fine," she told François with a grateful smile. Then she turned to Louis, who immediately returned her daughter to her. "A finer little girl I've never seen," he told her with a beaming smile.

"*Merci*," Noèle whispered, torn between savoring the moment, savoring her daughter's presence, and the need to inquire after Ian. Had they seen what had happened? She wondered, looking from sailor to sailor, many of whom were gazing after the merchant vessel as it slowly grew smaller upon the horizon. Had Ian been shot? Was he still...?

Noèle swallowed, closed her eyes and then lifted her head. "I heard a shot," she said, drawing all their eyes to her. "Before Ian dropped us." She tried to meet their eyes but found most averted. "Was he shot? Is he...? Did anyone see?"

Louis's gaze met hers as he placed a hand upon her shoulder. "We do not know," he told her honestly. "We heard the shot as well, but cannot say what happened." He swallowed before he placed his other hand on her other shoulder, his eyes meeting hers more firmly. "You both need to get dry." He looked down at Ophélie, who in that moment began to squirm and cry, agreeing with him.

Only now did Noèle notice that she was shivering, her clothes soaked through to the skin. She nodded her head, knowing that Louis was right, and allowed him to steer her down the docks and toward the *Chevalier Noir*. "But we cannot simply leave him behind," she murmured, not daring to look up, uncertain what would happen now. What would the crew do now that their captain was gone? Would

Louis as first mate take command? What decision would he make? Would he sail the *Chevalier Noir* back home, returning her and her daughter to the Durets as planned?

A disbelieving scoff fell from Louis's lips. "Of course not, *madame*." Noèle looked up and their eyes met, a devilish curl lifting the corners of Louis's mouth before he called over his shoulder to the crew following upon their heels, "Will we leave our captain in the hands of the devil, lads?"

As one, Ian's crew voiced their opposition to such an idea loud and clear, their eyes fierce and lit with determination. Noèle felt her heart warm at their support, their loyalty to their new captain.

To Ian.

"Go below deck and see to the babe," Louis told her as he assisted her up the gangplank. "I'll have hot water brought down to you and see that someone milks the goat." A smile touched his face as he looked at Ophélie, still squirming in Noèle's arms. Then he turned to his crew, bellowing orders and seeing the ship readied without delay. "Who is our fastest rider?" Noèle heard him call out as she made her way to the hatch.

"Jean!"

"*Bon*," Louis exclaimed, approaching the sailor. "Go and ride to La Roche-sur-Mer and tell *Capitaine* Duret what happened here. Tell him we'll be in pursuit."

"Aye, Sir!"

Returning to the captain's quarters, Noèle paused in the doorway, for a moment taken aback by the look of it...without Ian. Then, however, she determinedly pushed that thought away, knowing that it served no purpose. She looked down at her precious daughter, cold and squirming, and knew that she could not lose her head now. *Non*, she was needed. Her daughter needed her, and she better remember that!

Closing the door behind her, Noèle gently laid Ophélie upon the cot in the corner. She tried her best to murmur soft, comforting words as she peeled the wet clothing off Ophélie. She tried to smile at her, tried to feel joy over their reunion, and a part of her truly did feel it. "Hush, hush, little one," she murmured, brushing a wet curl from her daughter's forehead. "All will be well. I promise you, Ophélie."

Once wrapped in warm blankets, Ophélie calmed a little bit. And yet as Noèle changed out of her own soaked clothes, she continued to sing a lullaby she knew from her own childhood. Her voice and the soft melody soothed the girl as well as her own frayed nerves. Still, only when Noèle finally picked Ophélie back up, setting her cheek against her daughter's and breathing in the soft scent of her, did Ophélie truly calm down, reassured by her mother's presence.

"I missed you so much," Noèle murmured, holding her daughter close as she paced around the cabin. Back and forth, her feet carried her as she whispered to her child, telling her all that had happened, all the heartache she had lived through and the joy she now felt at having her back in her arms. She promised Ophélie that they would never be separated again, that from now on only happy days would follow. Still, deep in her heart, something twisted painfully at that promise, for Noèle knew that any happy days that might await her could only truly be happy with Ian in them.

Holding her daughter close, Noèle stepped up to the window, her gaze sweeping out over the sea as the *Chevalier Noir* slowly made its way across the churning waves. The floorboards beneath her feet moved, threatening to throw her off, but Noèle now felt at ease upon the sea. Indeed, it was a matter of familiarity, of routine, of practice. Had it been the same for Étienne? She wondered, surprised by the thought. Once again, she all but saw his smiling face in front of her, his kind eyes, and remembered the way he had always felt compelled to ease the suffering of those around him—whether he knew them or not.

A soft knock sounded on the door, and Noèle turned toward it. "Enter".

François appeared, himself changed into dry clothing. "Is there anything else you need?" the young man asked kindly as he set down a bucket with hot water upon the floor and then carefully placed a jug of goat's milk upon the table.

Noèle smiled at him. "There is not. *Merci*, François, for all you've done." He nodded his head in acknowledgment of her words, and yet Noèle could see that they caused him some unease. "Is there any news?" Noèle asked quickly, both for François's sake as well as her own.

His jaw tightened. "Not yet, *madame*. The merchant vessel has a head start, but we will do what we can to catch up." He inclined his head to her. "You have our word." Then he quickly took his leave, hastening back up on deck.

Holding her daughter in one arm, Noèle offered her a bit of the goat's milk, and the girl drank greedily until her belly was full and her eyes closed with deep slumber. Rocking Ophélie in her arms, Noèle thanked Alexandra silently for thinking ahead. If Antoine's wife had not insisted on them taking a goat along, Noèle would not have known how to feed her child.

Seating herself on the cot, Noèle held her daughter in her arms as she slept, her own eyes directed out the window at the darkening sky and the rolling waves. Again, she thought of Étienne, of the night he died, of the moment she had learned of his loss. And then, she thought of Ian, of the way he had come into her life, of the pain she had seen in his eyes. *Oui*, they were a lot alike. They had both gone through life hoping for the best and then finding their dreams dashed. Still, the first thing that came into Noèle's mind when she thought of Ian was the way he had held her, his eyes for once free of pain and regret but filled with a deep wonderment and, perhaps, even a touch of hope.

Even now, that memory brought tears to Noèle's eyes. She knew that Ian had given up all hope of finding happiness for himself long ago. She knew that because she had done so as well. She had loved and lost—as had he—and somehow she had always thought that that was it. That the rest of her life would simply be...

Noèle sighed, and her gaze drifted down to touch upon her daughter's peaceful face. Instantly, she felt her heart grow and strengthen, the mere look of her child filling her with longing and hope. *Non*, life was not enough. She wanted love. She wanted her child. She wanted...

...Ian.

A tentative smile teased Noèle's lips. "I love him," she whispered to her sleeping child. "I did not know until now. Or I suppose I did not dare admit it to myself. But now I do." Gently, she placed a kiss upon Ophélie's head, and the girl's mouth drifted into a gentle smile.

Closing her eyes, Noèle rested her head against the wall behind her. "Étienne," she whispered into the stillness, "I've loved you from the day we met and I will love you until the day I die." Tears pricked her eyes, and she exhaled a shuddering breath. "But I love Ian as well. I don't know how it happened. I think I was afraid of acknowledging that truth because..." Tears rolled down her cheeks, and she hung her head.

"Can you forgive me?" Noèle asked as her eyes traced the gentle curve of her daughter's closed eyes. "I never meant for any of this to happen, but I cannot regret loving you both."

The dark clouds outside the windows parted, allowing a single ray of sunshine through, bright and glistening, full of promise and hope.

And forgiveness.

Noèle smiled. "*Merci*, Étienne." She knew she would never forget him, but now, she needed to look to the future.

To Ophélie.

To Ian.

Chapter Twenty

DUBOIS

For a long time, Ian had been somewhere where time and place did not exist or where they simply did not matter. In truth, he could not say how long he had been there. It could have been years or months or perhaps only hours. All that mattered was that he wished to remain.

Unfortunately, he had no say in the matter.

As much as Ian tried to hold on to that blanket of detachedness that held everything else at bay, he could feel the drowsiness slowly disappear, as though the blanket was slipping through his fingers.

Time resumed, and the place he found himself in was hard and uncomfortable. He smelled wood and salt, recognized the familiar sea air as well as the soft up-and-down of the ship dancing over waves. Dimly, he heard voices and footsteps above deck. Aye, the sounds were familiar and felt soothing...at least, at first.

Then memory returned, and with it, a sharp, searing pain in his right shoulder. Ian groaned, rolling onto his other side, and cursed under his breath. His shoulder throbbed, and he felt his shirt sticking to his skin.

Blood.

Gritting his teeth, Ian fought against the pain and slowly pushed himself upright. He glanced down and saw red stains upon his shirt, the darker fabric of his vest concealing how much his wound had bled. Still, the lightheadedness he felt suggested significant blood loss.

Leaning back against the hull of the ship, Ian closed his eyes and breathed in deeply a couple of times. He did his best to push away the pain and focus his thoughts. Then he looked at his surroundings, his gaze drifting over barrels gathered in one corner and crates in another. A small oil lamp swung on a beam overhead, and Ian wondered how long whoever had brought it down here had been gone. The ship swayed gently, and he could see traces of sunlight streaming in between boards here and there.

Sighing, Ian once more leaned back and closed his eyes, welcoming the blackness. Yet it did not remain. Instead, memories surfaced, forcing him to relive the moment he had dropped Noële and her daughter into the sea.

Ian cringed at the image, at the memory of a bullet piercing his shoulder, of his muscles going slack and the sickening sensation of releasing someone he wished to hold on to. Of course, it had been his plan to drop Noële and her daughter overboard. It had not been a perfect plan, but the best one he had been able to come up with under the circumstances. A plan that would keep them out of Dubois's clutches.

Here and now, though, Ian could not help but wonder if he would have been able to release Noële had that bullet not taken the decision out of his hands. Was she all right? She and the child?

Of course, they were! They had to be! After all, he had seen the wolf charge after them, and his crew had been nearby, below on the docks. Aye, they were all right. They had no doubt received quite a shock upon being dropped into the sea, but now, they were all right. Louis would take them back to La Roche-sur-Mer, and the Durets would ensure that they would forever be safe from Dubois.

Ian smiled at the thought.

Aye, he had succeeded. He had returned Ophélie to her mother and seen them both safe. A part of him had feared that life would once again turn against him, that they would be hurt because of him, that he would fail them.

But he had not.

Relief swept through Ian despite the pain in his shoulder, even dulling it to a bearable degree. Indeed, he had nothing left to lose but his own life...and that was not worth much to anyone.

Least of all, him.

After all, his own family already thought him dead. Ian prayed that with him gone, they had been able to find happiness, their lives no longer overshadowed by his anger. Aye, upon coming to France, it had felt good to be part of *something* again.

Of a crew.

A family even.

The Durets were not unlike the MacDrummonds. They stood together and came when called. Yet Ian had never truly belonged to either. Why, he could not say. He had certainly tried. Perhaps it had simply not been meant to be. Now, it no longer mattered.

Over the next couple of days—how many, he could not say!—Ian drifted in and out of consciousness. He woke up once to feel a half-hearted bandage upon his shoulder and another time to find a jug of water and a crust of bread dropped by his side. Yet he never saw anyone, voices drifting down the hull all that proved he was not alone out on the open sea.

And then, one morning, Ian woke to the sound of heavy footsteps approaching from above. Instantly, his head snapped up and then whipped around before the hutch was flung open, and sunlight poured in. Ian blinked his eyes, keeping them fixed on the boots appearing in his view as someone descended the ladder into the hull of the ship.

Dubois.

"Ah, I see you've decided to continue gracing us with your presence, *Capitaine*," Dubois sneered mockingly. "The Durets seem to be giving away that title to just anyone."

Ian was surprised to feel a slight sting at Dubois's words, quickly reminding himself that he ought not care. He had done what had been asked of him, served his purpose and that was all that mattered.

"How is the shoulder?" Dubois asked as he sauntered over, twirling a small blade in his hands. He stopped in front of Ian, then leaned down and prodded a finger at the wound.

Ian groaned as pain exploded in his shoulder. Bright spots blurred his vision, and he felt that blackness from before return, slowly drawing closer. Perhaps he simply ought to give in.

"A clean exit," Dubois remarked, as though to praise his own marksmanship. "Missed all major blood vessels." He chuckled deviously. "After all, I cannot afford to lose my last piece of leverage." Anger rang in his voice as well as reproach, as though Ian were an unruly child, who had disobeyed his father.

Ian scoffed. "Dunna pretend ye *missed* on purpose," he taunted the other man. "Ye failed miserably! Noèle and her daughter will soon arrive in La Roche-sur-Mer, and the Durets will ensure that ye will never get yer hands on them again."

For his slight, Ian half expected Dubois to prod his wound again or perhaps skip that step entirely and simply shoot him right here and now. The other man, however, merely grinned that same, self-satisfied grin Ian had always loathed with every fiber of his being. "I still have you," Dubois declared triumphantly, "*n'est-ce pas?* I admit your loss will not hit the Durets as dear Noèle's would have; however, they will not simply abandon you." He scoffed derisively. "They come for their own. They always have. It's their greatest weakness."

Ian laughed, oddly grateful for the chance to ruin the man's day. "That's where ye're wrong, Dubois. The Durets dunna—"

"Ah! Have you already forgotten how they sank my ship—MY SHIP!—only to save that English whore?" Dubois snarled, his voice rising with each word he shouted into Ian's face. "Mark my words. They will come. They will take that whore to safety, and then they will come after me." He leaned back, placing a thoughtful finger to the right corner of his mouth. "But where to lure them?" he mused, eyeing Ian curiously, as though waiting for him to supply the answer. "Especially with winter approaching soon? Ought we make them wait?"

Ian shook his head, then flinched when the movement sent renewed pain through his shoulder. "Ye misunderstand, Dubois. They came for Lady Juliet because Henri loves her." He lifted his brows meaningfully. "They willna come for me. I'm no one to them. I'm a hired hand, capable but expendable." Ian almost cringed at his own words, surprised at the pain they caused him. Aye, a part of him wished he were lying.

Dubois eyed him through narrowed eyes, and for the first time since waking on board the merchant vessel, Ian felt a sense of unease crawl over his skin. "How the hell did ye survive in the first place?" Ian demanded, trying to redirect their conversation to a less treacherous topic. "Ye were on board when the Durets blew yer ship to pieces, were ye not?"

Dubois laughed, that triumphant glint back in his eyes. "*Oui*, I was," he admitted, slapping his leg in delight. "But men like me are not so easily killed."

"So, ye were on board," Ian repeated. "Then how did ye escape after the blast?"

Again, the man laughed, clearly enjoying the moment. "I have hide-outs in places you haven't even heard of and men loyal to me in every harbor." He shrugged. "I always find a way."

Ian remembered the string of uninhabited islands dotting the sea where the Durets had cornered Dubois's ship. Had the man truly taken precautions for such an eventuality? Had he had a dinghy stashed away somewhere? He had to have had or he would not be sitting across from Ian now.

"It took me a while," Dubois recounted as his lips pressed into a thin line, "but eventually I found my way back to my island." He scoffed. "I knew the Durets would betray a fellow privateer, and when I spotted French soldiers arriving, I was ready."

Ian remembered well the fortified island Dubois had made his own. Deep inland, he had built himself a small fortress, connected to the sea through a cavern. There, he had stashed treasures taken from enemy ships, treasures that rightfully belonged to France. "How?" Ian inquired. "What did ye do?"

Dubois's smile widened. "Poisoned food," was all he said, his words quickly followed by a mad chuckle. "I suspect they're still there, my food stuffed in their mouths. I took their ship, signaled to my men—those that remained—and returned to France to repay those that wronged me."

Ian heaved a deep sigh, for Dubois's words suddenly conjured a different memory. One from before.

From before he had become Ian Stewart.

From when he had still been Ian MacDrummond.

"I used to think as ye do," Ian told the other man without a second thought. After all, what did it matter? "Whenever my life didna go as I desired, I found fault with everyone but myself. I blamed others for my own failures, instead of taking responsibility for my actions."

Dubois's jaw clenched, his eyes hard and murderous. "You know nothing of what you speak," he snarled, reaching for the pistol at his belt and pointing it at Ian. Perhaps to silence him? "I deserved everything and more, everything they took from me. You may have failed in your responsibilities, but not I."

"And what of yer family?" Ian dared him, raising a challenging eyebrow. "Did ye not feel a duty to them?"

Anger blazed in Dubois's eyes. "I always thought of them," he snarled into Ian's face. "I always took care of my own. I always −"

Ian barked out a laugh. "Is that truly what ye believe?" he demanded, wondering if perhaps it would be wise to bait Dubois into shooting him now and have this over with, once and for all. "Ye killed them! Only a few days ago," or weeks perhaps? "I watched ye stab a knife into yer wife's belly." Still shocked by Dubois's ruthlessness, Ian shook his head, allowing his disbelief to play across his face. "And what of yer brother? Ye shot him! Ye care for nothing and no one but yerself. How can ye claim that −?"

"I meant to shoot *her!*" Dubois hollered, his face now bright red and his arms waving about frantically, one still holding the blade while the other clutched the pistol. "I meant to shoot that English whore! I never meant for any harm to come to my brother, but he stepped in the way and−"

"Aye, he did!" Ian interrupted, fixing Dubois with a penetrating stare, wondering if there was any chance for that man to realize what he had done. "He knew the kind of man ye were, and he disapproved. He did his best to protect someone innocent, including giving his own life to stop ye from harming her." Once again, Ian shook his head at Dubois, noting the way this gesture of disapproval made the pulse in the man's neck thud violently. "Yer brother felt guilty for not seeing the truth sooner. However, once he did, he did all he could to set things right."

A furious growl slipped from Dubois's throat. "He betrayed me," he snarled, pointing the knife at Ian as he leaned closer slowly, incrementally. "He was my brother ,and he owed me loyalty."

"And what about yer loyalty for him?" Ian demanded, trying his utmost not to see Noële's face before his inner eye as he continued. "Ye attacked the woman he loved. Ye –"

Dubois surged forward, and Ian felt the tip of the blade pierce the skin upon his cheek right below his left eye. "She deserved it! She refused to listen to reason. I tried to persuade her, to get her to accept my brother. What I did I did for him! And how did he repay me?" His lips twisted into a snarl as he leaned back with a deep huff. "He betrayed me!"

Staring at the other man across from him, Ian realized that no matter what he might say nothing would have any effect upon Dubois. For too long, the man had been living in a world all his own, his idea of right and wrong contorted by his need for power and control. He had never once seen anything wrong in his own deeds but constantly found fault with others. Was there anything at all Ian could say to make him understand?

Ian doubted it very much. More than that, it did not matter. Everything had turned out the way it should be. Dubois was now a traitor to his country and would be arrested and executed the moment the French got their hands on him. And Noële and Ophélie were safe—finally safe!—and on their way back home.

"Ye lost everyone," Ian said with a sigh...to Dubois as well as to himself. "Everything ye did brought ye to this very moment right here." He shrugged, then winced when pain shot through his shoulder. "Quite far from where ye hoped to be, isna it?"

Pressing his lips into a tight line, Dubois glared at Ian. Then he slowly, menacingly raised his pistol and pointed it at Ian's forehead. "And what of you?" he snarled, and yet for a brief moment, a slight tremble shook the hand that held the pistol. "I could shoot you right here, right now, and no one would care."

Ian exhaled a slow breath. "Aye, ye could." He held Dubois's gaze. "So? Will ye? I for one dunna care, for I have nothing left to lose."

A slight frown came to Dubois's face as he regarded Ian carefully. "No one would even know," he murmured as though to himself. "No one would even take note of your absence."

Ian nodded. "True," he replied in the same soft voice, as though they were speaking of a rather philosophical matter. "However, the same can be said for ye. If ye died today, would anyone mourn ye? If anyone took note at all, 'twould only be to rejoice. Is that the legacy ye wish to leave behind?"

Again, the hand that held the pistol was seized by a tremor. Dubois's lips thinned, the color of his face turning darker and darker as he stared at Ian.

Exhaling one last deep breath, Ian closed his eyes and whispered a silent goodbye to his children and to Noële. He did not mind dying today, for they would live on, and that thought gave him peace of mind in a way he had not known in many years.

Aye, he was ready for the end. In fact, he welcomed it. It was—

An earth-shattering *bang* reverberated through the ship, making it lurch, as though a heavy storm had suddenly come down upon them. Ian felt something pop in his ears, and his eyes flew open. He expected to look down the barrel of the pistol Dubois still had trained on him. Yet what he saw was Dubois losing his footing and stumbling sideways, struggling to regain his balance, the pistol still clutched in his hand but no longer directed at Ian.

Seeing his chance, Ian lunged himself at Dubois. What possessed him in that moment, he did not know. He could not remember catching a single clear thought, and yet he moved with purpose, the pain in his shoulder all but absent, pushed to the back of his being by a single-minded intent: to kill Dubois.

Once and for all.

Chapter Twenty-One
FAMILY ABOVE ALL

S tanding up on deck of the *Chevalier Noir*, Noèle looked out at the far horizon. And yet all she saw was blue; a blue sea and blue skies as far as the eye could see despite the harsh, colder winds blowing strong from the north. There was not even the tiniest dot anywhere upon the horizon that could have been a ship. Had they truly lost them?

Noèle looked down at her daughter's tiny head, her curls still as black as the day she had been born, and placed a soft kiss upon her hair. Her arms wrapped around Ophélie, who lay peacefully sleeping in a sling fashioned out of an old piece of linen, while Noèle swayed from side to side, from one foot onto the other, gently rocking her daughter to ensure that her sleep was peaceful.

A deep sigh left Noèle's lips, for her own sleep these days was filled with horrible images. As though to torture herself, her mind continued to picture all manner of harm coming to Ian at Dubois's hands. Where was he at this moment? Was he even still alive? After all this time? Did he feel abandoned?

Gripping the railing with one hand, Noèle returned her gaze to the far horizon. Surely, Ian knew that they would come for him. Of course, they would! And yet a voice deep down reminded Noèle of the way Ian saw himself. *Oui*, he did not think himself worthy of love. She had seen that in his eyes, had read between the lines whenever he had spoken of himself and his family, and of her and Ophélie. Did that mean that he did not think himself worthy of rescue? He had given everything, risked everything to save her, to save Ophélie; and yet she had no doubt that he would be surprised to learn that they had not hesitated to go after him.

"How is the little one?" came Louis's voice as he stepped up next to her, both hands coming to rest upon the railing. He crooked a half-smile at her, his full beard giving his face a kind expression.

Noële smiled at him in return, grateful for his company. "She is sleeping," she replied, glancing down at her daughter. "She likes to sleep in my arms, and I admit I enjoy holding her." Tears pricked her eyes, and her arm tightened around Ophélie. "It has been too long."

Louis nodded, and his gaze briefly dropped to Ophélie before his eyes met Noële's once more. "She will not remember what happened," he told her in a soft murmur; yet it rang with conviction, with absolute certainty. "All she will remember is feeling safe with you, you being here, holding her. Always."

Noële felt the sudden urge to hug Louis. "*Merci*," she whispered instead, smiling at him gratefully. "It is good to –"

"Sail ho!"

At the cry from the crow's nest, Noële flinched. She saw Louis's eyes widened ever so slightly before he looked up, raising his gaze to the top of the mast, one hand shielding his eyes from the glare of the sun. "Where?" A moment later, he was racing down the deck toward the bowsprit, and Noële was rushing to keep up with him.

Her heart beat frantically within her chest, threatening to break her ribs with each forceful thud, while her arms clutched Ophélie tightly. "Do you see anything?" she panted, careful not to lose her footing.

Pulling to a halt, Louis brought out his spyglass, sweeping it across the horizon. "There!" he exclaimed, his voice tense, cautious.

"Is it the merchant vessel?" Noële demanded as she came to stand beside him, her one free hand gripping the railing.

Again, Louis squinted, looking through the spyglass, his jaw set tightly. Then, he seemed to still before, all of a sudden, his posture relaxed. A wide smile came to his face, and he lowered the spyglass and turned to her. "*Non, c'est la Voile Noire.*"

Noèle's heart skipped a beat. Henri? "Are you certain?" she asked breathlessly, squinting her eyes at the dot upon the horizon.

Louis nodded. "*Oui*, black sails. It's Henri."

"How did they find us here?" Noèle murmured, her head spinning, trying to piece together how this was possible. "How could he possibly know? How long would it have taken Jean to reach—?"

Louis placed a calming hand upon her shoulder. "We shall have our answers in due time, *madame*." He nodded toward the hatch. "Go and rest, and I shall send for you the moment they are here." As Noèle hesitated, he glanced down at Ophélie and added, "She needs you to be well rested."

Giving in, Noèle returned below deck, settling upon the cot with Ophélie still in her arms. These days, she could not bear to be separated from her daughter for even a few minutes. But that was normal, was it not? After what had happened. With time, she hoped she would feel more at ease again.

Although sleep would not come, Noèle's thoughts drifted off and grew fuzzy, unfocused, and when a knock finally sounded upon her door, she did feel a bit rested, after all.

After quickly changing Ophélie, Noèle settled her back into the sling and then hurried up on deck. To her surprise, she did not only see the *Voile Noire* floating nearby, but a British vessel as well. For a moment, her heart paused in her chest, fear freezing her limbs. Then, however, Noèle spotted Violette Duret, Antoine's adopted daughter, standing side by side with her father and husband as well as Henri and Juliette upon the *Chevalier Noir*'s quarterdeck.

Violette was Alexandra's daughter from her first marriage to an English lord. However, that marriage had been less than happy, to say the least, and when Antoine had happened upon the beach below Silcox Manor one night and stumbled upon Alexandra, the young woman had taken her daughter and left her home and country behind. Violette had grown up as Antoine's daughter, her heart belonging to the sea as much as his did. Eventually, she had found her way back to

England and fallen in love, marrying a man with her same sense of adventure, for now they sailed the world together upon their own English privateer.

Still, the Durets' motto always prevailed: *Family above all.* Even country. French or English, they were loyal to one another and came when called upon, never hesitating to protect the ones they loved.

Noële rushed forward, her heart now a thousand times lighter at the mere sight of them. "Oh, it is so very good to see you! But how do you come to be here?"

Smiling at Juliette, Henri stepped forward, slipping an arm around her shoulder. "Ian sent a message before leaving Monpont, informing us of what had happened. We thought it prudent to be ready." Then his gaze dropped to Ophélie, and an awed expression came to his face. He barely breathed but only stared at her daughter as though lightning had struck him and he could no longer move.

Noële looked up at him. "Do you wish to hold her?"

Clearing his throat, Henri blinked. Then he chuckled, his gaze rising to meet Juliette's. A meaningful smile came to the young woman's face, and all of a sudden Noële understood that awed look in Henri's eyes. "Are you to be a father then?" she whispered, loving that glow in his green eyes. Indeed, she had always wondered if he would ever find someone who could possess his heart, all of it. But Juliette had fought and conquered it, and Noële knew she had never seen Henri so happy.

While Violette and her husband Oliver stood back, Juliette and Antoine also embraced her, holding her close and voicing their relief that she and her daughter were safe. "We were so worried," Juliette whispered, brushing a tentative hand over Ophélie's head. Her eyes had that same awestruck expression as Henri's. "But she is well?"

Noële nodded, smiling as Ophélie curiously observed the many people suddenly crowding around her. "Oh, she is adorable," Juliette exclaimed when Ophélie grasped her finger, clutching it tightly within her hand.

As much as Noële loved this moment, felt like she was coming home, it was far from perfect because there was someone missing.

Someone who ought to be here.

"Have you heard?" Noèle began, eager eyes turning to look at Henri and Antoine. "Has Louis told you—?"

Both men nodded.

"We have to—!"

"And we will," Antoine assured her before he turned to speak with Louis as well as Violette and Oliver.

"What now?" Noèle asked, looking up at Henri, as she was unable to make out the words that were spoken by Antoine. "We have to find him! We—"

Henri's hand settled upon her shoulder, a curious expression in his gaze. "We will. Louis already told us everything. I know that merchant vessel." Noèle felt her heart pause. "It trades with America. With heavy cargo, it will not be quick enough to outrun us. Our ships are lighter and, therefore, faster." He held her gaze. "We will catch them. I promise."

Noèle nodded, feeling tears prick her eyes. "*Merci*, Henri. *Merci beaucoup.*"

Henri smiled at her and then joined the others. "Is there anything you need?" Juliette inquired gently as she wrapped an arm around Noèle's shoulders. "Is there anything I can do?"

Sniffling, Noèle shrugged, then met Juliette's eyes. "I pray he is still alive," she whispered, realizing that thus far she had never once quite allowed herself to admit how deeply she feared for Ian. "What if Dubois—?" Her voice broke off.

Murmuring words of comfort under her breath, Juliette pulled Noèle into her arms, embracing her gently, careful not to upset Ophélie. Oh, it felt good to lean on her! It felt good to trust that Henri would do what needed to be done! It felt good not to be alone in this!

Brushing a strand of hair from Noèle's face, Juliette looked into her eyes. "I overheard that Antoine will again take command of the Chevalier Noir. Will you...Will you come aboard the *Voile Noire*? We could talk."

With a deep sigh, Noèle nodded. "*Oui*, I'd like that."

After another few minutes of conversation, the captains broke apart, each returning to their own vessel. Noèle and Ophélie joined Juliette and Henri on the *Voile Noire*, and Noèle felt something impatient hum beneath her skin. She tried to sit comfortably and sip the tea Juliette placed in front of her. Still, her gaze moved to the window and the sea beyond again and again as all three ships turned into the wind, cutting through the sea as though they possessed wings.

"You worry for him," Juliette observed with a thoughtful look in her eyes, watching Noële from the other side of the cabin.

Noële blinked. "Of course, I do! How could I not?"

Nodding, Juliette stepped closer and then seated herself in the chair opposite Noële's. Her green eyes swept over Noële's face, lingering there, as though waiting for some sort of answer. "That is not what I meant," she murmured softly, still watching and waiting. "You... You care for him, do you not?"

Glancing down at her sleeping daughter, Noële finally nodded before once more meeting Juliette's eyes. "I don't know how it happened, but he... He is..."

With a smile, Juliette reached out and grasped Noële's hand. "There's no need to explain. I can see how much he means to you." She squeezed her hand. "Does he know?"

Noële gnawed on her lower lip, completely caught off guard by this simple question. "I do not know," she murmured, remembering the moments they had shared with one another. "I don't think he does."

Oui, while another might have been able to read her face, to see in her eyes how she felt for him, Noële was almost certain that Ian had not. *Non*, he did not know. He would never have allowed himself to believe so. And if Dubois killed him, then he would never–

"And you and Henri?" Noële inquired, determined to push these awful thoughts aside. After all, they served no purpose and would only reduce her to a weeping mess.

A deep smile claimed Juliette's face. "We are married," she whispered, a radiant glow lighting up her eyes. "He came to England and..." She shrugged, and for a brief moment, her eyes closed, a blissful sigh drifting from her lips.

"I am so happy for you," Noële replied, struggling to keep her thoughts focused. "You are to be parents soon."

A look of surprise showed upon Juliette's face. "Did he tell you that?"

"He did not have to, for it was written all over his face." Noèle squeezed her hand. "As it is upon yours." She sighed. "I'm so very sorry to be interfering with your life, to draw you out here and away from your home. I wish—"

"Don't be," Juliette insisted. "None of this is your fault. It is no one's fault, except for Dubois." Her hand closed more tightly around Noèle's, her green eyes meeting hers determinedly. "We will always stand together because we're family. It's what makes us strong. Never forget that."

A deep and heartfelt smile came to Noèle's face because, in that moment, she truly knew Juliette's words to be true. Even though Noèle was not related to any of them, did not share their family name, she *was* family. Somehow, she belonged to them as did Ian.

And they would fight for him as he had always fought for them.

Oui, family.

If only Ian knew that he was not alone.

Chapter Twenty-Two
NOT ALONE, AFTER ALL

Grappling with Dubois, Ian cringed at the pain in his shoulder. Oddly enough, he was no longer ready to die. Something had happened! Something had changed! What that was, he did not know. All he knew was that he could not give up. He could not allow Dubois to kill him because...because...

A memory of Noële rose in his mind, her blue eyes wide and honest as they looked into his, a soft smile upon her lips. She looked beautiful, breathtaking, and yet what touched Ian most was that look of understanding in her eyes. She knew him, did she not? She knew him like no one else ever had, and...and she cared...for him. Was that possible? Or was he deceiving himself? Was it a beautiful thought he allowed simply because he was standing at death's door right now?

Ian did not know nor did he truly wish to know. Right here in this moment, it did not matter. All that mattered was that he could not allow Dubois to get his hands on that pistol.

Activity broke out up on deck, and Ian could hear voices shouting indistinctly and footsteps rushing back and forth. He wondered where the shot had come from, for it truly sounded like a cannon ball had been fired at them, had it not? Had it been a warning? Of course, there was the possibility of them being boarded by an English privateer. Was that what was happening right now?

Not waiting another moment, Ian shoved Dubois against a barrel, elbowing him in the ribs, then the other man suddenly jabbed a finger at his wound, flinging him back.

Ian groaned, and for a moment, he thought he was done for. His vision blurred, and he could not tell up from down, his sense of direction all but lost. Would Dubois shoot him now? Would he—?

An iron fist connected with Ian's jaw, and his head was jerked backward. He crashed to the floor, crying out in pain...when his hand suddenly felt something cold and smooth upon the floorboards.

Dubois's blade!

"You will pay for this!" Dubois snarled, wiping a trickle of blood from the corner of his mouth. He lifted the pistol in his hand, pointing it at Ian, when another loud *bang* echoed to their ears.

Another cannon ball!

Startled, Dubois flinched...and Ian did not hesitate.

From where his strength came, he did not know. However, his body moved as though of its own accord. Kicking the pistol out of Dubois's hands, Ian rolled sideways, gritting his teeth at the renewed pain in his shoulder. His left hand grasped the knife and then he swung around, once again elbowed Dubois in the ribs, and in one swift movement held the blade to his throat.

Dubois froze.

Panting, Ian stared at the other man, knowing full well that he would not last long. He could already feel darkness encroaching upon him again. If he wanted to act, it had to be now. "Over there!" Ian instructed, nodding toward the ladder.

With grumbled curses flying from his mouth, Dubois did as commanded, his posture tense, his eyes flashing with the desire of retribution.

Keeping his eyes fixed upon the other man, Ian bent down and picked up the pistol he had kicked out of Dubois's hands. "Up!"

An almost painful-looking snarl appeared upon Dubois's face, for he clearly despised receiving orders from another. Had he truly never been bested in a fight? Had he never been at another's mercy?

Slipping the blade into his belt, Ian grasped the pistol with his right hand, cringing as his injured shoulder rebelled against the move. Still, he needed his good arm to climb the ladder and he could not very well allow Dubois out of his sight.

With a glance over his shoulder, Dubois made his way upward while Ian stood below, the pistol still pointed at him. Then he, too, began to climb, careful not to fall behind, not to allow Dubois up on deck with him still stuck below. His shoulder throbbed painfully, and he had to blink his eyes against the bright spots that appeared in his vision. Still, Ian kept moving, forced himself to keep going, leaning out of the hatch only a moment after Dubois's feet touched the deck.

"Stop!" Ian called the second Dubois spun to dive for cover. The man hesitated, but the desire to disobey was all but visible in the tension upon his face. Ian's finger upon the trigger tightened, and when Dubois finally did move, Ian fired.

For a moment, everyone on deck froze as sailors whipped around, only now becoming aware of the happenings around the hatch. Dubois's eyes opened wide, and he looked down at his right shoulder with a somewhat bewildered look upon his face. Then time resumed, and a groan slipped from his lips. He clutched his left hand to his shoulder as blood seeped out of the wound, staining his clothes.

"Now, we're even!" Ian ground out as he clenched and unclenched his right hand, needing the pain to keep him conscious as the dark began to encroach upon his vision yet again. Still, he watched with a sense of satisfaction as Dubois sank to his knees, a loud groan rising from his lips.

Panting, Ian leaned against the mast, the pistol still trained upon Dubois as he lifted his gaze, sweeping it across the deck. Sailors stood with gaping jaws, staring out to sea as another ship pulled alongside the merchant vessel. Aye, it flew an English flag!

A privateer!

An English privateer!

What now? Ian's mind spun with what to do. Technically, he was a Scot; yet England and Scotland had never been on the best of terms. Also, he could not simply return home even if such an option were offered to him. He had no life in Scotland any longer. He was dead to all those who had once known him.

And then a shadow fell over Ian from behind, suddenly blocking out the sun, and his head whipped around.

Black sails blocked his view!

And Ian's heart leaped with joy before his mind had even had a chance to comprehend what was happening.

"Ian!"

At the sound of his name, Ian flinched, another groan slipping from his lips as his shoulder protested against the sudden movement. He pinched his eyes shut and breathed in deeply before opening them once more.

The black sails were still there, and his gaze flew over the ship, taking in the familiar shape, the crew standing armed, ready to fight, up on deck, their faces taut and determined.

Familiar faces!

Men he knew!

Ian stared when a dark-haired man suddenly swung across the gap between the two vessels and then landed with a thud right in front of him.

Henri!

"Are you all right?" Henri asked, clasping Ian's left shoulder, as Ian continued to stare at him, certain that this was some kind of mirage. Henri's gaze moved to Ian's right shoulder, and his jaw tightened as he quickly inspected the wound. Then he signaled to his crew.

Instantly, more men joined him on the merchant vessel, swords and pistols in hand as they quickly took control of the ship.

"It's good to see you," Henri said with his usual grin, his green eyes flashing with adventure as always. However, at the sound of a groan from behind, he spun around and his posture stiffened when his gaze fell on Dubois.

"How dare you board us?" the captain of the merchant vessel suddenly demanded as he strode over, flanked by two of Henri's men. "We sail under a French flag. This is treason!"

Henri grinned. "We're not boarding you," he said calmly, his gaze still fixed upon Dubois now squirming upon deck. "They are!" He nodded toward the English vessel, and Ian belatedly realized that it was the *Freedom*.

As though on cue, Henri's cousin Violet pulled herself up to stand on the railing of her vessel, one hand on the rigging. Despite her golden hair billowing in the sea breeze, she looked like a true privateer, armed to the teeth and a look of conquest in her eyes. Her husband, Oliver, stood only a step behind her.

"Or they're about to," Henri amended, meeting the captain's nervous gaze. "*I* am here to apprehend a criminal." He nodded at Dubois. "I assume you were unaware that you granted passage to a man wanted for treason, *n'est-ce pas?*"

The captain stilled, then cast a nervous glance at Dubois, who glared at the man with seething rage, still clutching his injured shoulder. "*Oui,*" the captain stammered suddenly before turning his attention back to Henri. "I-I had no i-idea."

"You traitorous rat!" Dubois hissed, his face turning dark red, giving him the appearance of a volcano about to explode.

The captain flinched, but he did not dare look at Dubois. "Th-Thank you for b-bringing this m-matter to my a-attention," he said to Henri, then glanced at the *Freedom*.

Henri flashed a grin at his cousin before addressing the captain of the merchant vessel once more. "If you allow us to take this traitor and his men back to France, I'm certain that the English can be persuaded to...turn a blind eye, *vraiment?*"

The captain nodded eagerly.

As a string of curses flew from Dubois's lips, Henri nodded to his crew. They quickly rounded up the men loyal to Dubois. Then he approached the vile man himself, grasping him by his shirtfront and yanking him to his feet. "You will pay for what you did!" Henri snarled into his face, ignoring the groan of pain slipping from Dubois's lips. "I assure you, the day you'll breath your last, I'll be there...and I'll smile." Then he tossed Dubois to two of his men. "Lock him up!"

Ian felt himself begin to sway, but Henri grasped him carefully, steadying him. "Ye finally have Dubois," Ian murmured, blinking his eyes to focus upon Henri's face. "I should've known that ye would come after him."

Henri frowned at him. "I'm relieved beyond words to have finally apprehended Dubois," he said slowly, his green eyes fixed upon Ian's, "but we came for you." His brows rose meaningfully. "You didn't think we would leave you behind, did you?"

Ian could do little else than stare at Henri. He heard the words, but his mind was too busy trying to convince him that he had imagined them. "H-How...?" he stammered, then swallowed and began again. "How did ye know?"

Henri grinned, then nodded to something beyond Ian's shoulder.

With Henri's hand upon his shoulder still steadying him, Ian slowly turned...and his eyes fell upon the *Chevalier Noir* floating nearby. And there, at the railing of the quarter deck stood Noële, tears in her eyes and a tentative smile upon her face.

Ian's heart leaped with joy...

...and then the world went dark.

Chapter Twenty-Three
LOVE AND ALL ITS PREDICAMENTS

Noèle vividly remembered the moment she had watched Ian's eyes roll back and his knees give in. She also remembered her heart stopping in her chest. For a terrifying moment, she had thought him lost to her for good, and all of a sudden, the world had seemed bleak and lonely and heartbreakingly sad. She had looked down at Ophélie, sleeping peacefully in her sling, and in that moment, the joy she had felt at the sight of her daughter had been dampened by that sense of loss that had suddenly washed over her.

"*Oui*, I love him," she had whispered to her daughter, doing her best to blink back the tears that had threatened before she had lifted her gaze once more and looked across the waters at the merchant vessel.

Henri had caught Ian before he could hit the deck, easing him down gently and then feeling for his pulse. Noèle's breath had lodged in her throat as she had waited, watched and waited for what seemed like a small eternity. And then, Henri had looked up and met her gaze, the hint of a smile upon his face as he had given a short nod.

Instantly, Noèle's breath had rushed from her lungs, and for a moment, her knees had felt so weak that she had had to grasp the railing for balance. "He's alive," she had whispered to Ophélie as much as to herself. "He's alive."

It was the one thing Noèle clung to. Nothing else seemed to matter beyond it. She had stood and watched from across the water as Ian had been taken from the merchant vessel and brought to the *Voile Noire.* She had seen François, Henri's surgeon, rush below deck to see to him while Henri's crew had rounded up Dubois and his men, bringing them onto the *Chevalier Noir* and locking them up in the brig. For a short moment, Noèle had felt uneasy, knowing that she was once again upon the same vessel as *that man.* Yet, Henri had quickly approached her, insisting she and Juliette instantly return to his own vessel now that the battle was done and no more danger awaited.

Later that day, after François had sent her from the sick bay so he could see to Ian's wound, Noèle stood upon the deck of the *Voile Noire,* breathing a final sigh of relief as she watched Antoine turn the *Chevalier Noir* back toward France, to Paris to deliver the traitors to the authorities.

The sun was slowly setting, casting an orange glow across the sky, and a strong wind blew, making Noèle's hair swirl around her head like a being all its own. She wrapped her arms tightly around her daughter as a chilling wind brushed over them, rocking her gently from side to side, and kept her eyes fixed upon the *Chevalier Noir* until it disappeared from sight. *Oui,* it was over now. She was finally safe again, and she finally had her daughter back in her arms.

Looking down at Ophélie, tracing the curve of her closed eyes as she slept, Noèle finally felt a sense of peace herself. For the past year and more, life had been dominated by so many dark emotions—pain, fear, regret, guilt—that Noèle had all but forgotten what it felt like to be happy and carefree, to breathe easily, to look forward to the next day and not dread it. Once, she had been happy...with Étienne. Then she had lost him and been convinced that she would never feel like that again.

Only now, Noèle *did* feel slight stirrings in her heart that felt familiar, that made her smile and hope and wish and dream. Noèle knew deep in her heart that Étienne would never have wanted her to suffer for the rest of her days. He would have wanted her to find joy again as she would have wanted the same for him had their roles been reversed. And she had found joy again, had she not?

"Are you all right?" came Juliette's voice as she stepped up to the railing, coming to stand beside Noèle. Her auburn tresses danced upon the breeze, and her wide green eyes shone with adventure. *Oui*, she was a perfect match for Henri, and Noèle loved seeing them together. It made her hopeful that despite obstacles happy endings could be found.

Swallowing, Noèle nodded, casting her friend a tentative smile. "Part of me cannot believe it is truly over," she whispered, her voice carried away upon the wind. "I never truly believed it could be possible."

Juliette's hand closed over hers. "But it is," the young woman assured her with a steady gaze. "Antoine is taking Dubois back to Paris. He will be tried for treason and executed. Soon, he will be gone from this world."

Inhaling a deep breath, Noèle nodded. "He will be gone from this world," she echoed Juliette's words, feeling them sink into every fiber of her being.

"What will you do now?"

Noèle shrugged, for in truth she had never once given any thought to what would come after retrieving Ophélie. "Return home, I suppose," she murmured despite the sense of reluctance that settled upon her at the thought. Indeed, dark memories linger there. *Home* was no longer the place it had once been.

"And Ian?"

Noèle chanced a glance at her friend, seeing the contemplative twinkle in Juliette's green eyes. "I care for him," she said softly yet boldly. "However, we hardly know one another. I don't know how he feels about me, not truly." She brushed her hand over her face, heaving a deep sigh as her heart urged her to his side once more. "He is a rather guarded man, in case you have not yet noticed."

Juliette chuckled. "Yes, I have noticed." Then the expression upon her face sobered. "He might not have said anything of the kind; however, sometimes deeds speak louder than words, do they not?" Again, she squeezed Noèle's hand. "He risked his life for you and Ophélie. What does that tell you?"

"I truly want to believe that he cares for me," Noèle murmured, torn between the deep sense of conviction she could feel in her chest and that tentative tingle of fear that crawled up her back. "Yet what he did he might have simply done out of duty. He had given his word to Antoine and Henri, and he is not a man who would break it…ever."

"Then you should speak to him," Juliette suggested, not a hint of doubt in her voice. "In my experience, men do not always know how they feel, and even if they do, they often come up with some sort of ludicrous reason not to admit to it." She grinned at Noèle. "Believe me, if you wish to know, you need to first make him realize how he feels. He might truly not be aware of it, unwilling to admit that his happiness now depends upon another. I believe, for men especially, it is a most fearful thought. They do like to be self-sufficient, often running from what they truly want out of fear of getting hurt, not realizing that running away is the very thing that hurts them."

Noèle nodded, hearing the wisdom in Juliette's words. Indeed, from what she had heard of the young woman's own story, Henri had been most insistent in keeping her at arm's length. He had been so fearful of losing her, of her coming to any harm that he had sent her back to England despite having lost his heart to her. Indeed, it had taken a lot of convincing for him to admit that he wanted her.

Loved her.

"You should go see him," Juliette suggested gently. "François says he's still sleeping and will be for some time, but he will know that you are there." She smiled at Noèle and then brushed a tender hand over Ophélie's head. "She is such a sweet little girl."

Noèle sighed, hugging her daughter closer. "*Oui*, that she is." She looked up and met Juliette's eyes. "Soon you shall have your own little angel."

Placing a hand upon her belly, Juliette nodded. "Yes, I cannot wait." She squeezed Noèle's hand. "Now, go and see to Ian. Everything else can wait."

Smiling at her friend, Noèle stepped below deck and carefully made her way toward the sick bay. François sat in a corner at a table. He looked up as she stepped inside and nodded to her, a kind smile upon his face. Then he turned his attention back to cleaning the instruments he had used stitching up Ian's wound.

With darkness falling, an oil lamp had been lit, no light filtering into the cabin through the window. However, it only cast a dim light, and Noèle had to carefully pick her way toward the cot where Ian slept, the wolf lying on the floor by his side, watchful as always.

Ian looked pale, frighteningly pale, his blonde hair almost white in the glow from the lantern. Yet his chest rose and fell slowly with each breath, reassuring Noèle that, *oui*, he was still alive.

As Noèle carefully tried to sit down on the side of the cot, Ophélie's eyes blinked open and she waved her little hands in a way that clearly suggested she was no longer tired or content resting in her mother's arms. Noèle tried to calm her, rocking her gently, but Ophélie had other ideas.

"Let me take her," came François's voice from the table as he pushed to his feet. A delighted smile graced his features as he looked at Ophélie. "Clearly, she needs a little excitement."

Noèle chuckled. "What sort of excitement can a baby long for, I wonder?"

François grinned. "Oh, we all start out small." He held out his hands to take Ophélie. "If you do not object, I will take her on deck and let her feel the wind."

Still a bit hesitant, Noèle nodded, then settled Ophélie in François's arms.

His eyes were serious as they met hers. "I promise she will be safe with me." He smiled at her reassuringly, then glanced down at Ian. "As I'm certain that he will be safe with you."

After placing a kiss upon her daughter's forehead, Noèle watched François carry her out of the cabin, his footsteps echoing upon the boards as they made their way toward the hatch. Then Noèle turned and once more seated herself beside Ian.

Her eyes swept over his features, taking in the pale glow of his skin. She wondered how much blood he had lost and what he had been through upon Dubois's ship. Her hand tentatively reached out and grasped his, relieved to feel the warmth of his skin. As Ian continued to breathe evenly, Noèle felt herself calm. Her gaze moved to the bandage upon his shoulder and then to the large bruise upon his chin. Had Dubois struck him? What other explanation could there possibly be?

Noèle did not dare think of what Dubois had done to Ian. No doubt he had been furious with him after losing his greatest bargaining chip so unexpectedly. The moment Ian had dropped her and Ophélie into the water, Noèle had known that Ian would be the one to pay for this, for their escape. Part of her had feared that Dubois would shoot Ian on the spot. Had Dubois truly missed? Or had his mark simply been off?

Whatever the reason, Noèle was grateful that Ian's life had been spared. That she still had the chance to tell him how she felt. That there still was a tomorrow.

As tense and serious as Ian always looked, right here, in this moment, Noèle looked at him and saw none of the strain that had come to look so familiar to her. Despite his paleness, he seemed almost relaxed, free of the burdens that had been placed upon him. He lay still, even breaths moving his chest, and she wondered if he was dreaming. Perhaps not, though, for he seemed so peaceful.

Had there once been a time in his life when Ian had been full of joy? Noèle wondered. Had an easy smile ever graced his lips? She wished she knew, for a part of her thought that, just like herself, Ian had once known how precious life was, that he had once not seen it as a burden but something to be cherished. Could he come to look at it like that again? Noèle wondered. Could they perhaps make a life together?

Long into the night, Noèle sat by Ian's side, holding his hand and imagining what tomorrow might bring. Once again, she found she had hopes and dreams, suddenly determined not to simply let them slip away. She had lost Étienne. Saving him had been beyond her control. But Ian was right here. He was alive, and he would be well again, and she knew she would forever regret it if she simply allowed him to walk out of her life.

But what if he chose to do so?

Chapter Twenty-Four

LOST

For a long while, the world remained largely distant, barely there, its sounds and sights almost nonexistent. Ian's mind felt sluggish, clear thoughts beyond his ability. He could not even open his eyes although he tried once or twice. Yet his strength failed him, and his mind quickly slipped back into the black void where nothing and no one existed.

Not even him.

And yet, there were moments—short, fleeting moments—when Ian felt *something*. He could not quite say what it was, but it felt warm and soothing and comforting. Was it a touch or a sound? It did not matter. It was simply there, reminding him that he was not alone.

As time passed, Ian became aware of muffled sounds nearby, voices and the clatter of objects, objects he could not identify. He felt a soft swaying, as though he were being rocked like a babe in his mother's arms. Was he still aboard ship? Was that what he was feeling?

Dimly, Ian recalled what had happened after he had dropped Noële and Ophélie into the water. He remembered being shot. He remembered losing consciousness. He remembered darkness. Was that the same darkness he felt now?

No, it could not be.

Raking his mind, Ian found images of Dubois lying upon the deck, a wound in his shoulder and blood dripping onto the wooden boards. He remembered a sense of satisfaction at the sight...and he remembered a sense of surprise flitting through him. What had caused it, though?

And then, all of a sudden, something seemed to explode in Ian's mind. Images soared to the surface, crowding his thoughts and speeding up his heart.

Henri! Aye, he remembered seeing Henri. And the *Voile Noire*! They had come, had they not? To apprehend Dubois. No! They had come for...

...for him!

Warmth flooded Ian's being, and he exhaled a deep breath. His hand tingled with the sense of another's touch, and an image of Noële appeared before his inner eye. The very sight of her made him ache, and he almost lifted his hand, desperate to reach out and feel her close.

"Ian?" came a tentative voice, no longer distant but close. So very close. Ian could feel it like a caress against his skin, and his eyes flew open.

And there she was.

Noèle.

Tears clung to her eyes, and yet a look of awe lingered upon her features as she stared down at him, her wide blue eyes looking into his. "Ian," she murmured, a touch of disbelief in her voice. "Are you truly awake?"

Ian blinked, uncertain how to answer. Was he awake? He swallowed, and his throat felt dry and scratchy. He tried to clear it, but the dryness lingered.

"Here," Noèle exclaimed as her hand slipped from his and reached for a cup upon the table by the bed. No longer aboard a ship, Ian thought. A chamber. But where? "Drink." She helped him sit up a little, moving another pillow behind his head before holding the cup to his lips.

Ian drank greedily and then coughed, his body suddenly uncertain how to manage a simple task such as swallowing. He tried to draw in a deep breath, to calm himself, and then lay back down.

"Are you all right?" Noële asked, a touch of alarm in her voice. "I can go and fetch someone. I can—" A startled gasp escaped her as Ian's hand clamped down upon hers.

Indeed, the thought of her leaving even if only for a moment was one he could not bear. Not after everything that had happened. Not after—

"Dubois!" Ian shot upright, and instantly, his head began to spin. "Where...is...Dubois?"

Gentle hands pressed him back down until his head once more lay upon the pillow. "Everything is all right," Noële assured him. "Antoine took Dubois to Paris. He is being tried for treason." Her hand squeezed his. "He's gone for good."

Ian exhaled a deep breath. "Gone for good," he murmured, savoring that sense of relief that washed over him, making his limbs feel languid and exhausted.

Comfortably exhausted.

Breathing in, Ian felt his mind slip away once more to a place where no danger lurked in the shadows. No, this time, he felt completely at ease, warm and safe, and the next time he opened his eyes, he felt more like himself than he had in a long time.

Once again, it was Noële's face he saw first. He did not know how much time had passed, and yet as he lifted his gaze he knew it could not have been a mere day or two. "Where are we?" he asked, sweeping his gaze around the room.

Noële squeezed his hand, a wide smile upon her face. "We're back in La Roche-sur-Mer," she told him, scooting closer. "We are in the Durets' home." Her blue eyes swept over his face. "How do you feel?"

Swallowing, Ian glanced at the table beside the bed. "Thirsty."

Quickly, Noële offered him another drink, and this time he forced himself to drink slowly. Sip by sip. "You look better," Noële commented, brushing a stray curl from his forehead, the tips of her fingers brushing against his skin. "You looked so awfully pale, and now...now there's color back in your cheeks."

Ian barely heard what she was saying as he stared at her, savoring this moment, a moment he had thought would never come. "And ye? Are ye all right?" His hand tensed upon hers. "Yer daughter?"

A deep smile graced Noèle's features. "Ophélie is fine. She is all right. Be assured of that. Thanks to you."

Ian eased the grip upon her hand. "I'm so sorry I dropped ye into the water. I know I shouldna have, especially not a babe of only a few months, but I couldna think of anything else to do. I couldna allow ye to—"

Noèle pressed her fingers to his lips, silencing him. Blue eyes held his, tears clinging to her lashes. "You saved us," she whispered, her voice choked. "You saved us both, and I will be forever grateful to you for that." Her fingers brushed over his lips until her hand came to rest upon his cheek. "I am so relieved that you are all right." A tear snaked down her cheek. "I was so afraid... I..."

Ian loved the feel of her touch, and without thought, he closed his eyes to savor it. Instantly, fatigue pulled on him, and yet he seemed to possess the presence of mind to close his hand more tightly around hers, to keep her with him, to not ever let her slip away.

Unfortunately, though, the next time Ian opened his eyes, it was not Noèle's face he saw. Indeed, standing by the windows, with his back to him, was Henri. His gaze was directed out toward the sea, the expression upon his face thoughtful.

"Noèle?" Ian said nonetheless, as though her name could conjure her somehow.

Henri turned toward him, large strides carrying him over to the bed where he sat down upon the chair situated there. "Awake again, I see," he chuckled, his green eyes serious despite the cheerful tone in his voice. "You've been sleeping for quite a long while." He paused, something flickering in his eyes. "You had a terrible fever. Noèle was afraid for you. We all were." He nodded as though to emphasize his words. "How are you?"

Ian swallowed. "Quite well," he replied, surprised to realize that he was speaking the truth. "How long?" he suddenly wondered. "How long have I been out?"

"Almost a month," Henri replied, his words chilling Ian's being. "You were in and out of it again and again. One day, we thought you'd recover, and the next..." He shrugged. "It seemed you were not quite certain if you wished to return to us." His brows rose in question.

Ian averted his gaze, suddenly feeling guilty. "Where's Noèle?" He knew he ought not ask. He knew he ought not long for her the way he did. It would only make it harder to let her go once the *Voile Noire* set sail again.

"In bed, sleeping. She's been here day and night," Henri told him with a meaningful look in his eyes, half teasing and half serious. "She refused to leave your side for more than a few minutes." He chuckled. "I wonder why that is?"

Rather uncharacteristically, Ian felt a flush rise to his cheeks, and he wished desperately that Henri did not see it. However, the amused look upon the Frenchman's face told Ian that he was not so lucky. "But she and Ophélie are well?" he asked quickly, searching for something to say that might, just might, distract Henri from teasing him further.

Henri waved a hand to brush Ian's concerns away. "They are more than well." He frowned briefly. "Well, except for Noèle's lack of sleep." Again, his brows rose meaningfully. "Other than that, they're perfectly well. Everyone is overjoyed to have them back home again, fighting over whose turn it is to feed Ophélie, to change her, to play with her, to rock her to sleep." He shook his head, chuckling. "It is as though they've never seen a babe before."

Ian sighed, relieved to hear that Noèle and Ophélie were safe and happy and finally where they belonged. Of course, the Durets would forever watch over them, ensuring their well-being and safety. "I am... glad to hear it," Ian replied, then reached for the cup of water. "And Dubois?" Aye, merely thinking of the man sent an ice-cold shiver down Ian's back. He remembered too well the way that monster had looked at Noèle, his vile thoughts written all over his face. For that alone, Ian could have killed him.

The expression upon Henri's face sobered. "Antoine sent word from Paris. Dubois is being tried for treason, and it looks favorable." He scoffed. "Well, for us, not so much for him."

Ian nodded. "That is good. She will feel much safer with him gone."

Henri regarded him curiously. "And you? What will you do now?"

Frowning, Ian shrugged, then sucked in a sharp breath at the pain that assailed his shoulder. "I suppose I am not much use like this." He glanced toward his injured shoulder. "However, I would like...nothing more than to rejoin your crew after I'm fully healed."

Leaning back in his chair, Henri crossed his arms, still eyeing Ian with a touch of surprised curiosity. "Is that so? You wish to be my first mate again?"

Ian nodded, trying to settle his shoulder in a comfortable way. "I do." He met Henri's gaze. "I don't know how soon—"

"Not this year," Henri interrupted, a slowly deepening frown upon his face. "Winter is fast approaching, and the ships are brought in for repairs."

"Next year then."

Henri shook his head, a languid sigh drifting from his lips. "I would've never pegged you for a fool." He suddenly leaned forward, bracing his elbows upon his legs, and met Ian's eyes. "Do you not care for her?" he asked directly. "Is that it? Are we all wrong in assuming that you've lost your heart to her?"

Shock froze every inch of Ian's body as he stared at Henri, unable to move, unable to utter a single word, unable to even catch a clear thought.

"*Oui*, you heard me correctly," Henri confirmed, once again leaning back in his chair and recrossing his arms. "Why would you run from this?" He heaved a deep sigh, then ran a hand through his hair. "Listen, not long ago, I was exactly where you are now. I knew, deep down, that I loved Juliette, but I was also terrified of what might happen if I admitted to it. I was terrified of losing her, of her losing her life!" He shot to his feet and stalked around the room, his hands raking through his hair. "And yet, in the end, I simply could not stay away. My father helped me realize that some risks are worth taking." He moved to stand at the foot of the bed, his green eyes meeting Ian's. "She cares for you. You have to know that. You cannot be so blind as to not know that." His brows rose meaningfully, his gaze drilling into Ian. "When Dubois took you, she did not hesitate. She insisted they go after you. She was terrified of losing you." He heaved a deep breath, then chuck-led. "Why do you think she has been at your side all this time?"

Henri's words continued to echo through Ian's head, and he could feel himself wanting to reach out to them, to believe them, to hold them close. And yet there was this part of him that could not help but doubt everything he had just been told. No, it could not be. Noèle could not possibly care for him. She still loved her husband, and she would love him until the end of her days. Love was nothing that simply went away. It survived death and separation and even heartbreak. Ian knew so from experience. Aye, long ago, he had believed differently, and that belief had ruined his life. He would be a fool to do so again!

"Think about it," Henri counseled. "If you care for her, you need to make that clear." He stepped away and toward the door, then paused and looked back at Ian. "And do not lie to yourself. I know it is tempting, for it seems to make things far easier. Yet in the end, it never leads to anything good." He reached for the door handle, and then paused yet again, a wistful smile coming to his face. "My grandfather always says, *The sea brings those together that belong together*." Shrugging, he looked back at Ian. "I never quite took him seriously...until I met Juliette." Then he left, closing the door behind him.

Ian did not know what to do or think, and for the first time, he wished for that blackness to return and take him.

Unfortunately, it refused.

Chapter Twenty-Five

THE DARING

"Have you spoken to him yet?" Juliette asked as they stood high up on a cliff overlooking the small village of La Roche-sur-Mer. Below them, the sea churned against the rock, waves rolling in from far out. A cold wind swirled around them, and both women tugged their cloaks tighter around themselves.

Noèle hung her head, shifting her eyes to the child in her arms, her cheeks rosy from the cold. "I have not," she said, watching as Ophélie tried to catch the strands of her hair that were billowing in the wind.

"Why not?" Juliette pressed, one hand resting upon her rounded belly. "It's been months since our return." She stepped into Noèle's line of vision, her green eyes relentless and yet gentle. "If you say nothing, he will leave as soon as he is able. You know that."

Noèle nodded. "*Oui*, I do."

"Then what is holding you back?"

Noèle heaved a deep breath. "I don't know," she said with a shrug, feeling that helpless sensation sweep through her once more. Indeed, over the past few months she had tried more than once to speak to Ian, to reveal how she felt and ask after his own heart. At each and every time, *something* had stopped her. Surely, they had spoken...about Ophélie, about the Durets, about privateering, about the weather and the sea. About everything and nothing. Yet despite the longing she had glimpsed in Ian's gaze every once in a while, he had remained distant, that wall around his heart now more fortified than ever. Why? What did he fear? What thoughts had been on his mind as he had lain in fever? What was it that now stood between them?

"*Oui*, I believe that he cares for me, and yet I feel as though," Noèle began, trying desperately to put into words what she sensed every time he looked at her, "no matter what I say, he will not believe me. He will not risk it." She shook her head helplessly. "Every time I try to broach the subject, he...pulls away. I can see it in his eyes. He is afraid to believe me, to even hear me say the words."

"That is all the more reason to speak to him," Juliette insisted with an annoyed eye roll. "Believe me, Henri was much the same. He was so stubborn and insistent that he did not care, that there was no future for us. You have to be *more* stubborn than him!"

Noèle paused, thinking back to the last time she had spoken to Ian. "I don't think that will be enough. There is something else. I feel as though he is living under some kind of dark cloud overshadowing everything. Something from his past, perhaps."

Ophélie giggled as her little hands continued to reach for Noèle's hair, giving it a painful yank every now and then.

"He told me he has a wife," Noèle said without preamble, knowing that this fact was something that occupied her thoughts a lot.

Juliette's eyes widened. "He does? But...?"

"He says she always loved another, and as much as he tried, he could never win her heart." She swallowed hard, retrieving a curl of her hair from her daughter's clutches. "I think he never truly believed himself worthy of her love nor does he believe himself worthy of anyone's love."

"Do you think he still loves her?" Juliette inquired carefully.

Noèle shrugged. "I have no way of knowing that," she replied, feeling her heart twist painfully in her chest. "I never knew her. I never knew them together. Yet I cannot help but wonder, what if he met her again today, would he..." She looked at Juliette with pleading eyes and shrugged. "What am I to do? How can I know if his heart will ever truly be mine?"

Juliette's lips thinned as she breathed in deeply of the cold air, a thoughtful look coming to her eyes. For a long time, she gazed out to sea before she met Noële's eyes once more. "Perhaps he should return home," she finally said. "Perhaps in order to move forward, he needs to confront his past."

Noële stilled.

In the moment Ophélie had been returned to her, she had known deep in her heart that Ian could not continue on for the rest of his days without once again laying eyes upon his children. *Oui*, this was about more than the wife he had left behind, the wife who could not love him. This went to the core of his being, and for as long as he ran from his past, Ian would never be at peace, never able to open his heart to another.

Not truly.

And Noële wanted him to.

Needed him to.

"Perhaps you're right," she mumbled, then frowned when Juliette suddenly stepped forward, hands reaching to take Ophélie from her arms. The girl had been struggling to get down, eager to explore the world on her own, now that she had figured out how to crawl.

"Then talk to him now," Juliette insisted, and her gaze rose and indicated something beyond Noële's shoulder. "Do not wait any longer." Then she tickled Ophélie under the chin and walked away, down the slope from the cliff and back toward the house. She nodded to Ian as he made his way upward, his gaze not quite daring to settle upon Noële's.

Yet he kept walking.

Bracing herself, Noële watched his slow ascent. It almost felt as though he knew what subject she intended to broach. Still, he could have turned and walked away.

"It is a beautiful day, is it not?" Ian greeted her, his gaze barely meeting hers before it slid off and went out to the far horizon. "Freezing, but beautiful." Snowflakes began to drift down from above, swirling through the air.

Noële moved to stand beside him, her gaze following his, thinking that perhaps this would be easier if they did not look at one another.

"There is something I wish to speak to you about," she began, feeling him tense beside her. In an odd way, she had become accustomed to all the subtle signs that spoke to his mood, to where his heart and mind were.

"Are ye concerned about something?" Ian asked, still determinedly keeping his gaze upon the far horizon. His arm was still in a sling, but Noèle knew that it would not be much longer before he was fully recovered. He already showed signs of deep annoyance when others insisted he rest his shoulder and not participate in the work around the house. It made him feel uneasy, reliant upon others, for he still thought of himself as a guest, an outsider, a stranger, who was granted something he had no right to.

"*Oui*," Noèle replied, knowing that there was no turning back. "I am concerned about you."

As a reply, Ian's eyes briefly shifted down to her, a slight frown creasing his forehead. "Me?" he asked in a disbelieving voice before his eyes dropped from hers once more. "I'm all but healed."

Noèle inhaled a deep breath, savoring the soft tingling of the fresh sea air reaching down into her lungs. "Because of you, I have my daughter back in my life," she said softly, remembering that one moment after endless months when she had finally seen Ophélie again aboard the merchant vessel. "I could not have gone on without her, without ever seeing her again. Without our children, we are barely half the people we used to be. There's a deep hole in our hearts that can never be filled by anyone else. It doesn't heal or mend in any way. It is just as gaping after years as it was that first day."

Beside her, Noèle could sense something heavy and sorrowful weighing down upon Ian's shoulders. Even though he tried not to let it show, she could see that he no longer stood as tall, his eyes now clouded with pain and longing.

Inhaling a fortifying breath, Noèle turned to look at him. She reached out and took his cold hands in hers, urging him to turn and face her.

Reluctantly, he did; and yet his gaze still would not meet hers.

"You will never forget them," Noèle began, her hands tightening upon his, needing him to understand that she would not walk away.

"You know this to be true. You know that their loss has overshadowed every step you've taken in the past few years, you know that will never change...unless you go back and fix what went wrong."

As though struck by lightning, Ian flinched in a way that almost yanked his hands out of hers. His blue eyes opened wide, shock marking his features, making it clear that he had never once, not even for a tiny second, considered returning home.

Not truly.

For the longest time, Ian simply stared at her, so obviously aghast that Noèle felt the urge to reach out and comfort him. Yet she resisted, knowing that he needed to feel this. He needed to feel this sense of loss and longing, of hope and possibility. He had pushed all thoughts of his family away, no doubt hoping that by ignoring all he felt he would eventually no longer feel it.

Only that was not how the world worked.

How the heart worked.

Love, especially for one's children, was forever.

"No." That one word slipped from Ian's lips, his jaw instantly hardening in resistance.

Noèle breathed in deeply, holding on tightly as he tried to pull his hands from her grip. "I will not let you run away from this," she told him, forcing steel into her voice. "You were there for me when I needed you. You helped me when—"

"I only did what ye asked me to do," Ian pointed out, a touch of anger in his voice. Yet it could not mask the panic she could sense within him. "Ye wanted yer daughter back. I only—"

"I did, *oui*, as do you," Noèle interrupted, determined to meet every one of his arguments with one of her own. "The only difference between the two of us is that you are not willing to admit it. I know you miss them. I know you long for them. Your heart wishes for nothing more than to see them again." She stepped closer, her gaze drilling into his. "Look me in the eyes and tell me I'm wrong."

Ian's eyes closed, and he bowed his head in surrender. "I left to protect them," Ian whispered to the wind, his voice barely audible, barely able to carry these words out into the world. "They're better off without me."

Noèle recognized his words as those he had no doubt spoken to himself again and again, hoping that one day he would truly believe them. And yet right here, in this moment, Noèle could sense an almost desperate need in him to hear them contradicted. "You know that is not true," Noèle answered his silent cry. "You were a good father to them. You—"

His head snapped up. "How would ye know that? How—?"

"I know!" Noèle insisted, her hands once more tightening upon his as she held his gaze. "I know!"

His gaze lingered, and she could see that he wanted to believe her, that a part of him already did, for the right corner of his mouth twitched, as though deep down he longed to smile. "Ye willna give up, will ye?" he asked then, and that corner of his mouth twitched yet again.

Noèle smiled at him. "You never gave up, either," she told him, reaching out to cup her hand to his chilled cheek. He stilled at her touch, and yet she could sense that he, too, longed to feel her closer. "I've never seen you happy," Noèle whispered, gently brushing her thumb along his bottom lip, feeling his warm breath against her skin. "I long to see you happy, Ian. Please!"

A tremor went through him, and then he lifted his hand and placed it upon hers still cupping his cheek. His gaze held hers, something weak and equally strong shining there, while the fingers of his other hand twined with hers, holding on. "Aye," was all he said, one word that was swept away upon the wind so quickly that Noèle momentarily doubted whether he had truly spoken it.

Yet joy gripped Noèle so abruptly that she flew forward, pushed herself up onto her toes and drew Ian down into a kiss. Her lips touched his, and she slung her arms around him, enjoying the feel of him so close.

Ian's response was immediate.

His embrace almost swept her off her feet as he returned her kiss with a fierceness she had not expected. He always seemed so restrained, his demeanor guided by reason, by rational thought instead of impulse. And yet every once in a while, his emotions overruled his thoughts. Noèle remembered well the last time he had kissed her. It had been a similar moment, a moment when he had given in to what he wanted.

Ignored that little voice that had no doubt told him that it would be most unwise.

Pulling back, Noèle looked up into Ian's blue eyes, dark with emotions. She wanted nothing more than to continue what they had begun, to tell him how deeply she had come to feel for him.

Only now was not the time.

Ian's demons still lingered, ready to pounce on anything she might say and twist her words into something that would serve *them*.

Not *her*.

Noèle could not allow that to happen. *Non*, she needed to be patient. She needed to fight his demons before pulling him back out into the light.

Still, she would never forget this kiss!

"Come," Noèle exclaimed, grasping his hand and pulling him down the slope after her. "There's a lot to do before we can be off!" Out of the corner of her eye, she thought to see Ian's face fall when he realized what he had just agreed to.

Too late, Noèle thought almost giddily.

Chapter Twenty-Six

A VOYAGE HOME

For the first time, Ian stepped aboard a ship with a tense feeling in his gut. Something deep inside told him that he ought not be here. Aye, it was a day like any other. The spring sun shone brightly overhead, and the winds looked favorable, a warming breeze traveling upward from the south. Seagulls circled here and there, swooping in close every once in a while. Ian breathed in deeply, savoring the touch of salt upon the air, feeling the familiarity of walking across deck, that soft swaying beneath his feet. Indeed, he knew how to be on a ship. He had become acquainted with this life, the life of a sailor. He felt capable here, in control even, his mind and heart at ease, working hand in hand not against one another.

Yet, today, was different. Ian felt it in every step he took, for his thoughts instantly rushed across the sea, traveled the distance and soared high over the shores of Scotland.

His home.

His old home.

Standing with his hands grasping the railing, his loyal companion as always by his side, Ian raised his head and looked at the men readying the ship. They did what they always did, and yet today they did it for him. He was the sole reason for this voyage. Even now, Ian could hardly believe that the Durets had agreed to let him use the *Chevalier Noir* in order to sail home and see his children.

Scoffing, Ian shook his head, remembering the moment Noèle had spoken to the family, had explained where they meant to go.

Where *she* meant to take him.

Aye, Ian had been certain they would turn her down. Not because they felt no compassion, for he knew they did. Yet he had simply assumed that they had other uses for their ship, now that the new year had come, that it was needed, that they could not simply afford to hand it off without anything in return. Still, they had.

Without hesitation.

And gladly.

"The winds look good!" Henri remarked as he strode up the gang-plank and moved to stand beside Ian. His green eyes sparkled with mischief, and Ian was certain that Henri was amused by the way Noèle had orchestrated this voyage. Aye, she had a mind of her own and a strong will, and she was not afraid to use either.

Ian gave a short nod, his eyes remaining fixed upon the horizon.

Beside him, Henri chuckled. "*Oui*, you look like a man conflicted," he remarked in a voice one would use to comment upon the weather. "Then again, you always have." A challenging note clung to Henri's voice, and Ian knew that the Frenchman was only waiting for Ian to take the bait.

Years ago, Ian would have done so without thinking twice about it. However, he was a different man today. Indeed, that thought calmed him, and he felt a small sense of pride at the notion.

Failing to elicit a reaction from Ian, Henri grumbled something unintelligible under his breath. Then he stood back and straightened his shoulders, taking a deep breath, as though years had passed since he had smelled fresh sea air. "You will always have a family here in France," Henri suddenly said, and Ian could feel the Frenchman's eyes upon him, "yet you cannot ignore the one you left behind in Scotland. You need to make things right...for your own sake as well as hers."

Ian drew in a shuddering breath, overwhelmed by the advice he had received in the past few weeks. Everyone seemed to think that this voyage was a good idea, that it was necessary even. But why? What awaited him in Scotland? What would it do to his family if he suddenly reappeared?

"Take good care of her," Henri ordered in a mockingly stern voice as he clasped his hand onto Ian's shoulder. "Do you hear me?"

Turning to look at his former captain, Ian met Henri's eyes...and saw a friend. Not simply his captain or a fellow sailor, but a friend. Someone he might, aye, think of as family.

With the weight and comfort of Henri's hand upon his shoulder, Ian nodded. "Aye, ye have my word."

Henri grinned, then slapped Ian on the back. "I always knew you were a good man, Ian Stewart...or whatever your name is." Chuckling, Henri inclined his head in a farewell gesture and then hurried back down the gangplank, joining the rest of his family who were at this very moment standing upon the docks, waiting to see them off.

Him...

...and Noële.

As well as Ophélie, of course.

As Ian's gaze swept over the Durets, he could not help but wonder how this all had come to be. Years ago, he had left Scotland with nothing, not even his own name, determined to keep to himself, to live out the rest of his life in solitude. And he had thought himself successful. He had found something to do, something that gave his life meaning, and yet, somehow, he had ended up *here*.

To Ian's utter shock, he realized that Henri's words had been the truth. He *did* have a family here in France. He never would have believed it possible, and yet it had happened. Did that mean that something else he thought impossible could also be achieved?

Ian was fearful of giving into these thoughts, and so, as Noële came to stand beside him, Ophélie in her arms, Ian once again swept his gaze over the family he had never sought to find. He saw Henri and Juliette, standing arm in arm, as well as Antoine and Alexandra and their four children, their sons Victor and Vincent as well as their daughters, Aime and Aurelie. He saw Alain, Antoine's brother, as well as their parents Hubert and Colette. They had all taken him in, and he had come to care for them.

As much as Ian had tried to guard his heart from any emotional entanglements, he realized that he had failed. He had failed, and yet... he could not say that he regretted what had happened. He had a family! A family who had been at his side these past few years, who had come when he had needed them, who had risked their own lives to protect his. Ian could scarcely believe it, and he felt tears misting his eyes as the *Chevalier Noir* finally pulled out of the harbor, leaving behind one half of his family.

But not for good.

No, he would return. He could not imagine ever not returning home. Indeed, this small French village had found a place in his heart. He felt comfortable here and at ease, cared for and...wanted.

That was it, was it not? Ian had never quite felt *wanted*. Back home in Scotland, he had had a family, and he had been happy growing up there. However, with his wife, he had always known that he was not her choice. At least, not her first choice. She had lost the man she loved and Ian had stepped in to fill that void, and yet he had never quite managed. Each and every day, he had known that he was not good enough.

After all, he was not *him*.

Gritting his teeth, Ian forced his thoughts away from something that had plagued him for far too long. Countless days and nights, he had spent asking himself what he could do, how he could make her happy, in what way he needed to change to be more like *him*. He had done all he could, and yet it had never been enough.

Stepping away from the railing, Ian strode across the deck, his eyes watchful as they swept across the horizon. His mind analyzed the winds pushing the *Chevalier Noir* forward, drawing her away from the French coast and out into open waters. He saw Laurent at the helm and Guillaume up in the rigging, bravely facing his fear after slipping and nearly falling to his death the year before. He saw François and Jean and each and every man who had been with him these many months past, a crew he could count on, a crew that had his back.

And then he turned and looked back up at the quarterdeck where Noèle stood, Ophélie in her arms, her raven hair billowing in the wind. A smile lingered upon her features, and something utterly irresistible shone in her blue eyes. How it had happened Ian did not know, and yet he knew without a doubt that his heart was hers. Somehow, yet again, he had lost his heart without his even noticing. Only now, too late, did he realize what had occurred.

Aye, he had made the same mistake all over again.

Chapter Twenty-Seven
FEARS THAT CRIPPLE

Noële knew that there was something on Ian's mind. How could there not be? Yet deep down, she thought it was not the return to his old home that currently preoccupied his thoughts. *Non*, the way he seemed to avoid her, barely able to look her in the eyes, spoke to a different matter. At first, she thought he might be angry with her for forcing his hand, for sending him on a journey he did not wish to undertake. And yet it was only in moments when the comings and goings of everyday life led them together that he behaved in this strange manner.

Almost avoiding her...

...and yet unable to stay away.

Making soft cooing sounds, Noële settled her daughter in a corner of the cot, wrapped snugly in a blanket given to her by Alexandra. Her little chest rose and fell with even breaths, and every once in a while, a soft smile stole across her features. Noële loved watching her daughter sleep. Simply looking at her little face made her feel peaceful and calm and brought hope to her heart.

Tonight, though, she had something else on her mind.

Tonight, she had asked Ian to join her in the captain's quarters.

As expected, he had been surprised by her request, and yet he had not argued but simply nodded in that taciturn way of his.

Brushing the pad of her thumb across Ophélie's forehead, Noèle smiled as the wolf snuggled in beside her daughter. Then she straightened and turned to meet Ian's gaze. He simply stood there across the cabin by the windows, his features somehow gentler after watching her put Ophélie to bed. Had this simple moment reminded him of other moments he had shared with his own children? No doubt, as a father, he knew the joys of holding a sleeping child in his arms. Now that Noèle did as well, she could not imagine finding sleep at night without holding her daughter for at least a few moments.

With one last glance at a peacefully sleeping Ophélie, Noèle stepped away from the cot and toward the tortured man she had come to love. *Oui*, returning to Scotland, facing the demons of his past was important, and yet Noèle wished to know more first. Ian had already told her a little bit about his past, his family. He had told her about his wife and that she had never been able to love him because her heart had always belonged to another. Yet Noèle could not help but wonder, how had Ian ended up in France? What had happened? And why had he never contemplated returning home?

"Is there anything ye need help with?" Ian inquired, the muscles in his jaw tightening as his gaze moved from Ophélie to her. "Anything ye require?"

Noèle looked at him curiously. "Can you truly not think of another reason for me to ask you here? Do you truly believe that people would only seek your company because they need something from you?"

The muscles in Ian's shoulders tightened even further, and yet he refused to say anything at all. He simply stood there in the glowing light of the setting sun...and waited.

A part of Noèle had expected him to turn around and leave—flee her presence! *Oui*, Ian liked avoiding these kinds of topics. He did not wish to discuss himself or how he felt, his life or anything that made him feel uncomfortable...which was almost everything. Yet he stayed. He stood stock still like a marble column...and waited.

The flicker of a smile tickled Noèle's lips. *He does not wish to go*, she thought to herself. *He would never admit it, but he wants me to make him stay. He wants comfort and closeness, and I will not disappoint him.*

Holding Ian's gaze, Noèle moved toward him, inhaling a deep breath as she squared her shoulders, reminding herself that this would not be easy. "How did you come to leave Scotland?"

As expected, Ian flinched. It was a barely visible movement, and yet to Noèle, it felt like a shockwave. She could feel it everywhere. She could feel his resistance, the way he shrank back from that topic, wishing he could run from it, but also knowing that if he did so, his demons would never go away.

Ian cleared his throat, linking his hands behind his back. "A fishing boat pulled me out of the waters," he told her in a voice that betrayed no emotion, as though he was speaking about another's life and not his own. "Sometime later, the *Voile Noire* came upon—"

Noèle held up a hand. "I know that story. *Non*, what I wish to know is how you came to be in the water in the first place. What happened that day? Why did you not simply ask them to return you to shore?"

Ian's eyes looked almost thunderous, and for a moment, Noèle thought he would inform her that it was none of her concern, that she had no right to meddle in his life. Yet he simply sighed, and then slowly, ever so slowly, the hard expression in his eyes waned. "'Tis a long story," he finally said, contradicting emotions filling his voice.

Smiling up at him, Noèle gently took his hand in hers. "We have all night," she told him, tugging him forward so her other hand could reach up and cup his cheek. "I want to know everything."

Although Ian seemed to lean into her touch, his jaw hardened. "Ye will think differently once ye hear what happened," he ground out through clenched teeth. "Once ye hear what I did."

Holding his gaze, Noèle shook her head. "We all have things we regret. We all make mistakes. Yet I know the man you are, and I refuse to believe that you did something unforgivable." Gently, she brushed the pad of her thumb across his cheekbone. "I know so because of the simple fact that even after all these years the thought alone still tortures you." Pushing herself up onto her toes, Noèle placed a gentle kiss upon his lips. "Please, Ian, tell me."

The expression upon his face grew gentler, and yet the pain in his eyes remained. For a long time, he simply looked at her, his eyes sweeping across her face, lingering here and there. Then he reached out a tentative hand, tenderly touching the tips of his fingers to her face, tracing the line of her jaw. He sighed, then nodded in acquiescence or perhaps defeat, and turned away. He moved toward the windows, his back to her, his hands linking behind his back. He stared out across the sea, the warm glow of the setting sun trailing across his features as he resigned himself to this moment.

Noèle felt a shiver flit across her skin when Ian began to speak. His voice was quiet and not angry as she had expected. *Non*, instead there was something heartbreakingly sorrowful in the way he spoke, the way he bowed his head.

"I dunna quite know where to begin," Ian murmured softly into the stillness. "Even now, after all these years, I'm not entirely certain how things came to pass." He cleared his throat. "I always loved my wife. I loved her from the first moment I laid eyes upon her." For a moment, his eyes closed and he inhaled a deep breath. "I know that she cared for me, but I soon came to realize that her heart would never be mine. I dunna remember a particular moment when that realization struck. It was more something that slowly seeped into my being over time. I remember anger rising. I remember resentment growing. I kept trying, yet...nothing happened."

Noèle felt her heart grow heavy. She could not imagine finding herself married to someone, loving them and knowing at the same time that that person did not love her back. Would *never* love her back. What would it have felt like if she had found herself married to Étienne in such a way? If he had married her as a friend while she had given him her heart? Noèle could not imagine such a fate, living day after day, fully aware that there would be no happily ever after. She could imagine growing angry, too, and resentful. It was natural to feel those things, was it not?

"I knew I had been a fool," Ian continued, his shoulders sagging, as though a heavy weight had descended upon them. "I love my children and I love my wife, and yet knowing that she didna love me back, that I would never be good enough, that I would never be *him*...changed the man I was." He bowed his head, and out of the corner of her eye,

Noèle saw the wolf's head rise, his watchful eyes directed at Ian. "I didna realize it at the time, but I felt trapped and angry and I needed someone to blame." He shook his head at himself, at his own foolishness. "And I found that person when Moira Brunwood came to live with her aunt at Clan MacDrummond."

Standing in the corner, Noèle watched him, watched a myriad of emotions play across his features. She could sense his reluctance to continue on, and so she stepped forward and placed a hand upon his arm. "Who was she?"

Ian's lips thinned. "People whispered that she had the Sight. Only she had used that gift against her own people. She had betrayed her clan, her family, and had been banished for it." His gaze returned from the vastness of the horizon and moved to meet hers. "The Brunwoods and the MacDrummonds had always been close, allies, friends." He heaved a heavy sigh. "And so, my friend, our chief, Cormag MacDrummond, agreed to take her in when the Brunwood chief requested it. Ye see, Moira was the Brunwood chief's cousin. They had grown up with one another, and despite her betrayal, he felt the need to look out for her. He knew he couldna allow her to remain with their clan, and yet he didna wish to banish her without any place to go." Again, his lips thinned, and he shook his head. "I was against it from the start, believing that she didna deserve this mercy. I feared what she might do to my clan, my people if given the chance."

All but holding her breath, Noèle slipped her hand into Ian's, holding it tightly within her own as she looked up into his eyes. "What did she do?" Noèle asked, fearful to hear the answer.

To her surprise, though, Ian scoffed. "She did nothing. She was no danger to anyone. In fact, she did her utmost to make amends, to help, to protect. She saved people whenever she could, my own daughter included." Ian's eyes closed, a look of utter shame upon his face. "I, however, became a danger to her."

Noèle felt her insides tense as a coldness swept through her, sending shivers down her back. This was not what she had expected.

Chapter Twenty-Eight

THE VILLAIN IN THE STORY

Ian knew that Noèle was determined to see the good in him. She simply was the kind of person who saw the good in everyone. And yet as those last words left his lips, he felt her still, her muscles tensing as she found her beliefs shaken by the truth.

For the truth was that Moira had never been the villain in this story. He had! Ian MacDrummond had been the villain.

The one who had been a danger to others.

The one who had acted out of rage.

The one who had betrayed his own people.

And now, Noèle knew it. Now, she would never again look at him with those eyes of hers, full of trust and hope and kindness. Now, she would be wary of him...and perhaps she ought to be.

Her small hand tightened upon his as she swallowed, courage and determination keeping her eyes from falling from his. "What do you mean?" she asked tentatively. "How did you become...a danger to her?"

More than anything, Ian wished he could simply disappear, stalk from the cabin and fling himself overboard. Aye, the sea ought to have taken him instead of Étienne that night!

"I heard the whispers," Ian continued, fighting to remain where he was, knowing that she deserved to know, "and I started to believe them. I looked at her, and I saw someone cunning. I became suspicious of her, and then one day, I saw her speaking to my wife." A disbelieving scoff left his lips. "Saying it out loud now makes it sound ludicrous. Yet in that moment it felt like proof."

Noèle frowned at him. "Proof of what?"

Closing his eyes, Ian inhaled a deep breath, steeling himself for what lay ahead. "Proof that she was a witch, a witch who had turned my wife's heart against me." He met Noèle's eyes, wondering if she would laugh at him now.

Instead, a flicker of understanding lit up her eyes and she nodded. "*Oui*, the heart has a way of protecting itself. It finds ways to lift burdens that are too heavy."

Aghast, Ian stared at her. "Ye canna truly excuse what I—"

"I am not excusing anything," Noèle interrupted him, her blue eyes still holding that same sense of trust he had come to cherish. "All I'm saying is that you found yourself in an impossible situation and that sometimes when that happens we do things we wouldn't otherwise do. We do what we need to do to survive." Tears came to her eyes, and all of a sudden, she looked frighteningly vulnerable. "When I lost my husband, I felt..." Shaking her head, she stared up at him. "I don't know if there is a word to describe how I felt. I was so lost and it hurt so much that there were days when I thought...I could not continue on." Clearing her throat, she forced her tears back, her lips thinning as she fought for composure. "I know what it's like to stand at that abyss and reach for anything to keep from falling in. Anything at all."

Most days, Ian looked at Noèle and thought her delicate and vulnerable, an immediate need to protect her sweeping through him, the need to see her safe; yet here, in this moment, she possessed a silent strength Ian envied.

Without thinking, he reached out and wrapped her in his embrace, not for her but for himself. He needed her strength, her certainty, her understanding. She felt warm and alive and real, grounding him to this moment, and her arms came around him as he had known they would.

For a long time, they simply stood in each other's embrace as the ship swayed gently, dancing across the waves. The golden sun dipped lower, bit by bit disappearing into the sea, and the streaks of red and purple across the sky made the world seem more peaceful than it ever had been.

At least, to Ian.

With her arms still wrapped around him and her head resting against his shoulder, Noèle whispered, "What happened then?"

Involuntarily, Ian tightened his hold upon her, drawing comfort from her presence. "I spoke out against her. I told Cormag that he had made a mistake. I urged him to reconsider." He felt her hand settling over the rapid beating of his heart. "When he wouldna listen, I lashed out at her. I told her to stay away from my family, from my wife and children. I..." He gritted his teeth against the memory that resurfaced. "I even attacked her."

That day, so many years ago, returned to him as though it had been only yesterday. "Blair had gone to pick some sort of flower, but she fell into a pool of water and nearly drowned." He still remembered the blue tinge of her lips and the paleness of her face. Never in his life had Ian been more frightened. "And when I learned that my daughter had gone to pick flowers for *her*, I completely lost control of all my senses. I sought her out in her own home, wrapped my hands around her throat and threatened to crush the life from her." A wave of shame and regret flooded his heart. "If Cormag hadna interfered, I—" He swallowed the lump in his throat. "I dunna know how he knew, but he was suddenly there. He came and he stopped me."

Noèle shifted, and Ian felt her looking up at him, her head still resting against his shoulder. "He loved her, did he not? Cormag?"

Surprised by her words, Ian moved so he could look down into her eyes. "Aye, he did. He married her not long after." Ian remembered well how he had thought Moira had put a spell on Cormag as well. He remembered his frustration that no one saw what he could see so plainly in front of him.

"And then? How did you come to be in the sea?"

"I kept warning everyone, and yet no one listened. I saw those around me listening to her, instead, looking at her as though she were a friend, someone to trust. My own wife befriended her. My daughter could speak of little else but her." A frustrated sigh left his lips. "No matter what I did, no one would listen. I saw them all slipping away... and so I thought the time to act had come."

Releasing Noèle, Ian stepped away. He could no longer bear her touch, not when he was so close to revealing his darkest secret to her. He moved closer to the window, his gaze fixed outside at the last smidgen of light remaining. "I watched her, and when I saw her leaving the castle early one morning, I followed her. I struck her down, tied her to a horse and took her across the land toward the sea."

Behind him, Ian could sense Noèle move closer, her soft footsteps upon the floorboards echoing to his ears. A part of him wished she would once more reach for his hand while another wanted her to stay as far away from him as possible.

"Only when we reached the cliffs," Ian continued, determined to speak the truth and have it done with, "my daughter found us." To this day, he could not believe that Blair had been there, that she had come. "She said she had seen some sort of danger in her dreams. She said she had been worried about me and, thus, she had followed us." He closed his eyes, once again seeing Blair's little face, her eyes so full of love and devotion, so innocent and yet so wise. "I knew then that she, too, possessed the Sight, that she had dreams that spoke to her of the future, just as Moira did. I looked from my daughter to the woman who had taken everything from me, and I couldna bear it any longer."

Now, Noèle's hand did reach out, settling upon his arm, a soft pressure, reassuring and yet urging him on at the same time. "What did you do?"

Ian met her eyes. "Honestly, I dunna know what I would've done... and 'tis that thought that frightens me most."

Noèle frowned. "What you...*would* have done? What do you mean?"

"It was in that moment that a wolf charged out of the undergrowth," he told her with a wry smile, remembering the moment he had first laid eyes on his loyal companion. As though the creature knew he was being discussed, a soft yip left his throat, his watchful yellow eyes still fixed upon them both.

Noèle's eyes widened as she looked from Ian to the wolf and back. "That is how you met?"

Ian nodded. "He was thin and malnourished and desperate for food, and he looked at my daughter and saw easy prey." He lifted his head and met the wolf's eyes across the cabin. "He charged, and I couldna get to her." His gaze moved and returned to Noèle's. "But Moira could." Fighting the tears that threatened, he pressed his lips into a thin line, his thoughts traveling backward in time to that one moment. "Even though I had attacked her in countless ways, even though I had been close to drowning her in the sea, she didna hesitate. She protected my daughter, risked her own life by stepping into the wolf's path armed with no more than a branch."

Noèle's eyes were wide and instantly moved to her own sleeping child. As a mother, she understood the horror he had gone through better than anyone.

"As Moira struggled to hold the wolf at bay, I snatched up Blair and put her on a horse, sending her to safety." In that moment, Ian had known that he would never see his daughter again. "And then I turned back to Moira and the wolf. I pulled my dagger and threw myself onto the wolf. We fought, rolling around on the cliff top, and I could feel my senses beginning to slip away. I'd hit my head, and I could feel blood running down my temple." He remembered the way darkness had settled over him, threatening to close his eyes and loosen his hold.

"I remember," Ian whispered, as Noèle looked up at him with a tear-streaked face, "seeing Cormag arrive in the clearing. How he came to find us I dunna know. Perhaps Moira had a way of calling him to her." He shook his head. "And then the wolf and I rolled off the cliff, and for a split second as Cormag raced toward us, our eyes met and I found myself looking at my old friend. And in that moment, it hit me what I had done. I remember my mind clearing with such force that it felt like a dagger had been plunged into my heart. I hurt all over." He bowed his head. "And then the moment was gone, and I fell." He met Noèle's eyes. "I remember the cold of the water, the shock...and then nothing. I dunna know how I came to be on the fishing boat. I dunna remember being pulled from the water."

Noèle's hands grasped his, warm and soft. "You saved her life," she whispered, her blue eyes searching his. "You—"

"I *threatened* her life!" Ian objected, trying to pull his hands from hers, but she would not allow him. "Her life wouldna have been in danger if it hadna been for me."

"True," Noèle agreed, yet the gentle look in her eyes did not wane. "You made a mistake; *oui*, more than one," she amended when he opened his mouth to object, "but once you realized the truth, you did what you could to make amends." Her eyes were wide and imploring as they looked into his.

Ian sighed. "Some things canna be undone...or forgiven."

"Is that why you never returned?" Noèle inquired, eyeing him in a rather shrewd manner. "Why you never even considered it? Are you afraid she will not forgive you? That your friend will not?"

Ian scoffed. "How could she? After what I've done—"

"I believe she's already forgiven you."

Shocked by her words, Ian stared at her. "W-What? Why would ye...? How could ye possibly...?"

One of those terribly disarming smiles tickled Noèle's lips. "Because if there is anyone in this world who understands, it is her. Has she not been down the same path? Did she not also receive a second chance?"

Ian knew the answers to her questions, and yet deep inside, he thought them unconnected to his own life. What he had done and what Moira had done...

She had never...

Yet he had tried to...

"Believe me," Noèle whispered as her hands reached out and cupped his face, "you and Cormag will not meet as enemies but as friends, for that is what you always have been. Trust me. He will understand because she does."

Tears blurred Ian's vision, and then he felt himself sink to his knees, his arms wrapping around Noèle as she cradled his head against her belly. She held him as he wept for the past, for all he had suffered and lost, for all he had foolishly given up without a fight.

Yet if he had not...

...he would never have met her.

He would never have met Noèle.

It was a thought Ian did not wish to consider. Meeting her had been worth every bit of pain he had endured.

Aye, perhaps there was a reason for everything that had happened. Perhaps.

Chapter Twenty-Nine
ONCE A FATHER

Ever since the night Ian had revealed the demons of his past to her, he had been different. He no longer tried to avoid her, a shy smile touching his lips whenever their paths crossed. Noèle delighted in the change in him. He still seemed apprehensive, almost fearful, and yet every once in a while she caught a glimpse of the man she believed he had once been.

A man who knew the meaning of a smile.

A man who cherished laughter.

A man who loved life.

Noèle had also taken note of the way Ian often eyed Ophélie, his blue eyes wistful and full of longing. Yet he never stepped too close, a shadow falling over his face whenever the little girl stretched out a hand toward him.

One day, three days after that night, Noèle remembered what Étienne had often told her: *Fate favored the daring.* And so, early that morning when Ian came to the captain's quarters to inquire after her, Noèle simply placed Ophélie in his arms. "Will you watch her?" she rushed to say on her way out the door. "I promised to help out with breakfast."

And then she was gone, climbing up the hatch and up on deck.

A wide smile came to Noèle's face as she met the early morning sun, her hands settling upon the railing. The air felt fresh and invigorating, and somehow Noèle felt certain that they were nearing their destination. Squinting her eyes, she wondered how much longer before she would spy Scotland upon the horizon.

Of course, it was not recommended for a French vessel to simply sail up the English coast and into enemy waters. However, Henri had a good bit of experience, sneaking in and out of England to see Violette and her family, and he had passed on invaluable suggestions, regarding "opportune" fog and caverns that could hide a ship until nightfall.

Noèle smiled as she breathed in deeply, savoring the sea air, the way it tugged upon her curls and brushed across her skin. Before, she had never spent much time aboard a ship. She had never truly understood Étienne's fascination with the sea. Now, however, Noèle had to admit that there was something almost magical about standing upon the deck of a ship cutting across the waves, the wind swirling wildly around her and the horizon far out there in the far distance. She felt truly at peace, her past no longer a burden and her future a string of endless possibilities.

Her eyes swept over that thin line where sea met sky, and yet again Noèle wondered when she would catch her first glimpse of the Scottish coast. What would it look like? Would it seem familiar? Or utterly foreign? She tried to imagine the tall cliff face from which Ian and the wolf had fallen into the sea. She tried to picture it in her mind: the rock, the trees, the clearing.

And then, her mind suddenly galloped off in an entirely different direction!

Noèle no longer saw an image of the countryside but instead of the family Ian had left behind. She saw a young eight-year-old girl with blue eyes and blonde curls, standing hand-in-hand with a boy two years her senior, his hair a wild red and his eyes as green as...his mother's.

Ian's wife.

Ian had a wife, and, at least, three years ago he had loved his wife deeply. It had almost destroyed him to know that she had never been able to return his affections. But what of today? Noèle knew she ought to have contemplated this question sooner. Perhaps she would have if she had not been afraid of its answer. Did Ian still love his wife? The same way he had back then?

The same way she had loved Étienne?

Tentatively, reluctantly, Noële tried to picture the slender young woman with red hair and brilliant green eyes who had conquered Ian's heart so long ago. A part of Noële wanted to dislike her, and yet she knew it would not be right. After all, Margaret MacDrummond had never truly done anything wrong. She had lost the man she had loved, had had her trust in him betrayed, and had then hoped for another chance at love with Ian.

Noële wondered if, at the time, Margaret had truly believed that given time Ian would surely conquer her heart. Had she been hopeful? And had the fact that Ian had been unable to sway her heart felt devastating to her as well?

Had his wife perhaps found that, at least, a part of her had come to love Ian now that he was gone? That she thought him dead and lost to her for good?

Noële swallowed hard at that thought, for it entailed another that was almost too painful to consider. What if somehow Ian and his wife found their way back to one another after all these years? What if they reached the Scottish shore and he wanted to stay with his family?

Instantly, Noële chided herself. If Ian had any chance of finding his way back to his family, then she ought to be happy for him, ought she not? It was what he wanted. What he had always wanted.

Sighing deeply, Noële closed her eyes, wondering where that peacefulness had gone. All of a sudden, her heart felt heavy and she no longer hoped to glimpse Scotland upon the horizon. Was that selfish of her?

Oui, it was.

Yet it did not change how she felt. She cared for Ian, she loved him, and she wanted him by her side. She could not imagine living day after day without him. All of a sudden, he felt as essential to her as the air she breathed.

But how did *he* feel?

If only she knew.

Rather dumbfounded, Ian stared down at the little girl in his arms. Her wide blue eyes looked up at him in a similar fashion before she reached out a hand and grasped a loose strand of his blonde hair. Her little fingers curled around it, and he felt a soft tug upon his scalp. Perhaps he flinched or made some kind of grimace, for Ophélie suddenly giggled, clearly delighted, and immediately tugged upon the strand of his hair again.

When Noèle had simply handed her daughter to him and then flown out the door, as though it were something perfectly normal, Ian had not known what to think. For a moment, every fiber of his being had stilled, uncertain what to do next, unable to cope with this new situation. He had wanted to call after her, to call her back, to tell her that she could not simply leave Ophélie with him. Yet no sound had passed his lips. He had simply stood there in the middle of the cabin, his eyes wide, and looked down at Noèle's little daughter.

Ophélie's hair was raven-black like her mother's, and her blue eyes reminded Ian of the dark sea on a stormy day. At barely a year old, Ophélie's gaze spoke of curiosity, of a fascination with the world around her, of a burning desire to explore each and every aspect of it. Her little fingers curled with eagerness, reaching out and tugging upon his hair and collar, her eyes sweeping over his face, as though she wished to memorize the look of him.

Ian felt his heart constrict in his chest, for he had known such an expression before. He had seen this look, this very expression, upon his own children's faces. Niall and Blair both had once looked at him like this, had once lain in his arms, their eager hands reaching for him.

"Ye remind me of someone," Ian suddenly heard himself say as he shifted Ophélie and sat down upon one of the chairs, facing the windows, settling Ophélie upon his leg. "I havena seen them in a long time." Ophélie's blue eyes watched him intently, as though she understood every word. "I miss them," Ian admitted quietly, allowing his sorrow to sweep through him so he would feel it in every fiber of his being.

Ian found his mind stray elsewhere until Ophélie's hand once more tugged upon the strand of his hair to bring his attention back to her. He smiled seeing the expression upon her face. "In fact, we're on our way to see them right now." Ian closed his eyes and shook his head. "It feels odd to say this, wrong somehow. Years ago, I swore I would never return. I swore I would never again risk their happiness. I knew they were better off without me, without my anger."

Ian was surprised to hear himself speaking thus, and yet it was that wondrous expression upon Ophélie's face that kept him talking. It felt good to pour out his soul to another, and yet she knew not of what he spoke. It was simply the rhythm and the tone of his words that fascinated her, that made her pause and listen.

Ian smiled at her. "I do want to see them again, and yet I'm afraid of how they'll look at me. Will they turn away? Most, though, I'm afraid of the moment when I'll have to bid them farewell once more. And yet, I know I canna stay. No matter what happens, Scotland is no longer my home. My family is no longer my family." His thoughts trailed backwards to the life he had once had. "My family thinks me dead, and so they moved on without me. They have a life now that doesna include me, and I dunna have the right to upset it by returning." He stilled when a sudden thought occurred to him. "What if... Maggie remarried?"

Ian wondered if that was even possible. After all, even after years of marriage, her heart had still belonged to her first love. Would she ever enter into another marriage without love? No, Ian did not believe that possible. Maggie had always been a passionate person, loving fiercely and with all her heart. If only she could have loved him!

At that thought, Ian's mind instantly conjured an image of Noèle, and as though Ophélie could read his mind, a soft giggle fell from her lips. "Yer mother is verra special," Ian told her with a smile, feeling his heart lighten. "She's verra special to me." He reached out and twirled one of Ophélie's short strands around his forefinger. "And to ye as well, of course."

As though wishing to swat his hand away, Ophélie reached out her own. Yet her finger simply curled into his shirt and held on tight. Then she plopped her other hand into her mouth and sucked on her fingers, a dream-like expression upon her face.

Again, Ian found himself smile, remembering his own children at that age, wondering what they looked like today. Only now, he felt torn. A part of him, that old self he had once been, still longed to return home, to his family, to his own life. And yet, now, there was a new part, and that part wished to remain where he was with Noèle and Ophélie.

Oddly, in that moment, Ian realized that he *was* two men. Aye, deep down, he was still Ian MacDrummond, and yet he was also Ian Stewart. Somehow, rather unexpectedly, he had come to love this new life he had made for himself. He had not realized it until this moment when all of a sudden he *wanted* again.

Before, he had merely existed from day to day, trying to keep his head down and his attention focused on the tasks placed before him. He had tried his utmost not to think and feel and wish and hope and dream. In fact, he had done very little of all of these in the past four years. And yet, the past few months had changed everything.

"I love yer mother," Ian whispered to little Ophélie, amazed at the feeling that swept through him at saying it out loud. A dazzling smile came to the girl's face, as though she wished to give her blessing.

Ian laughed. Tears pricked his eyes, and yet he laughed. He could not remember the last time he had, and yet it felt perfectly natural.

If only he knew what to do!

Chapter Thirty

SCOTLAND, AT LAST

Noèle froze outside the captain's quarters as Ian's laughter drifted to her ears. At first, she had been unable to identify the sound. It felt oddly foreign and somehow out of place. Never before had she heard him laugh, and the moment she realized what that sound was, Noèle stilled.

She simply stood there, just outside the door...and listened.

It was a moment that she knew would forever remain with her. A moment like the first time she had seen Ophélie smile. A moment that was breathtaking and overwhelming and beautiful...and so very unexpected.

Unable to stay away, Noèle quietly and slowly pushed down the handle to open the door. She inched forward, afraid to interfere, to break the spell; yet she could not pause her feet. They stepped across the threshold, and her eyes were drawn to the tall blonde-haired man by the window. He stood there in a posture that made her think he was not the same man she had left behind earlier that morning. Indeed, he seemed relaxed as he gently held Ophélie in his arms, speaking to her in a soft melodious voice as he pointed to the waves pushing the ship onward. He spoke of Scotland, of his childhood, of things he had seen and things he had done.

For a long moment, Noèle simply stood there and watched them, watched her little girl look up eagerly into Ian's face, listening intently. *Oui*, Ian knew how to be a father. He was a natural at it, and perhaps Ophélie could sense it. They did look like father and daughter, and that thought squeezed Noèle's heart in both a wonderful and painful way. Oh, how she wished they could be a family!

And then Ian looked over his shoulder and their eyes met, and for one precious moment, Noèle thought that he, too, wanted as she did.

"Your daughter is a good listener," Ian remarked with a touch of humor in his voice that caught Noèle off guard. His blue eyes twinkled with...mischief?

Noèle blinked, trying her best to clear her sight, for she truly could not believe that he...

That Ian...

Smiling at him, Noèle closed the door behind her, then moved farther into the cabin. She kept her eyes fixed on Ian, examining every line and crease upon his face, those little dimples at the corners of his mouth and the slight twitch that came to his lips now and then. Had she just not seen them before? Had they truly been there? Or had returning to Scotland, returning home brought them back?

Stepping closer, Noèle brushed a gentle hand over her daughter's head. "I've always thought so," she replied with a smile. "Are you not, *ma petite?*" she asked Ophélie, tickling her under the chin.

Delighted, Ophélie giggled, closing her eyes and pinching her chin closer to her chest in order to chase away her mother's teasing fingers.

Then Noèle looked up into Ian's eyes. "You have a way with children," she remarked, wondering how he felt holding Ophélie in his arms. No doubt it made him think of his own children. How could it not?

Sighing, Ian nodded. "I'd forgotten," he murmured as his eyes swept back to Ophélie, "how wonderful it feels to..." His lips suddenly thinned, pressing into a tight line, and then he returned Ophélie to her arms.

Cradling her daughter, Noèle wondered what was on Ian's mind. He had clearly enjoyed the time with Ophélie, and yet there was a dark cloud. Was it longing that burned in his heart? Or still a sense of guilt? A sense of not being worthy?

"No doubt, we shall be there soon," Noèle said, trying to prompt him to reply, to say something, to reveal how he felt about what lay ahead.

Sighing deeply, Ian hung his head. "And then?" he asked, turning to look at her for a moment before stepping away, his gaze directed out at the sea. "What then?" He shook his hand. "My clan does not even live near these cliffs. It is at least a day's ride to MacDrummond Castle." He turned to look at her. "What am I to do? They think me dead. I canna simply..." Again, he shook his head, completely at a loss. "I canna imagine what it would be like for them to suddenly...see me again after all this time. Do I even have the right to return now, this way?"

Noèle understood the fear that lingered within him; yet she could not allow it to take him over. "*Oui*, your return will come as a shock to them, certainly," she said softly, gently rocking Ophélie in her arms as she stepped toward him. "Yet that sense of shock will not linger. I assure you, it will quickly vanish and be replaced by joy and relief."

For a long moment, Ian stared at her, as though she had assured him that the sun would not set that night, that it would continue to shine until the next morning. Then, he slowly shook his head, and yet Noèle thought to see a spark of hope light up his eyes. Of course, he wanted his family to welcome him back. How could he not?

"Land ho!"

Those two words suddenly echoed through the stillness in the cabin, and they both flinched, as though it had been a gunshot. Ian's eyes widened, and Noèle could see that his breath had lodged in his throat, his chest suddenly so still, almost immovable.

Settling Ophélie into one arm, Noèle stepped toward him, reaching out a hand and gently touching Ian's face. "All will be well," she assured him, holding his gaze and willing him to believe her. "Whatever happened, whatever you fear, all will be well."

Then, slowly, they made their way up on deck. Not a word passed between them, each lost in their own thoughts. Each battling contradicting emotions of dread and hope.

Louis tossed Ian a spyglass, and he moved up to the railing of the quarterdeck, and then, with a heavy sigh, put it to his right eye. Following his gaze, Noèle could not quite make out land in the distance. It was still too far away, and yet part of her felt as though she could sense it. "Is this it?" she asked, gazing up at Ian as the wolf moved to their side. Ian once again seemed so still, barely aware of those around him. Only the wind managed to toss about strands of his hair and tug upon his clothes. "Is this the place?"

Slowly, Ian nodded. Then he lowered the spyglass and turned to look at her. "Aye, it is." His gaze returned to the land in the distance and then once more moved back to her. "As far as I remember there are caves nearby, big enough to hide the ship. 'Tis the same way Henri always conceals the *Voile Noire* when he sails to Norfolk." He shrugged. "But then what? As I said, I canna simply walk back into MacDrummond Castle and..." He shook his head, a look of horror upon his face at the thought. "I have no way of knowing what happened in my absence. I have no way of knowing..."

Noèle could see fear and apprehension upon his face. As much as he tried to hide them from those around him, casting uneasy glances at the crew bustling about deck, the fear was there.

The wolf sensed it as well, his eyes watchful and his body tense.

"I don't know," Noèle admitted. "However, we cannot simply turn away. We've come this far, you've come this far, and you owe it to yourself and your children to see this through." She stepped closer, and reached out a hand, placing it upon his arm. "We'll take this one step at a time and see what happens."

Swallowing hard, Ian finally nodded. "Verra well."

Standing side by side, they watched as the *Chevalier Noir* drew closer to the shore, no more than a small speck upon the horizon that slowly grew bigger and brighter. Soon, they could make out cliffs and trees and a pebbled beach down below near the water's edge. It was a land wild and untamed, beautiful and promising adventure. What did it feel like to Ian? Noèle wondered as she looked up at him.

His face looked stony, expressionless as he stared and stared, his thoughts his own. Then he lowered his gaze and looked down at the wolf. It was as though a shared memory resurfaced. After all, this was the place where everything had begun.

As the ship drew closer, Noèle craned her neck to see up the tall cliff face. From what Ian had told her, she knew that a large clearing was up there surrounded by trees and beyond them open land. It had been in that clearing that the wolf had first attacked. It had been in that clearing that Ian had tried to take Moira's life. It had been in that clearing that everything had changed.

Gone differently.

Noèle wondered if to Ian everything felt like it was in the haze. He moved and spoke, gave commands and saw the ship securely concealed in a large cavern below the cliff face. Although his eyes remained distant, the pulse in his neck giving away his inner turmoil.

And then, Noèle was following Ian off the ship. She stepped carefully, Ophélie in her sling, as they made their way out of the cavern and onto the beach. As distracted as Ian was, Noèle could still feel his hands hovering nearby, always ready to catch her—her and Ophélie!—should she slip and lose her footing. It brought a smile to Noèle's face and warmed her heart.

A small path led upward from the pebbled beach. It snaked up the hill, overgrown with wildflowers and tall stemmed grass, gently swaying in the breeze blowing in from the sea. At times, Noèle could barely see, for her hair was tossed so wildly about her that she felt almost blind.

Ian walked in front of her, slow step by slow step, hesitation in every fiber of his being. Yet he continued on, not stopping once.

Until he did.

Only in the last moment did Noèle notice that Ian had drawn to a halt. Her hands reached out to shield Ophélie as she all but bumped into his back. She was about to ask what was going on when she glanced past him and her eyes fell upon a young girl with blonde hair and deep blue eyes standing in the middle of the path.

For a moment, Noèle felt confused. Was there a settlement nearby after all? She wondered. Was that where the girl had come from? Then, however, she took note of Ian's rigid posture, the way he did not even dare draw breath, and although she could not see his face, Noèle suddenly knew precisely who the girl was.

Chapter Thirty-One
RETURNED FROM THE DEAD

Ian knew he ought to turn back the moment he stepped off the ship. Indeed, this was a foolish idea! They were at least a day's ride from MacDrummond Castle, and without horses, even farther. What were they supposed to do? Traipse across the country-side? He glanced at Ophélie as Noèle settled her gently in her sling. With a small child not even a year old?

Yet Ian knew that Noèle would never allow him to turn back now. She was a fierce one, and for some reason, she believed that he needed this.

Was she right? He wondered as they moved across the beach and toward the hill that sloped gently upward. Aye, something seemed to be tugging him onward. He could feel it deep inside, a part of him that wished to return. Yet his mind continued to doubt if this was wise. How often in his life had he acted upon his instincts? And how often had he been wrong?

Hopefully, Noèle would come to realize that this was a foolish endeavor once they stood up on the clearing and she saw nothing as far as the eye could see. Nothing but trees and meadows.

Wilderness.

No doubt, then, Noèle would change her mind. She would think of her daughter and make the right choice. They would sail away again and...

Walking up the trodden path, Ian closed his eyes and whispered a silent goodbye to his children. Deep down, he knew he was never meant to see them again. He knew that this was for the best. Surely, they were happy now, free from the burden of his anger, barely able to remember the father they had once had.

After all, years had passed...and they had still been so young.

And then Ian's eyes opened again and right there, in front of him, only a few paces up the path, stood Blair.

Jarring to a halt, Ian stared at his daughter.

Blair looked different, older, and yet she looked completely the same, exactly as he remembered her. Her blonde curls danced in the wind, and her blue eyes looked at him as they had countless times before, full of wisdom...and mischief. And yet what shocked him most was that *she* did not look the least bit surprised to see *him*.

A smile stole onto Blair's face as she watched him, and all of a sudden, an almost desperate plea surged through Ian's mind, *Please, remember me! Please, love me!*

As though Blair had read his mind, her smile blossomed into something Ian could find no words to describe. "Father! I knew ye'd come!" she exclaimed with such joy that Ian felt certain his knees would buckle. Yet in the next instant, his daughter flung herself into his arms and he caught her as he had a thousand times before.

For a moment, time was suspended. It meant nothing. Present, past and future all blurred into one, and Ian felt his heart open as he all but crushed his daughter to his chest. Tears blurred his vision, and he dimly noticed that he sank to his knees. Yet he never let go, reveling in the way she held on to him, her embrace just as fierce.

"I knew ye'd be here, Papa," Blair whispered in his ear. "I knew ye'd come."

Ian stilled as his daughter's words echoed through his mind. Then he reluctantly pulled back and looked up into her beloved face. "Ye knew? How could ye know?"

Blair smiled as her small hand reached out to brush a billowing strand of hair out of his face. "I saw ye in my dreams," she replied, as though he ought to have known. "I saw ye return."

Ian's breath rushed from his lungs, and he remembered that day in the clearing almost four years ago. That day, Blair had found him here as well. That day, her dreams had led her here. "Do ye often see things in yer dreams?" Ian asked tentatively, his hands firmly settled upon her shoulders, afraid to let go.

Blair nodded. "Sometimes 'tis confusing, but Moira helps me to make sense of what I see."

Ian flinched at the mention of Moira's name.

Instantly, the expression in Blair's eyes changed and she placed a gentle hand upon his cheek. "She isna angry with ye, Father. She never was." Her blue eyes beckoned him to believe her. "She knows 'twas not yer doing. 'Twas the shadow."

Dimly, Ian recalled his daughter's words from four years ago. After he had kidnapped Moira, she had followed them because she had been afraid for him. *The shadow. I saw it in my dreams. It walks behind ye. It wants to hurt ye.*

Then, Ian had not known what Blair had meant. He had only seen her words as proof that, after his wife, Moira had bewitched his daughter as well. Later, though, in quiet moments upon the *Voile Noire*, Ian's thoughts had occasionally returned to that moment and he had realized the truth.

Blair had been afraid of his anger, of what it did to him, Ian, of the way it threatened to change him, turn him into a man he did not want to be. Aye, his anger had ruined everything. It *had* hurt him.

It had made him hurt others as well.

It had been a shadow upon his life.

Ian smiled up at his daughter. "Ye've always been a wise one, little Blair. I should've listened to ye."

Blair shrugged, as though his choices had not upended her world. "I know ye did yer best, Father. Dunna feel sad." She placed a kiss upon his cheek.

In that moment, the wolf moved toward her, driven by curiosity, and although he had once attacked her, Blair showed no fear. "Ye were a good friend to him," she told the beast with a nod. "Thank ye." After patting the wolf's head, she reached out her hand to Ian. "Come."

Following his daughter, Ian glanced over his shoulder at Noèle. Tears streamed down her face as she smiled at him. He held out his other hand to her and she took it. Together, they crested the hillside.

With his heart thudding wildly in his ears, Ian at first did not hear the voices. Only when he saw Noèle frown did he pause. His feet stilled, but Blair tugged him onward, a knowing smile on her face. "They dunna know yet," she whispered with a giggle that finally made her seem like the young girl she was. "I didna think they'd believe me. Sometimes, people have a hard time believing what they canna see or touch." She shrugged, then suddenly drew closer to him and, with a mischievous twinkle in her eyes, said, "So I lied. I told them I was sad and I wanted to come here to feel close to ye." She squeezed his hand. "That last bit wasna a lie after all." Then she was tugging him onward again.

Another step, and then another, and Ian felt as though he was wading through a dream. A part of him still could not believe that he was truly holding his daughter's hand, that he was back here in Scotland, that...his family and friends were right there in the clearing only a few paces away.

The sight of them nearly brought Ian to his knees, and he stared and stared. And this time, Blair allowed him, standing patiently by his side.

Horses stood grazing near the trees, and tents had been set up around a large campfire. Ian spotted a group of small children playing near the fire, their faces unfamiliar as they had no doubt been born after *that day*. He saw Claudia and Emma, a babe in her arms, their eyes watchful and trained on the children as they spoke to one another. And then his gaze fell on Garrett and Finn, their husbands and two of his childhood friends, chopping firewood at the edge of the clearing.

Ian swallowed, realizing how much he regretted not having been here. Life had truly gone on without him. He knew none of them today and—

Ian blinked as he spotted Cormag.

Seated by the fire with Moira by his side, his old friend slowly rose to his feet. He stared at Ian in shock before running a hand over his face, as though to chase away the mirage. He blinked and blinked again and then looked down at Moira.

With a smile upon her face, Moira nodded, her blonde hair billowing in the breeze, before she turned her head and met Ian's gaze. Her green eyes held no hatred, and she nodded at him in greeting.

Ian feared he was crushing his daughter's hand as well as Noèle's. Yet he could not release them.

And then Cormag was striding toward him, and for a moment, Ian feared his old friend meant to strike him down, meant to exact revenge for what Ian had done to his wife.

Then, however, he felt Noèle squeeze his hand reassuringly, and from one moment to the next, everything changed. His heart felt suddenly lighter. Gone was the fear that had walked with him these past years. The day seemed brighter, and he looked into Cormag's face and saw...joy.

Disbelief, but also joy.

"Ye're alive!" Cormag exclaimed a second before he embraced Ian, thumping him on the back and holding him in a tight embrace. "I canna believe it!" He suddenly pulled back. "How?"

Ian was at a loss, but fortunately, Blair was not. "I kept telling ye all that he was fine," she said to Cormag with a chiding look, "and yet ye didna believe me. Ye simply patted my head as though I was a child."

Cormag chuckled, a rare sight for he was a rather taciturn and serious man. "Ye are a child, little Blair. But I admit...I should've listened. Will ye forgive me?"

Grinning, Blair nodded.

"Wait!" Cormag exclaimed, his gaze going back and forth between Ian and his daughter. "Did ye know he'd be here? Is that why—?"

Blair nodded. Then she tugged on Ian's sleeve. When she had his attention, she nodded toward the cliff where Ian and the wolf had fallen into the sea. Up on the highest boulder, overlooking the churning waters, sat Niall.

His red hair gleamed in the sun, and his green eyes were wide and unblinking as he stared at his father. All blood seemed to drain from his face, and for a frightening moment, Ian feared his son might faint and go over the edge. Then, however, Niall swallowed, slowly shaking off the momentary paralysis that had fallen over him and climbed down. Once his feet reached the ground, he turned around, and the moment his gaze fell on Ian, his eyes widened once more.

Ian knew how his son felt, for he, too, could hardly believe that this was truly happening. That he was here, holding his daughter's hand and seeing his son stand only a few paces away.

"Ye've grown tall," Ian murmured, barely aware of the silence that had fallen over the small campsite, all eyes turned to him, jaws dropping in shock.

Niall nodded, then hesitantly took a step toward Ian, that doubtful look still in his eyes. "I'm ten now," he replied, his words lacking strength as though he was uncertain if he spoke the truth.

Ian felt his heart thundering in his chest, making him grow light-headed when he suddenly felt the wolf brush past him, an eager yip leaving his throat.

Instantly, Niall's eyes widened and he shrank back. So did everyone else. Shouts of alarm drifted to Ian's ears, ripping away the spell that had fallen over him. He turned his head and saw Garrett and Finn swing their axes as they rushed forward, their faces grim and their eyes fixed upon the wolf. Cormag spun, swept a little boy into his arms and quickly deposited him into Moira's arms before he drew the dagger at his belt.

At the open hostility shown him, the wolf tensed, then bared his fangs. He slowly backed away until he stood positioned in front of Ian and Noèle, determined to protect them.

"*Non*, wait!" Ian heard Noèle call out before she surged forward, wrapping her free arm around the wolf.

Ian instantly stepped into Cormag's path, holding up his hands to appease his friends. "Please, there's no need to be concerned. The wolf is with us. I promise he willna harm anyone."

Cormag stilled, a deep frown upon his face. His gray eyes were wide, full of doubt, and yet Ian could see that he was listening. His gaze lingered upon Ian's face and then moved down to the wolf. For a long moment, Cormag seemed to consider him before he finally nodded and resheathed his dagger.

Behind him, Garrett and Finn lowered their axes. Their faces, though, showed confusion as they gathered their wives and children close, drawing them behind themselves.

Stillness fell over the clearing. No one spoke as all eyes were directed at the wolf. Ian lowered his hands, then stepped back and moved to Noèle's side. He, too, crouched low and placed a hand upon the wolf's head, then scratched behind his ears.

Instantly, the wolf relaxed and then sidled closer to Ian, rubbing his head against Ian's shoulder in an affectionate gesture. "I assure ye all that ye have nothing to fear from him."

Garrett stepped forward, raking a hand through his hair as he eyed the wolf doubtfully. "But was he not a moment ago ready to charge?" His gaze moved to Ian, and despite the tension upon his old friend's face, Ian still saw a touch of wonderment in Garrett's eyes.

Ian rose to his feet, his gaze moving around the small circle of old friends, meeting their eyes one by one. "Aye, he was...but only to protect us."

Suddenly, gasps flew from everyone's lips and Ian saw the eyes around him widening. He turned to look over his shoulder, and a smile came to his face when he saw little Ophélie reaching out her hands and tugging upon the wolf's fur. She giggled delightedly as she raked her little hands across his face, even sticking a finger into his mouth. In turn, the wolf started to lick her face, making her squeal and bat his muzzle away.

Noèle laughed, stroking the wolf's fur. "He is harmless," she said to everyone. "I assure you. There is nothing to fear."

With a smile, Blair stepped forward and knelt down beside the wolf. She let him sniff her hand and then scratched him below the chin. "He's like a dog," she exclaimed delightedly. "A big dog." Then she turned to wave the other children over, and one by one, they came, their curiosity getting the better of them. Ian saw their parents hesitate, close to forbidding their approach. In the end, however, they stayed back and watched in amazement as the children grouped around the *big dog*, instantly delighted with their new furry companion.

"Father?"

At the sound of Niall's voice, Ian turned toward his son. He still stood where he had before, hesitation upon his features. Yet the look in his eyes almost broke Ian's heart.

Exchanging a quick glance with Noële, her arm still slung around the wolf, Ian waited until she nodded. "Go," she whispered. "Talk to your son. We'll be fine."

Striding forward, Ian approached his son, uncertain what to say or do. So much time had passed, and Niall had never been one for easy affection. With Blair, it was simpler. She said what she thought, and she bestowed hugs with ease. Niall, however, had always been different. Would he shy back if Ian tried to embrace him?

Almost shy, Niall stood before him, wringing his hands in a nervous gesture. His eyes were still wide, and yet they did not dare meet Ian's... not for long, at least.

"I dunna quite know where to begin," Ian admitted honestly as he stood before his son. "A lot of time has passed, and...I never truly expected to see ye again."

Niall looked up at him, his mouth open, as though he wished to reply. Then, however, he thought differently and took a step back instead.

Ian raked his mind for something to say, some kind of gesture that would bridge this gap between them. Of course, his son felt no connection between them. He had been so young when Ian had left, when he had thought him dead. Niall had lived so many years without Ian, his memory of the father he had once known growing dimmer. Still, Ian knew that the years that stood between them were not all that hampered their connection now. Even before, Ian knew that he had not been the kind of father Niall had needed, had deserved. Aye, Ian had been too distracted by his hatred to pay closer attention to his son. Was it too late now?

"Ian?"

At the sound of her voice, Ian whipped around.

Over the course of the past few days, Ian had tried his best to picture the moment he would see his children again. He had imagined what he would say, what they would say. He had pictured his greatest hopes and his deepest fears. Of course, he had also thought of his wife from time to time, and yet the moment he had set foot back on Scottish soil, Maggie had been nowhere on his mind.

Now, she stood across the clearing, her unruly red hair dancing in the wind. She looked precisely as Ian remembered her, her delicate frame offset by a fierce will and passionate heart, both of which sparked in those brilliant green eyes of hers. She was as beautiful as she had always been, and Ian remembered the moment he had first seen her. He remembered how he had known from one second to the next that she possessed his heart.

Chapter Thirty-Two
ANOTHER LIFE

The moment the red-haired woman stepped out from between the trees and into the clearing, Noèle knew who she was. Although Ian had spoken to her of his wife, Noèle had never truly asked for a description of the woman. It had not felt appropriate. Yet one look at the woman's face told Noèle everything she needed to know.

There was shock there, of course, but that was not all. Far from it. Her green eyes seemed to glow a little more with each second that passed, with each second that her mind absorbed this news.

Ian's return.

Disbelief slowly waned, mixing with sparks of relief and joy. A smile tugged upon her lips as she slowly moved into the clearing, her gaze fixed upon Ian alone.

Ian, too, seemed mesmerized, and Noèle could feel her heart breaking a little more with each step the two of them took toward one another. She all but knew that the moment they met, every chance for a future with Ian would be lost to her.

And so, she averted her gaze, turned her attention back to the children crowding around her. Little hands reached toward the wolf from all sides, and Noèle could tell that he was becoming a little overwhelmed. She turned to look at Blair. "Can you help me a little?" she asked Ian's young daughter, the girl's blue eyes remarkably like her father's.

Blair nodded. "Does he like fetching things?"

Noèle shrugged. "Honestly, I don't know. I've only recently met him myself, and there has not quite been the opportunity to explore games."

Even though Blair could not yet have reached her nineth year, she called the children to attention with a sure voice and then led them over to the clearing's edge near the forest, picking up a small boy who could not yet walk. Together, they gathered sticks and all the while Noèle watched as Blair continued to speak to them, now and then pointing back to the wolf before once again looking around the small circle of children.

Beside Noèle, the wolf watched them with just as much curiosity. Every once in a while, he would almost dance on the spot, as though wishing to be off, but uncertain if that was wise. A low whine rose from his throat, and then he looked up at her with questioning eyes.

Noèle smiled and nodded. "Go ahead! Go play!" In a flash, the wolf was off, bounding across the clearing, momentarily shocking the adults while at the same time delighting the children.

"'Tis the same wolf, is it not?"

Noèle rose to her feet and turned to look at a tall, blonde woman. Her blue eyes were watchful, and she had that look about her that made Noèle think that there were very few things this woman did not notice. "You're Moira, *n'est-ce pas?*"

A smile teased the other woman's lips. "Ian told ye about me," she said, and it was not a question. "Aye, I'm Moira."

"My name is Noèle Clément," Noèle introduced herself and then nodded toward the wolf. "*Oui*, it is the same wolf."

Still smiling, Moira shook her head in awe as she observed the wolf playing with the children. Her own perhaps two-year-old son stood beside her, his hands curled into her skirts, eyes wide as he stared across the clearing. "The last time I saw him, he wanted to rip out my throat." She shifted on her feet and then turned to look at Noèle. "He doesna seem so angry anymore."

Noèle paused, aware of the shift in their conversation. Indeed, Moira was not speaking about the wolf but about Ian instead. "A lot has happened," was all Noèle replied, uncertain how much to say without betraying Ian's trust.

Moira nodded knowingly.

"You are not angry with him?" Noèle inquired openly, turning a curious glance to the other woman.

"No, I'm not," Moira replied, drawing in a deep breath as a distant look fell over her face. "For a time, I feared him. I saw his anger and knew 'twas directed at me, and yet..." She blinked and met Noèle's gaze. "I always knew that it was fueled by pain, and I often wondered what would happen if, somehow, that pain went away." Something curious sparked in Moira's eyes.

Something inquisitive.

Noèle frowned, uncertain what it was Moira wished to know, what thoughts currently occupied her mind. "He missed his children dearly," Noèle finally said as the other woman's gaze began to make her slightly uncomfortable, "and yet he never intended to return. He feared he would not be well received." Quite unintentionally, Noèle's gaze moved across the clearing toward the spot where Ian and his wife had vanished behind a large boulder. She burned to know what they were speaking about!

Heaving a deep sigh, Noèle shifted Ophélie in her arms. The little girl had fallen asleep, and her weight was slowly becoming too much for Noèle to hold for a prolonged time.

"Would ye like to settle her somewhere?" Moira asked, gesturing toward a tent near the fire. "As ye can see, we're all well practiced in caring for young children."

Noèle returned her smile and nodded. "*Oui*, I would appreciate that." Following Moira, she ducked her head and stepped into the small tent. There, she settled Ophélie gently upon a thick blanket. She brushed a gentle hand over her daughter's sleeping face and then stepped outside once more. Moira beckoned her forward, patting the log beside her. "Come and sit."

Noèle did so, and yet her gaze once again moved to that boulder behind which Ian still remained. She felt her insides tense and willed her thoughts elsewhere. "Niall seemed quite overwhelmed to see his father again," Noèle remarked as she settled herself next to Moira.

The other woman nodded. "Aye, he missed him desperately." She looked up to where Niall sat in a darkened corner of the clearing, a stick in his hand which he drew across the packed dirt ground. The expression upon his face was fallen, and Noèle wished there was something she could do for him.

"Do ye see that man over there," Moira suddenly said, nodding her head toward the other side of the clearing where her husband stood with three other men. Two of them had been chopping firewood upon their arrival whereas Noèle could not recall having seen the third one before. "The one with the short blonde hair, who doesna quite look like a highlander but rather like a misplaced Englishman." She chuckled.

Noèle nodded. "Who is he?"

Moira's gaze held hers for a moment longer before she said, "He is Maggie's husband."

"Maggie?" Noèle asked with a frown before understanding dawned and her jaw dropped. "You mean...?"

Brushing a blonde curl behind her ear, Moira nodded. "Aye."

Noèle's head whipped around again, and she stared at the Englishman. As though he could feel her gaze, he turned to look at her and their eyes met. Although Noèle could not deny that she felt a certain sense of unease, the look upon his face was friendly...but tense. Of course, it was! With Ian returning home, his own marriage was suddenly threatened. Did he feel as she did? Noèle wondered.

Drawing in a deep breath, Noèle turned back to Moira. "Are they...?" How did one ask these questions? Noèle wondered. "I mean, their marriage, was it...?"

"They're in love," Moira said with a smile. "They have been for a long time."

Noèle could not quite say what emotions she felt in that moment. However, the dark cloud that had settled above her head the moment her eyes had fallen on Ian's wife slowly seemed to move away, allowing the sky to brighten. Yet...

A deep frown drew down Noèle's brows as her thoughts tried to make sense of what she had just learned. "But I thought...," she murmured. "Ian said that her heart always remained with her first love." A spark of anger ignited in Noèle's heart. After breaking Ian's heart day after day for so many years, how was it possible that she had now lost her heart to another?

Moira smiled, then reached out and reassuringly patted Noèle's hand. "Things are not always what they seem," the blonde-haired woman said with a wisdom that reminded Noèle of Blair. "Maggie lost her heart to him," she nodded toward the Englishman, "long before she ever met Ian. Yet a misunderstanding kept them apart." She sighed deeply. "Until about a year ago."

Noèle stared at Moira. "This...This is *him*?" Moira nodded. "But... But how?"

"'Tis a long story."

Hope warred with fear, and Noèle buried her face in her hands, heaving a deep sigh. "Isn't it always?"

"Aye," Moira chuckled knowingly.

Chapter Thirty-Three
HUSBAND & WIFE

Ian saw the way Maggie met the man's gaze. He saw the look that passed between them, and in that moment, Ian's insides twisted painfully and he felt an unexpected sense of rage bubbling up in his veins. Had she truly lost her heart to another? After he had tried for years to win her for himself!

"Come with me," Maggie said to him after glancing over her shoulder. "I think there's a lot we need to talk about." And then without waiting for a reply, she moved away, walked across the clearing and then disappeared behind a large boulder near the cliff face.

Ian hesitated for no more than a second. His limbs hummed with energy, with the need to speak to her. He had spent the past few years reliving every moment, imagining how things could have been different, never expecting to have the chance speak to her again, to ever be able to ask a question.

And now, here they were.

It felt...odd.

Stepping around the boulder, Ian looked toward the sea where the sun slowly drifted lower. The sky was painted red and violet, darkening slowly, the dimming light illuminating Maggie's features.

At his approach, she turned toward him. Her wild hair still danced around her face, and despite the seriousness of her expression, the corners of her mouth twitched as though she wished to smile.

"Who is he?" Ian asked, curious. Aye, he also felt anger, and yet he felt no sense of jealousy. He did not feel crushed to learn that his wife had lost her heart to another. No, the anger he felt was for the years of their past. Why could she not have loved *him*? Why did it have to be like this between them?

A contrite look came to Maggie's face, and yet she met his gaze unflinchingly. "He's my husband."

Ian felt her words like a punch to the gut, and for a second, he feared he might topple over the edge and once again plummet into the sea. "Ye...Ye married again."

Maggie nodded. "I did." Licking her lips, she stepped toward him. "Please, let me explain."

"Do ye love him?" Ian growled out, feeling as though years of his life had been wasted, as though he had lived without meaning...for nothing.

Maggie drew in a slow breath. Her green eyes settled upon his, and for a second, she waited, not saying a word. "Aye, I love him. I've always loved him, ever since the day we first met...so very long ago when I was a young girl."

Ian stared at his wife as her words slowly sank in. "Are ye jesting?" he snapped, and his hands shot forward and grasped her by the shoulders. "After everything he did to ye, ye took him back? He betrayed ye! He—!"

"He didna!" Maggie objected, and her delicate hands curled into his shirt front, giving him a sharp tug. Aye, she was a fierce one! Always had been! "'Twas a misunderstanding! My mother lied to me! He never married! And it broke his heart when he learned that I had!"

Looking down into his wife's face, Ian suddenly felt all his strength leave him. Had he truly spent years of his life in misery because of a simple lie? A misunderstanding?

Ian hung his head. If Maggie could have married the man she loved back then, then he, Ian, would still have had his heart broken, aye, but he would have recovered, would he not have? After all, he would never have allowed himself the illusion of winning her heart one day. Instead, he could have moved on, perhaps found love elsewhere. And yet if they had never married, there would be no Blair and Niall.

The thought was devastating!

Aye, if they had never married...

Ian froze as thoughts he had entertained before returned with a swiftness that took his breath away.

He would never have met Noële!

Indeed, he would never have held such anger toward Moira. He would never have kidnapped her and taken her to this clearing. The wolf would never have attacked. They would never have gone over the edge and plummeted into the sea. He would never have ended up on the *Voile Noire*!

At the mere thought, everything within Ian shied away from that possibility. He could not imagine not knowing the Durets. He could not imagine never having met Noële. He could not imagine—

"Ye no longer love me," Maggie suddenly whispered, awe ringing in her voice. Her green eyes swept his face, as though she were searching for evidence to support her theory. "'Tis her, is it not?"

Ian swallowed, then took an abrupt step backward, releasing her shoulders. "What?"

A smile claimed Maggie's features. "Ye love her, do ye not?"

Ian felt heat shoot into his face. "We were speaking of—"

"But 'tis true!" she exclaimed, taking a step toward him. "Ye no longer love me! Ye love her!"

Panting, Ian stared at her as the world came crashing down around him. Aye, he loved Noële! He knew he did, and yet the thought of admitting to it here and now made him feel foolish. It made him feel vulnerable, and the last time, he had allowed himself to be vulnerable, he had come to regret it.

Dearly!

Maggie's face sobered. "I'm sorry," she said, honest regret marking her features. "I have no right to pry into yer heart." She heaved a deep breath. "I still canna believe that ye're standing right here in front of me, and at the same time, it feels perfectly normal to speak to ye." She stepped toward him and reached for his hands. "I never meant to hurt ye. I'm so sorry for everything that happened. Believe me, when I learned that Nathan had never married, that my mother had lied to me, it felt as though the ground had been pulled out from under me. Everything suddenly felt futile. Every struggle had been for nothing. And yet, if..." She sighed, and a smile came to her face. "We wouldna have Niall and Blair."

Surprised to hear Maggie echo his own thoughts, Ian felt himself calm.

"I think," Maggie began with a tentative voice, "'tis only reasonable to feel regret for something we lost, for something we had to endure." She shook her head. "But I dunna want to feel like that the rest of my life. I've chosen to be happy, and I am." She reached out a hand and cupped it to Ian's cheek. "And I want ye to be happy as well."

Maggie's touch felt...odd. Not like the touch of a wife. Not the way he had imagined it. How often had Ian hoped she would reach out to him? A simple touch. A sign of affection. Now, though, it felt like the touch of a friend. Was she right? Did he no longer love her?

"Ye needna worry," Ian told her, uncertain how to proceed. However, he knew he could never endanger her happiness. "I have no intention of staying. Ye needna worry for...for yer marriage. Ian MacDrummond will remain dead, and Ian Stewart will return to France."

"France?" Maggie asked with a frown. "Is that where ye've been?"

Ian nodded.

"Tell me about it."

And he did.

Side by side, they sat on the edge of the cliff, their legs dangling high above the water, and spoke to each other as they never had before, sharing all that had happened in their respective lives. To Ian's surprise, it soon felt natural, and they even shared a laugh or two.

"What an adventure!" Maggie remarked with a smile. "I never knew ye loved the sea."

Ian chuckled. "Neither did I."

With her hands braced behind her, Maggie leaned back, her gaze directed at the sunset. "And her?" she asked with a sideways glance at him.

Ian shrugged. "I will take Noële and her daughter back to France.

The Durets will see to them."

"Is that what ye want?" Maggie inquired. "What she wants?"

Ian gritted his teeth, then fixed her with a hard gaze. "I willna make the same mistake twice!" he growled, then pushed to his feet. "I willna—!" His voice broke off as he stalked along the cliff's edge.

Jumping to her feet, Maggie came after him. "Why would ye think it a mistake?" She grasped his arms and pulled him around, looking up into his face. "Why does it seem so impossible that another might... love ye?" She paused. "That's it, is it not? What...I did to ye made ye believe that...no one could ever love ye." Tears collected in her eyes. "Oh, Ian, I'm so sorry! I never meant for this to happen. I..."

Ian watched as her tears spilled over and ran down her cheeks. Her green eyes were so wide and so sorrowful that he suddenly no longer felt angry. Somehow, all his anger evaporated into thin air, as though it had never been. He saw Maggie's heartbreak, echoing his own, and realized, perhaps for the first time, that she, too, had had hopes. Aye, she had married him, hoping that they would find love, had she not? Unfortunately, her heart had never softened toward him. He sighed. It had not been her fault.

"'Tis all right," Ian told her, not wanting her to carry this burden with her into the days to come. She deserved better. "'Twas not yer fault. I should never have asked for yer hand. I knew how—"

Maggie's hands tightened upon his. "If I hadna already given away my heart," she whispered in a calm voice, yet one that allowed for no argument, "I could easily have loved ye, Ian. Ye need to know this. Ye've always been a wonderful man, and I truly and honestly, would have loved ye. Do ye hear me?"

Ian *did* hear her; and yet, it was not Maggie's voice that echoed through his head. No, it was Noële's. Had she not said similar words to him not long ago?

You're so easy to love.

Those few words echoed through his mind again and again no matter how hard Ian tried to ignore them. He feared them because they made him hope and want. And wanting was a dangerous thing. Ian knew that from experience.

"Niall feels as ye do."

Ian blinked, and his gaze focused upon Maggie's once more. "What?"

She nodded. "He didna say anything," she began, a concerned look coming to her face. "Yet when I look at him, I see such sadness. At first, I wasna sure what it was, but then I began to suspect. He never dares reach for another, not even me and Blair. I think on some level he knows that we love him, and yet I think there might be a part of him that doesna quite believe us." She wiped a tear from her cheek. "Is that how ye feel?"

Ian almost nodded; still, the need to hide, to mask how he felt, to conceal any vulnerability stopped him.

"Please," Maggie implored him. "If ye can help him..." She grasped his hands tightly, painfully. "Ye're his father, and he needs ye."

Ian could not say why or how it had happened, but for some reason—specially over the past few years—he had come to believe that no one truly needed him, least of all his children. More than once, he had told himself that they were better off without him, that his anger had been like a poison and that now they could finally be happy. Yet was that true?

Ian swallowed. "I will speak to him."

Maggie exhaled a deep breath. "Thank ye." She stepped back, brushing a loose strand from her face. "Sometimes he seems happy, truly happy, and then there are moments when I feel as though I dunna know him at all, as though he hides his true self from me." She cast him a sad smile. "I'm glad ye're back. We missed ye." She chuckled as fresh tears rolled down her cheeks. "Yet yer daughter has been insisting for a while that we were not to worry about ye, that ye would be fine." She reached out and placed a hand upon his cheek. "I should've listened, but I never thought..." Sighing, she shook her head, disbelief still lighting up her eyes. "'Tis so good to have ye back."

Ian did not know what to say. He had not expected this, not even in his most wonderful dreams. But now he needed to speak to his son. If Niall truly felt as he did...

Ian gritted his teeth. No, he could not allow his son to walk down the same path he had. Niall deserved better.

Far better.

Chapter Thirty-Four

ANOTHER WIFE

Noèle tried hard to listen to the stories told around the fire.
As the day slowly drew to an end, Ian's friends gathered together, telling stories about his childhood, about growing up together. Laughter echoed across the clearing as they all sat by the warm fire, its flames dancing in the cool breeze drifting in from the sea. Most of the children were already asleep, and Noèle smiled as she looked over her shoulder into the tent to see Ophélie still sleeping peacefully next to Liam, Moira and Cormag's little son.

"He was always the most daring one of us," Garrett recounted laughing, looking around their small circle of friends. "When we were young he would always say, *No risk, no gain.*" He slapped his knee. "He got us into so much trouble!"

While Finn laughed loudly, sharing his friend's joy, Cormag was more of a quiet type. He listened carefully, and every once in a while, Noèle thought that he was watching her. Yet he never quite looked at her. Still, Noèle got the distinct feeling that somehow she was being weighed and measured. *Oui,* friendship still connected them. Cormag still cared for Ian. He cared so much that he worried as friends were wont to do. Could he somehow tell how deeply Noèle cared for Ian? Did he wonder if she was good enough for his friend?

Again, Noèle's gaze flitted back to the large boulder behind which Ian and his wife had disappeared. A small eternity had passed since, and restlessness began to hum in Noèle's limbs. More than anything, she wanted to jump to her feet, cross the clearing and demand an explanation. She wanted to know what was happening, what was being said. Was Maggie truly in love with her husband? Of course, Noèle had no reason to doubt Moira's words, and yet she could not imagine how anyone could choose another over Ian.

It seemed impossible!

Her eyes shifted to Nathan. He, too, looked rather uncomfortable, his eyes distant and his jaw working, as though he were grinding his teeth together. Was he worried? Did he not have faith in his wife's love for him? Or was he merely concerned about the circumstances? After all, technically, Ian was Maggie's husband. Was he worried that their marriage would now no longer be considered valid?

All these questions and more raced through Noèle's head. She wished she could articulate them, discuss them and have someone soothe her fears. Yet she knew she could not say a word. Ian's friends were celebrating his return, rejoicing in seeing their friend again when they had thought it impossible.

Noèle heaved a deep breath, and then as she looked up, her gaze caught on Maggie's flaming head of hair as the woman strode past the boulder. Ian walked only a few steps behind her, and Noèle almost shot to her feet but caught herself in the last instant. Indeed, she had no place here, nor the right to demand any sort of explanation. Nathan, on the other hand, did. The second he saw his wife returning, he surged upward, large strides carrying him to her.

Noèle saw whispered words passing between the two of them, what looked like a reassuring smile upon Maggie's face. Ian strode past them with no more than a furtive glance. He approached the fire and exchanged a few words with his friends before asking, "Have ye seen my son?"

Moira nodded toward the cliff face, a soft smile upon her face.

"Thank ye," Ian said, and Noèle could not help but feel as though these two words were meant to express a lot more than simply his gratitude for being informed of his son's whereabouts. Their gazes held for a moment longer, and again Moira nodded, something silent passing between them.

Noële almost fidgeted in her spot, missing the days when it had been so easy to draw closer to Ian, to exchange a few words, to look into his eyes. Then, it had seemed so natural. She had not even thought about it much. Now, however, that she feared these moments were gone for good, she longed for them to return, knowing how precious they had been.

And then Ian's eyes found hers, and her heart paused, as though holding its breath, too afraid to miss even a moment of this. Whatever it was. Noële certainly had no name for it. This connection. This bond. This instant awareness of another, of who they were and how they felt.

And then Ian turned away and strode over to the cliff face. Noële hoped that he would be able to comfort his son. Of course, she did not know the boy at all, but he had seemed troubled. More than that. He had seemed...sad and forlorn.

"Did he say anything?" Garrett inquired the second Maggie and Nathan returned to the fire. "Is he staying? Why did he come back now? Where has he been? How—?"

Claudia, Garrett's wife, placed a hand upon his arm. "Slow down," she told him with a chuckle. "You will not receive any answers if you keep talking like this."

Garrett chuckled and pulled her close, brushing a kiss onto her lips. "Ye're one to talk!" Then he turned back to Maggie, looking at her with expectant eyes.

Sighing, Maggie settled onto the log, Nathan beside her. "Apparently, a fishing boat pulled him out of the sea, him and the wolf." She reached for Nathan's hand and drew it into her lap, holding it tightly. "'Tis quite a long story." Her eyes swept the small circle of friends and then came to rest upon Noële. "He's been in France all this time, sailing aboard a French privateer under a captain that goes by the name Henri Duret."

"What?" Claudia exclaimed the second Garrett's jaw dropped. "Are you certain?"

Maggie chuckled. "Aye, I was surprised to hear the name myself. I dunna think Ian ever knew it. When Ian and Finn went to Glasgow to assist Garrett in yer pursuit," she looked at Claudia, "I think they never learned the name of that ship's captain."

Noèle frowned, completely at a loss. Was it possible that these people had met Henri at some point? It sounded as though they had. The circumstances, however, eluded Noèle.

"I remember ye telling me about the French privateer that boarded the ship ye were on," Maggie continued with a nod to Claudia. "I remember ye mentioning that name. However, it seemed that Ian was unaware of it. Only, once upon it, he recognized the black sails, of course." She laughed. "Well, he's been on quite an adventure."

"And now?" Finn asked with a sideways glance at Nathan. "Did he say what he intended to do now?"

Noèle saw Maggie's hand tighten upon Nathan's, giving it a reassuring squeeze. "He doesna intend to stay," she said with a thoughtful look. Shifting in her seat, she met Nathan's gaze. Then she suddenly turned and looked at Noèle. "May I speak with ye?"

Surprised, Noèle almost flinched. Indeed, this day had wrought havoc on her nerves. Not only was she worried about losing Ian for good, but over the past hour, she had become increasingly uncomfortable under his friends' rather scrutinizing gazes. Of course, they wanted to know how Ian was still alive, where he had been and everything else that had happened to him! She had seen it in their eyes. And yet they had not asked. And in that moment, Noèle wondered for the first time who his friends thought she was to Ian.

Maggie rose to her feet and walked over, offering Noèle her hand. "Dunna worry," Moira said, placing a hand upon Noèle's arm. "I'll keep an eye on your wee one."

Nodding, Noèle stepped around the log and fell into step beside Maggie. Oh, this felt odd!

Without saying a word, they walked along the tree line, and one of the horses snorted affectionately as they strolled past. "Do ye love him?" Maggie asked unexpectedly, and Noèle spun around, staring at her.

Maggie laughed. "I'll take that as a *yes*."

Noèle was overwhelmed by the familiarity in the other woman's voice. After all, they had never met before today and...there were countless other obstacles that stood between them. "I...I..." Noèle stammered, uncertain how to reply.

Maggie smiled at her, something kind and compassionate in her expression. "Loving someone can be terrifying," she remarked with a roll of her eyes. Turning toward the horizon, she sighed. "I know. I feel...as though the thought has been with me for many years." She looked back at Noèle. "Only once I decided to meet it head-on, did it lose its power over me." Her face lay in shadows, and yet Noèle thought to see something determined in the other woman's gaze. A moment later, Maggie asked, as directly as before, "Do ye love him?"

This time, Noèle did not flinch. Indeed, she felt rather calm and collected. She looked into Maggie's eyes and returned the question, "Do you?"

A slight curl came to Maggie's lips, and Noèle could not help but think that she approved of Noèle's boldness. "I do love him," she replied, "but not the way ye do. Ye have nothing to fear from me." The smile upon her face slowly waned, and she took a step forward, something serious in her gaze. "He doesna believe anyone could ever love him." Her words did not sound like a question, and yet there was a look upon Maggie's face that suggested that she was waiting for an answer.

Noèle nodded. "I know," she replied, and the other woman nodded. It was like a dance, questions and answers, challenges uttered and met. They were each trying to gauge the other's bond with Ian, to understand where they stood and where they could go from here. "I love him," Noèle forced herself to say, to speak openly and truthfully. "Only I worry that...he will never love me the way he loved you." She felt the urge to drop her gaze but fought it. She needed answers. She wanted reassurance. And Maggie was the only one to provide them.

With a smile, Maggie shook her head. "Aye, he might have loved me once...but he does no longer. I saw it in his eyes tonight. He was furious when he learned of my marriage, but not because he was jealous, rather because he felt all his efforts had been in vain." She sighed heavily. "'Tis not easy to realize that something we worked for, we strode toward will forever be denied us, was never within our reach.

Sometimes, too late, do we realize that perhaps we never truly wanted it in the first place."

At Maggie's words, Noèle felt relief washing through her like a tidal wave. For a moment, she felt as though her knees would buckle, sweeping her off her feet. All of a sudden, she felt exhausted and her eyelids drooped. However, Maggie's hands grasped her arms, steadying her. "I need to speak to him."

Maggie nodded. "I'd recommend that. But be prepared. Ian has always been a rather stubborn man."

Noèle chuckled. "*Oui*, I've noticed."

"He willna be easily convinced."

"*Non*, he will not." Oddly enough, the flame-haired woman suddenly seemed like an ally, and Noèle wondered if perhaps everything had happened the way it ought to have. Certainly, life was never easy, but in the end, it was always worth it, was it not?

Chapter Thirty-Five

FATHER & SON

Rounding the boulder's other side, Ian spied his son seated upon the cliff's edge. A moment of panic seized him at the sight, and he felt compelled to lunge forward and pull Niall back. And then he saw his face, barely illuminated by the last rays of the sun, and he knew that above all else Niall simply felt alone in the world.

Ian knew that feeling. For so long, he had felt alone. Even before he had gone to France, he kept to himself and avoided all contact with others. Even when he had still lived in Scotland with his family and friends. Even then, he had felt alone. He had fought a battle his family had not even seen, not even deemed necessary. They had not understood, no matter how many times he had tried to convince them, to explain himself. Aye, he had felt alone.

For many, many years.

Was that the way Niall felt, too?

Drawing in a deep breath, Ian slowly approached, wondering what he ought to say to his son or perhaps what he ought not. It had been a long time since he had been a father.

At his approach, Niall looked up and then back down, bowing his head. Sadness clung to his features, to his posture, to everything that made him who he was. "Ye will leave again, won't ye?" His voice was no more than a whisper, and yet Ian could hear tears lingering there. Had Niall been crying? Indeed, Ian could not recall ever seeing his son cry. He certainly had when he had been little and had stubbed his toe or bruised his knee. But not in moments like this. Had there ever been a moment like this?

Sighing, Ian seated himself beside his son, uncertain how to reply. "Do ye want me to leave?"

Niall's head snapped up, his eyes suddenly wide. "No!" was all he said, and the vehemence behind that one word made Ian almost lose his balance.

Never had Ian truly thought of him leaving as abandoning his children. Always had he thought them better off without him. The thought that Niall could blame him for what he had done had never occurred to Ian, and now that he knew he had to leave again, Ian felt devastated. "I wish I could stay," he murmured. "A part of me truly does. Yet I canna."

Tears gathered in Niall's eyes. "Why?" His lips began to tremble, and he pressed them tightly together. "If ye truly wished ye could stay, ye would." Anger laced his voice, and he scooted a little back, farther away from Ian. His eyes narrowed, and he wiped at the tears lingering there. "Ye left! Ye simply left!" Accusation swung in his voice. "Ye left me!" He sprang to his feet and backed away.

Shocked nearly senseless, Ian stared at his son. "No! I never left *ye.*" He surged upward, long strides carrying him after his son. He reached for Niall's arm, grasping it tightly and holding on. "I didna leave ye," he tried to explain after a few calming breaths. "It simply...happened. At first, I couldna return, and then... I thought I shouldna." He tightened his hold, pulling Niall toward him. "I thought... I thought staying away would be the best for all of us."

Niall's eyes widened as he stared up at Ian, an utterly aghast look upon his face.

Ian hung his head. "Do ye not remember what 'twas like? For so long, my anger poisoned every moment of yer life. Do ye not remember that? I was never quite there for ye, not the way I should have been because I was too preoccupied with—" How on earth was he to explain this? Niall had only just reached his eleventh year, how could he understand the pain and anger Ian had felt in his marriage?

"I know what happened between ye and mother," Niall suddenly said, his jawline hard as he held Ian's gaze. "I'm not blind. I never was. And I hated mother for what she did to ye, and when she found Nathan again, I yelled at her. I yelled at her! I didna want her to replace ye!" He jerked back his arm, retreating as he shook his head. "But *ye* replaced *us*! Ye went and found yerself a new family, did ye not? Why did ye come then?"

The first emotions to sweep through Ian at Niall's words were shock and disbelief. Yet swift on their heels came a glowing pride, warming him from the inside out. The thought of his son defending him, standing up for him made him feel cherished and treasured. Did his son truly love him so fiercely? Ian had never quite thought it possible simply because he never had thought himself worthy of such a love.

Yet perhaps it did not matter if he was worthy. Perhaps as full of flaws as he was, to his son, he would always be someone who loved him.

"I didna replace ye," Ian told him because it was the truth. "No one could ever replace ye." He heaved a deep sigh. "For years, I was so focused on what I couldna have that I completely forgot what I did have." He stepped forward and placed his hands upon Niall's shoulders. "Ye and yer sister."

"Then why did ye leave?" Niall's shoulder sagged.

Ian shrugged. "'Tis not easy to explain. I felt sad and angry and ashamed of what I had done." He could see in his son's eyes that Niall knew, at least, somewhat of what had happened up here on the cliff face almost four years ago. "I was ashamed of the man I had become, and I believed myself not worthy to be yer father. I thought I needed to leave to give ye the chance to live a happy life. The reason I left had nothing to do with ye and everything with me. There were demons in my past that I feared would claw into ye as well. And so, I left because I thought it was the only way to protect ye." Tears ran down Niall's face. "Perhaps I was wrong. I have been wrong about so many things. I spent most of the past four years out there, trying very hard not to think about anything, not to think about what I had done, about the man I had become...or about ye." Again, Niall began to tremble, and Ian tightened his grip upon his son's shoulders. "Because whenever I did, I wanted nothing more than to return here and see ye...only I knew I shouldna. I knew 'twould be selfish, and so I stayed away. I *made* myself stay away."

"I missed ye so much, Father," Niall sobbed, then threw his arms around Ian and buried his face in his shirt. "I missed ye every day."

Ian enfolded his son in his arms, crushing him to his chest, as tears ran down his cheeks. "I missed ye as well, Son. Every moment of every day."

"Dunna leave again," Niall wept, his words muffled as he kept his face hidden against Ian's shirt.

At his son's plea, Ian's heart broke. More than anything, he wanted to assure Niall, restore his trust in him, his faith in the world. Yet if he stayed, it would be the end of Maggie's marriage. She would be separated from the man she loved all over again. If he stayed, he, too, would lose the woman he loved.

And that woman was no longer Maggie.

Somehow, his heart had finally let her go and turned elsewhere.

To Noèle.

Ian closed his eyes. What was he to do? If only he could be both men, Ian MacDrummond and Ian Stewart! If only he did not have to choose!

"Take him with ye," came Maggie's voice, and father and son looked up, blinking back their tears.

Her red hair glistened in the last rays of the sun as she walked toward them, sadness darkening her eyes. Yet a warm smile illuminated her face.

"What?" Ian asked, keeping his arm wrapped tightly around his son's shoulders.

Maggie brushed a hand over their son's head, then cupped it to his cheek. "Take him with ye," she whispered in a choked voice as her eyes moved from Niall to Ian. "He needs ye right now, so take him with ye."

Ian stared at her dumbfounded. "Do ye truly...?" He could not quite finish the question.

Maggie nodded before her gaze returned to Niall. "I love ye, and as yer mother, I want nothing more than to see ye happy." She cupped Niall's face in both her hands, holding his gaze imploringly. "Yer father belongs out there right now," she nodded toward the far horizon, "and I belong here. Ye...need to find yer own path. But know that whatever ye choose, we both love ye and we always will."

Niall flung himself into his mother's arms, and she held him as he cried. Tears streamed down her cheeks as well, and she lifted her eyes to Ian's. "I know ye'll take good care of him," she told him with such conviction that Ian felt certain he had strayed into a dream. "But dunna stay away too long." She gave him a brave smile. "Come back and visit. No doubt Blair will let us know whenever ye draw near."

Ian nodded, then held out his hand to her and she took it. "Thank ye," he whispered, wishing they could have spoken like this long before today. "I knew we were meant for each other the moment I saw ye," Ian said with sudden insight. "Only I misunderstood. We were meant to be parents and have these two wonderful children."

"Aye, we were," Maggie agreed before she looked down into their son's face.

Niall's face was red and tear-streaked; and yet he seemed at peace, no longer tense, eaten up by the burdens he had carried for far too long.

"Well, then," Maggie said with a smile, "what do ye choose, Niall? Do ye wish to go with yer father for a while? Of course, the moment ye grow tired of his company, ye can always come back." She chuckled. "I'll always be happy to have ye here with me."

A smile came to Niall's face, one that looked almost foreign upon his features. Ian swore in that moment that he would do all within his power to make his son smile every day of his life. "Aye," Niall replied with a nod, his eyes going back and forth between his parents. "I want to go with Father."

"Good," Maggie replied, pulling him into her arms once more. "But ye must promise to write to me, at least, twice a day." She smiled down at him as he rolled his eyes at her. "Roll yer eyes some more and I'll make it three."

Niall chuckled and hugged his mother tightly.

Excitement swept through Ian at the thought of seeing his son every day, of teaching him to sail and watching him explore the world. Never once had Ian entertained the hope of being a father again.

"And ye," Maggie said suddenly, looking at him. "Ye need to speak to Noèle."

Ian flinched, and Niall looked up. "Who is Noèle?"

Maggie grinned. "Noèle is the woman yer father loves," she said simply, shocking them both. She brushed a hand over Niall's head. "One day, ye'll understand what it means to find yer other half. Sometimes ye have to be patient, but once ye find her, ye'll not want to be parted from her ever again."

Rather dumbfounded, Ian stood staring at Maggie as Niall turned to look at him. "Ye love Noèle the way Mother loves Nathan?"

An answer was beyond Ian. All he could do was stare.

"Aye, he does," Maggie replied for him. "She'll make yer father happy the way Nathan makes me happy. But no matter what, we'll always be yer parents, ye hear?"

Niall nodded.

"Verra well." Maggie tugged her son into her side, then looked up at Ian. "Ye need to go and talk to Noèle. Tonight! Now!" she instructed sternly.

"But—"

"Now!" she insisted, her forefinger raised in warning. "Ye know as well as I do that ye have a tendency to run from these things, and ye've run for long enough. 'Tis time to face what ye fear most." She reached out and squeezed his hand. "Dunna worry. Ye'll not be disappointed." Then she and Niall walked back toward the campfire, leaving Ian to stare after them, wondering if he had imagined this whole day.

Somehow, nothing felt real.

It was all too good to be true.

Chapter Thirty-Six

A CONFESSION

After stepping into the tent to see her daughter, who continued to sleep like a log, Noèle went back outside. The sun had disappeared by now, and the roaring fire was the only light source. Laughter echoed across the clearing as Garrett and Finn continued to tell stories about their childhood, about growing up in Clan MacDrummond. Whenever Ian was mentioned, Noèle listened intently, amazed at who he had once been.

So cheerful.

So carefree.

So daring.

Could he be all those things again? Noèle hoped it was possible, for he deserved no less.

Pacing near the campfire, Noèle once again cast many a glance in the direction of the boulder, hoping that Ian was able to reach his son. And then Maggie rose from her spot beside Nathan and went to join them.

Noèle's heart churned.

By now, she knew where everyone's hearts lay. She knew that Maggie loved her husband. She even knew that Ian no longer loved his wife. She hoped to know that he truly, truly loved her, Noèle.

Yet would he dare risk his heart again? After all, he had been burned! Severely! Would he be too fearful now? Or would she be able to find the words to convince him?

And then Maggie and Niall stepped out from behind the boulder, and their faces seemed...relaxed? *Oui*, they looked at ease, and it made Noèle's heart thud faster within her chest. She caught Maggie's eye, and the other woman winked at her, nodding her head in the direction of the boulder.

For a moment, panic surged through Noèle—This was it! The moment of truth!—but then she tamped it down and hurried toward the boulder. Now or never!

And *never* was not an option!

"Wait!" Moira called, and Noèle paused, looking back over her shoulder. "Here. Take this." The blonde-haired woman lit a small lantern and held it out to Noèle.

Casting a glance around the clearing, Noèle nodded gratefully. "Thank you." She took the lantern, fully aware of all the expectant faces turned toward her, and then hurried away, grateful for the small light guiding her steps.

Indeed, this far away from the campfire, the world seemed almost pitch black. A few stars shone overhead, and a sliver of the moon was visible in the sky. Yet their light seemed to barely touch the ground, making it treacherous—especially so near the cliffs.

Approaching the boulder, Noèle placed one hand upon it, feeling the rough stone against her skin. She inched forward, holding the lantern higher, her eyes straining to see the man she was looking for. At first, the other side of the boulder seemed deserted, large shadows falling over her, until something moved. One of the shadows separated from the others and came toward her.

"Noèle?" came Ian's voice, his approach almost silent despite the roughened stone beneath his feet. "What are ye doing here?"

Noèle held the lantern higher until she could make out his face in the dark. For a moment, it looked hollow and strained, an eerie color, as though he were not from this world. Then, however, Noèle saw something spark in his eyes, eyes that shone with a calm that went far deeper than usual, to the core of his being. *Oui*, he looked almost happy, a slight twitch drawing up the right corner of his mouth. Yet there was a thoughtful expression upon his face, and he eyed her most curiously.

"I came to see how you were," Noèle replied, uncertain how to begin. A myriad of words and phrases surged through her mind, jumbling her thoughts and making her hesitant. If only she knew the right words to say! The ones that would convince him of her honesty, of her genuine feelings for him! But what if she chose the wrong words? Would she lose him then?

An actual smile came to Ian's face. "I am..." He sighed deeply and then shrugged. "There are no words. I never expected this. Any of this."

Noèle could almost feel his joy spread to her. She breathed in deeply, returning his smile. "So, you were able to mend fences with your son?"

Ian's eyes closed, and his smile stretched to encompass his entire face. Noèle could not avert her eyes. *Oui*, she had never seen him thus before. "I never knew," he murmured, then looked at her again. "I never realized how he felt. I was truly blind to everything around me. I didna even see how he suffered." His jaw tightened, and he nodded determinedly. "But now I do see him, and I will never again make him feel abandoned." He took a step toward her, and suddenly his eyes lit up the night. "He wants to come with me. Back to France."

"Oh, that is so wonderful!" Noèle reached out her free hand and grasped his. "I'm so very happy for you, Ian. I know how much you missed your children, and I am so glad you will finally have some time with your son." Here, Noèle paused, her teeth sinking into her lower lip as she gathered her courage. "I'm curious to get to know him if you don't mind, of course."

Ian's gaze narrowed ever so slightly, making her think that he had detected the hint of nervousness that had come to her voice. "Of course not," he replied slowly, still slightly squinting at her, as though he were searching for something. "If ye dunna mind," he said then all of a sudden, "I would like to stay for a few more days to spend some more time with my daughter before we leave. Then, I shall take ye and Ophélie back to France and—"

Ian suddenly broke off, pressing his lips into a thin line. Even in the dim light, Noèle could see a muscle in his jaw twitch, his shoulders now hard, his posture rigid. For a long moment, he simply looked at her, his jaw working before his right hand flew up, and he raked it through his hair. Something impatient lingered upon his features. Something eager even. Yet it was tempered by a touch of fear that shone in his eyes.

Noèle felt utterly confused by the sudden change in his behavior. She had been about to object to him taking her and Ophélie back to France when this sudden change had come upon him. Why had he stopped himself? What had suddenly occurred to him that had changed what he wanted to say? Why was he looking at her like this now? Why—?

"I'm in love with you."

Noèle blinked, momentarily certain that she had merely imagined hearing his voice, imagined hearing him say these words.

A deep breath rushed from Ian's lungs. "I apologize for speaking so bluntly," he said in an apologetic voice, shaking his head as though at himself. "I simply...I simply needed to say it. I needed ye to know. I wanted to, at least, say it once."

Noèle felt her hands begin to tremble as she stared at Ian, completely overwhelmed. As much as she had hoped to hear these words, they shocked her, nonetheless. Perhaps even more so because she had not expected them. Not truly.

With shaking hands, she placed the lantern on a ridge jutting out from the boulder beside them. She was afraid the metal ring would slip through her fingers and plunge them both into darkness.

Almost shyly, Ian averted his gaze, glancing at the dark ground beneath their feet before looking up at her once more. Again, he raked a hand through his hair, clearly nervous. "Perhaps I shouldna have said anything," he remarked with a nervous chuckle. "I've never been...good with words or good at reading another." Closing his eyes, he chuckled darkly. "I never truly knew how my son felt. I never truly took note of my daughter's abilities. Aye, I was blind to so many things."

He clenched his hands at his sides, then took a step toward her. "I care for ye, but...I would never take advantage of ye." The muscle in his jaw ticked angrily. "I need ye to know that. I promise that I will return ye and Ophélie safely to France. Ye needna doubt that."

Ian's declaration had made Noële feel as though she were soaring through the sky. Her heart rejoiced, and she barely knew how to contain it. She wanted to fling herself into his arms. She wanted to kiss him. She wanted to tell him that she loved him as well because, of course, she did. How could he not know that?

And then...Noële paused, still listening to all the words that poured from Ian's lips, and wondered how anyone in this world could truly be this blind.

For he was! So very, very blind!

"Would that be all right?" Ian asked tentatively, a slight frown drawing down his brows as he watched her. "Or...would ye rather return to France right away? I mean, I suppose I could always return later...if that is what ye wish."

Feeling energy surge through her body, Noële stepped forward. As though of their own volition, her shoulders drew back and her chin rose as she met Ian's gaze. "*Non*, that is not what I wish."

Instantly, Ian's face fell. Yet before he could make any sort of ludicrous reply, Noële bridged the remaining gap between them. Swift steps carried her into his arms, and she pushed herself up onto her toes and planted a determined kiss upon his lips.

Quite obviously, her kiss shocked Ian nearly witless because he froze, as though he had suddenly been turned to stone. Only his heart picked up its pace, hammering wildly beneath the palm of her hand.

Noële, however, could not have cared less. She held onto him and kissed him for as long as she wished, for as long as was needed to prove her point. Then, she stepped back, looked up to meet his eyes and said, "I'm in love with you as well, and I do not want you to return me and Ophélie to France. I want to stay with you now and for the rest of my days. That is what I wish."

All of a sudden, life felt simple to Noële. She could not believe that only moments ago she had been worried and doubtful, uncertain of how to proceed, perhaps even uncertain of what she wanted. Perhaps it had been Ian's intention of returning her to France, the threat of seeing their path separated from one another. Whatever it had been, Noèle finally knew all that she needed to do, that she wanted to do.

After all, the question had never truly been whether Ian loved her or whether she loved him but rather whether he would ever *believe* that she did. Ian's heart was like a fortress with walls upon walls guarding it from the outside world. To reach him, one had to bridge all of these walls, tear them down and destroy his defenses. Noèle could see that her own declaration had caught Ian off guard. It had shocked him, rocked the foundation upon which he stood. And yet there was something in his eyes that betrayed a deep yearning.

He *wanted* to believe her.

Desperately.

But would he dare?

Chapter Thirty-Seven

A FOOL AGAIN

Perhaps his mind was simply overwhelmed, Ian thought as he stared down into Noële's face. After all, this day had been a day like no other. He had been confronted with countless moments he had not seen coming, moments he had not even dared imagine. He could barely tell what his heart felt, his emotions so entangled that he felt an almost desperate need to take a step back. Perhaps they would make more sense from a different vantage point.

He squinted, searching her face, unable not to, yet afraid to contemplate this one question. Did she truly mean what she had said?

"Don't look at me like that, Ian," Noële remarked in a rather chiding voice that rang with annoyance. "*Non*, you did not misunderstand me. *Oui*, I did say that I love you. Don't you dare tell yourself that I did not mean what I said." She lifted her right forefinger in warning, her eyes suddenly so intense that Ian felt the breath lodge in his throat.

What was going on?

Ian cleared his throat. "Ye've been through so much and—"

A furious grunt left Noële's lips, and in the next instant, her hands shoved him backward, forcing him to retreat a step in order to maintain his balance. "Why do you do this?" she snapped, that accusing finger once more in the air. "Why is it so easy for you to believe something awful that people say to you? But when I tell you that I love you, you treat me like a liar. Why?"

The light from the lantern flickered across her angry face. It lit up her eyes, made them glow like two embers. Aye, Ian knew that Noèle was fierce. She had fought for her daughter tooth and nail, had given everything, risked everything. And yet, he could not remember ever having seen her like this. She seemed so...not even angry, but...annoyed.

"Tell me!" she snapped. "If you call me a liar, then, at least, tell me why you doubt me!"

Ian shook his head. "I never called ye a liar. I never would! I simply—"

"*Oui*, you did!" Noèle insisted. "You do not believe me, and if you truly do not believe that I'm telling you the truth, then you must think that I'm lying. It's the only sensible conclusion." She almost glared at him, and Ian swallowed hard, caught off guard by this passionate nature of her. Never had he seen her like this before.

"I never once believed you would lie to me," Ian replied cautiously, lifting his hand in an appeasing gesture. "I simply think that perhaps you are confused about what you feel." He swallowed hard. "You've suffered so much, been through so much that perhaps you simply... overinterpret your emotions."

For a long moment, Noèle stared at him, an aghast look upon her face. Then she blinked and that accusing finger flew up once more and pointed at his chest. "Are you saying," she began in an eerily calm voice, "that you believe that I kissed you out of gratitude? Because you saved me? Because you saved my daughter?"

Ian remained silent, his gaze fixed upon the wildly thudding pulse in her neck. Aye, Noèle might appear collected; however, it was easy to see that she was outraged. Indeed, he ought to have chosen his words more wisely. Without meaning to, he had insulted her, suggested that she was willing to repay him by offering—

"How dare you?" Noèle snapped, her anger flaring. "Is this truly how you think of me?"

Ian gritted his teeth, torn between yanking her into his arms and pushing her far, far away from him. "I apologize for expressing myself poorly. I never intended to—"

"Would you please stop apologizing? Explain yourself!"

"There's nothing to explain. I simply think it would be wise if—"

"You said you loved me," Noèle exclaimed, throwing his words back into his face. She moved toward him, her eyes wide as they searched his face, desperately trying to understand. "Do you...Do you not want me?"

Ian knew that he was not making much sense or any sense at all. His own head was spinning, and he barely knew what he was saying. Never in his life had he felt so out of control, so much at the mercy of the comings and goings of life.

Yet looking down into Noèle's eyes right now, Ian almost forgot what he needed to say. After all, this could not end well! Even if she truly loved him—Did she?—her heart would always be Étienne's. As much as Ian wanted to give in to this dream right now, he knew it would not be wise. He knew he would regret it later. He knew it would yet be another mistake.

"It has nothing to do with ye," Ian finally said, hating that crestfallen look upon her face. Who would ever not want her? It was a ludicrous thought! She was wonderful and breathtaking and fierce and stubborn and kind and—

"How can it not?" Noèle demanded, a touch of bitterness in her voice. "You say you love me, and then you push me away." Her brows narrowed, and a touch of suspicion came to her eyes. "You told me you loved me, and yet you do not believe that I feel the same for you. Then why did you say it in the first place? Did you—?" She stilled, and her eyes widened ever so slightly.

Ian tensed, uncertain what was going on in her head.

"Tell me why!" she demanded harshly. "Now!"

"There is noth—"

"*Oui*, there is! Why did you tell me?"

"I don't—"

Noèle's eyes flared. "Do you want me to fight for you?"

Her words shot through him like a bolt of lightning. They shocked him. They threw him off balance. They caught him completely off guard. Yet, far in the most distant recesses of his mind, Ian could hear a faint little voice screaming at the top of its lungs, "Yes!"

"That's it, isn't it?" Noèle exclaimed, the frown gone from her face and a look of triumph lighting up her eyes. "You want me to fight for you!"

Ian shook his head, desperately trying to clear it, to rid himself of these thoughts. Of course, he did not want her to fight for him! The thought alone was ludicrous! He wanted—

Aye, that was the problem. Ian did not know what he wanted. He had fought hard not to want anything. After all, wanting led to feeling lonely and vulnerable. That led to loss and heartbreak. It was not wise to want anything at all. It was even worse to want someone.

Suddenly, Noèle surged forward, her hands rising, and then she grasped the sides of his face. Even in the dark, her blue eyes shone brightly, looking up into his. "I love you, Ian," she said softly and gently and with so much conviction that Ian felt the warmth of her words reach out and touch him. "I do. I do love you. It is the truth, and it will always be the truth whether or not you choose to believe me. And I promise you that no matter what you do I shall not leave. I shall not go away. I shall remain with you for always."

Ian felt his breath quickening. His hands clenched and unclenched at his sides as he fought the desire to reach for her and pull her even closer. "I'm not calling ye a liar," Ian said carefully, needing her to know that none of what he was about to say was meant as any kind of accusation. "All I'm saying is that ye gave yer heart away a long time ago, and that is not something that can be undone. Believe me, I've spent years trying and I failed." Reaching up, he gently grasped her wrists, determined to put more distance between them. "There's no use in pretending. Hoping against hope will not serve either of us." He tried to remove her hands from his face, but she would not let him.

Noèle's lips thinned and her eyes narrowed before she slowly began to shake her head from side to side. "You're wrong. How can you not see that?"

Ian scoffed, his hands tensing upon her wrists. "How can ye ask me that question?" he demanded. "Ye've seen my wife, spoken to my wife." He shook his head. "She still loves the man who first conquered her heart. Nothing was ever able to change that. Nothing!" He gritted his teeth against that wave of disappointment, of inevitability. "Is it not the same for ye and Étienne? Will ye not always love him? Can ye truly look me in the eye and tell me that ye no longer do?"

Ian held his breath as Noèle stared up at him, tears glistening in her eyes, illuminated by the soft flicker of the lantern. "I do love him," Noèle said quietly, sorrow and loss clear in her voice. "*Oui*, I do. You're right. I do still love him, and a part of me always will." Her hands tightened upon his face, and she moved closer. "And I know that a part of you will always love Maggie, but does that mean you cannot love me?" Holding his gaze, she shook her head. "Perhaps the reason you were not able to conquer your wife's heart was because she was never meant for you. Perhaps I was meant for you all along, because everything that happened led us to this very point, right here, right now." Tears ran down her face, and yet her voice did not waver.

Ian felt the yearning in his heart grow. She stood right here in his arms...or not quite. She would if only he dared reach for her. He could feel her warm breath against his lips, see honest emotions sparking in her eyes, and knew that more than anything he wanted to believe her. Only deep down that familiar voice whispered again, urging him to doubt her, urging him to be on his guard, reminding him that this would be yet another mistake. "And what of Étienne? Were ye not meant for him?"

Noèle sighed. "Perhaps I was. Perhaps I was meant to share these few years with him, but that does not mean I am not meant for you right here, right now...if you want me." Swallowing, she lifted her chin. "This is the choice you will have to make. It is yours, not mine. I've already made mine. I will not walk away. If you do not want me, you'll need to say so. Tell me you don't love me. Tell me you want me to leave...and even though it will break my heart, I will honor your wishes. But if you cannot," her voice grew in intensity, her fingers almost digging into the sides of his face, "if you do not, I will not leave your side. Ever."

Ian knew that he was in trouble. Somehow, that voice in his head slowly grew fainter until he could barely hear it. He could feel every sense of caution fade away, easily overpowered by a desperate want he had thus far kept under lock and key. Because the truth was that he *did* want. He had tried not to. He had almost succeeded in making himself believe that he did not.

Only it was a lie.

And he knew it now.

He wanted.

He wanted her.

He wanted Noële.

And she was right here, her hands upon his face, his own wrapped around her wrists. All he had to do was tug her closer and she would be in his arms. And she wanted to be…if he dared believe her. And he was beginning to. She did mean what she said, did she not? Had she truly come to love him?

Ian closed his eyes, and a long breath rushed from his lungs before he met her eyes once more. "I'm afraid," he admitted, surprised that he would dare share his vulnerability with another.

Noële smiled. "I know."

Chapter Thirty-Eight
TO RISK ONE'S HEART...AGAIN

At Ian's sign of surrender, Noèle felt her heart begin to dance in her chest. She could almost taste victory, certain that if she remained adamant, he would yield eventually. He would give in and give them both a chance.

"I'm afraid, too," Noèle replied, grateful for his honesty and determined to prove that he could trust her with everything, even his fears. "Believe me, this is not easy for me either. I am risking my own heart as well." She swallowed hard against the lump in her throat. "I'm afraid that no matter what I say I will not be able to convince you. I'm afraid that I will lose you because you're too stubborn to see what's right in front of you." She tried to smile at him, rejoicing in the soft twitch that came to his lips as though he, too, wished this moment could take a different turn. "I'm afraid to risk my heart and have you trample it into the dust, but I'm also afraid to let you go and regret it for the rest of my life...because I know that I would."

Even in the dim light from the lantern, Noèle could see the hard expression upon Ian's face soften. The tension in his hands waned, and they released her wrists and slid up her arms until they came to rest upon her shoulders.

Noèle smiled. He was reaching for her, reaching out to her. Slowly.

As much as he dared. He was trying. Trying hard. And she was grateful for it.

"This is not easy," Ian murmured as his eyes swept over her face and his hands slowly slid past her shoulders and onto her back.

"It is not," Noële agreed, moving closer and sliding her hand from his face to the nape of his neck. "It's a risk. Life is full of risks, but if we never take any, if we hide from them all, would it truly make us safer? Happier?"

Ian closed his eyes, a deep breath rushing from between his lips.

"You've tried, have you not?" Noële whispered, urging him to look at her once more. "These past few years, you've kept yourself apart, have you not? You've tried your hardest to be self-sufficient, to not connect to anyone, and while, *oui*, you might have kept your heart a little safer, it also felt lonely, did it not?"

Instead of answering her, Ian suddenly yanked her into his arms. His own came around her, all but crushing her to his chest as he buried his face in her hair. Noële held onto him with all the strength she possessed, knowing that he needed her right now, knowing that this was a moment of weakness for him, that he felt vulnerable.

He was taking a leap of faith...trusting that she would catch him.

"I want you," Noële whispered in his ear. "I want you now, and I will still want you tomorrow. Not because you saved me and my daughter. Not because I feel safer with you by my side. But because every day seems a little darker without you there. Because when you're not there, there is that terrible ache in my chest as though half of myself is missing. Because as much as you've tried to push me away, my heart feels safe with you. I love you, Ian, and I need you to believe me right here, right now. But if you cannot, then I will still keep fighting for you. I won't give up, and you will not be rid of me no matter what you do." She pulled away, blinking against the tears that ran from her eyes, and looked up into his face. "If nothing else, believe that."

Wiping a hand over his eyes, Ian chuckled, his voice choked with tears as well. "No one has ever fought for me," he said quietly, gently tracing his knuckles over her forehead and down her temple. "I suppose I did want you to. I never realized it, but..."

"I know," Noële whispered, finally understanding what had held him back, what had stood in their path. "It is crippling to feel alone and unloved." Again, she reached up to cup his face in her hands. "Yet you were never unloved. You need to know that. Maggie might not have been able to give her heart to you, but that does not mean that no one else ever could. Your children love you. They adore you. They want you as much today as they did the day you left. You found friends, family even, in France. You found a new home, a new place. There are a lot of people who want you in their lives, and I am only one of them." She smiled up at him, so utterly relieved to have gotten through to him.

"Ye are the most important one of them all," Ian whispered, and for a long moment, his dark gaze lingered upon hers before it slowly drifted lower and touched upon her lips.

Yet he hesitated.

"Kiss me, Ian," Noèle urged him, assuring him that he was not overstepping a line. "You have my permission. You will always have my permission to kiss me anytime you want because the truth is that there has never been a time when I did not want you to."

An adorably shy smile came to his face before he tipped his head and gently touched his mouth to hers. Noèle's arms came around him, holding him closer, and she gave herself up to the moment.

Finally, her heart and mind were at ease, no longer burdened by fearful questions. Every muscle in her body seemed to relax as happiness swept through her. She felt calm and excited all at the same time, eager for the future ahead, no longer worried what it might hold.

Ian's embrace felt wonderful. He was gentle and considerate, and she could feel that his words had been the truth. He did love her. He did want her. He made that perfectly clear with every touch, every kiss, every whispered word.

Arm in arm, they sat down with their backs against the boulder, the lantern overhead casting a warm glow over them. They looked out across the sea and up into the sky, savoring the darkness, for it wrapped them in a cocoon all their own. The rest of the world seemed to be gone, almost nonexistent, and for the first time, they felt as one, two people looking toward the same future.

"Where do we go from here?" Ian asked tentatively, his arm still wrapped around her, her head resting against his shoulder. "Life seems...rather complicated considering everything."

Noèle sighed, perfectly content in this perfect moment. "I suppose we can do whatever we want." She paused, considering his words carefully, and then sat up, trying to meet his eyes in the dark. "Is this a matter of what we want or of how we get what we want?"

A smile touched his lips. "Perhaps a bit of both." He held her gaze. "What is it that ye want?"

Noèle grinned at him. "You." He chuckled, shyly averting his gaze for a split second before looking at her once more. Noèle was coming to love this adorable sight of him. "My daughter, of course. But I also want to get to know your children. They're wonderful. I want to know more about your life here, but I also want to return to France, to our family there. I suppose I want a lot of things, but what truly matters is that we walk this path together."

Ian drew in a deep breath, and for a second, Noèle wondered if something worrisome was on his mind. He tensed ever so lightly, his hands wrapped around hers, before he opened his mouth. "I wish I could marry ye."

An instant smile came to Noèle's face. "I wish for that too," she replied joyfully. "Why ever should we not?"

Ian cleared his throat, a touch of discomfort upon his face. "Well, at least technically, I'm still married."

Noèle laughed. "And yet your *wife* has a new husband." She squeezed his hands reassuringly. "Perhaps we should ignore the technicalities and simply do what feels right. Maggie clearly belongs with Nathan, and you clearly belong with me." She leaned forward and placed a kiss upon his lips. "How can you deny that?"

With a low growl in his throat, Ian answered her question, claiming a kiss of his own. He held her close, his hands upon her back possessive, making it unmistakably clear that he agreed with her. She was as much his as he was hers.

"I told Maggie," Ian said when he finally pulled back, "that Ian MacDrummond would remain dead, that she need not worry about any implications for her marriage."

Noèle nodded. "Perhaps this is a perfect solution then. While Ian

MacDrummond will always be a part of you, perhaps right now, you can be Ian Stewart." She grinned at him. "And Ian Stewart is not married...as far as I know."

Ian chuckled. "He is not." He pulled her closer, his gaze fixed upon hers. "Not yet."

His eyes searched hers, and Noèle felt every part of her warm and tingle at the way he held her, the way he looked at her. "*Oui*," she finally said. "My answer is *oui*."

A slight frown came to Ian's face. "I havena even asked ye yet."

Noèle laughed. "Oh, but you did." She leaned back in, asking for another kiss, and he complied.

Noèle sighed as she sank into his embrace. Perhaps more than Ian knew, she, too, had been afraid of the future, of what was to happen to her. After losing her husband, everything had seemed dark and glum and painful. And then life had taken such an awful turn that Noèle had stopped believing that she would ever find even a smidgen of joy again. Somehow, she had resigned herself to simply existing from one day to the next, quite like Ian had done himself. Perhaps that was what made them perfect for one another, that knowledge of what it felt like to stand upon the abyss...and make it back. They had both seen their lives shattered. Both believed to have reached the end of everything that was good. And yet, now, here they stood, together as one, and the future seemed so bright that Noèle almost felt bathed in light despite the dark surrounding them.

Oui, hope never died, did it?

Chapter Thirty-Nine

DREAMS

Ian stood at the edge of the clearing, his eyes sweeping over the encampment. He had never believed he would ever be back here, that he would ever lay eyes upon his friends and family again. And yet here he was, his heart and mind at peace for the first time in countless years. With a smile upon his face, he watched his own children as well as his friend's children chase each other around the campfire. The sun shone overhead, and birds chirped in the trees nearby. A mild breeze blew across the clearing, and voices echoed everywhere. Cormag and Garrett were skinning rabbits they had caught hunting while Emma and Claudia saw to the youngest of the children. Nathan and Finn watered the horses and then led them over to a grassy patch.

And there, near the boulder, he saw Maggie and Noèle, both their faces joyful and animated, words flying back and forth between them, as though they had known each other for years. He saw no sign of animosity or jealousy, and his gaze once more moved to Nathan.

Years ago, Ian had hated the man. He had hated him for what he had done to Maggie or rather what he, Ian, had thought had happened between them at the time. More than that even, he had hated Nathan for his hold upon Maggie's heart. Yet, today, Ian could look at him and feel nothing of the kind. Aye, part of him, he supposed, would always love Maggie in some way. She was the mother of his children, and that was a bond that would last a lifetime. Yet he was no longer *in love* with her. When that feeling had changed, Ian did not quite know. Yet he was certain that it had been Noèle's doing. Somehow, in her quiet and tentative way, she had claimed his heart...and he had barely even noticed.

Not until it had been too late.

Ian smiled at the thought, grateful for the way things had turned out. After years of merely existing, he was actually right back in Scotland, surrounded by the people he loved the most. He saw Niall and Blair cutting vegetables by the fire, whispering to one another animatedly, as they helped Moira prepare a stew. Cheerfulness lingered in the air, and Ian felt reminded of wonderful childhood moments, festivals and celebrations amidst the entire clan. Aye, he had been happy long ago, and now, to his surprise, he was again.

While the crew of the *Chevalier Noir* had set up camp down below on the beach, Ian, Noèle and Ophélie stayed up here upon the clearing with his friends and family. They had agreed to stay on for another week, spend some time together and create new memories that would sustain them until the next time. Ian had taken his children hunting as well as gathering roots and berries. They had climbed trees and told each other stories of their years apart. They had ridden across the fields, feeling the wind in their faces, and he had watched as both Niall and Blair had played with Ophélie. The little girl was delighted with all the attention she got, and after a few days, Ian thought they looked remarkably like siblings, the way Niall and Blair always picked her up, carrying her along, always watchful, so she would not get hurt. Niall, in particular, had practice being an older brother, and he seemed to have no qualms in teaching his sister how to be an older sibling.

Ian was in awe of his children. The years had truly changed them. They were still as amazing as they always had been, and yet all of a sudden, they seemed so grown-up, able to do things they had needed help with before. Still, just being near them was a dream come true for Ian, and he savored each and every moment.

"Can we see yer ship?" Blair asked one day as she and her brother came running up to him the moment he stepped out of his tent. Both their eyes were wide, the expression upon their faces eager. "What did ye say it was called? The *Chevalier Noir?*" Blair was quite careful in pronouncing the words just right.

Ian chuckled, remembering his own attempts at speaking French.

"What does it mean?" Niall inquired as he carefully pronounced the name himself. "It has to mean something, doesna it?"

Ian nodded, grinning at Noèle, who had stepped out of the tent after him, Ophélie in her arms. "Aye, of course, it means something." He looked into his children's expectant faces. "It means *black knight.*"

While Blair's brows drew down into a slight frown, Niall's jaw dropped in awe. "Does it have black sails?" Blair inquired, putting a thoughtful finger to the corner of her mouth. "I remember someone telling a story about a ship with black sails once." She looked at her brother questioningly. "Was it not a pirate ship?"

"A privateer," Ian corrected before his children's imagination could rush off to unknown places.

"What's the difference?" Niall asked, grinning at Ophélie as she tried to grab a lock of his red hair.

"A privateer possesses a letter of marque from his government," Ian explained. "That means that a privateer sails under a country's flag, boarding enemy ships and obtaining their cargo as spoils of war. A privateer receives a share of the bounty but hands over the majority to his government. A pirate, on the other hand, is a criminal and will be tried as such if caught."

The five of them together slowly made their way down toward the beach while Blair and Niall fired questions at Ian that he was only too happy to answer. There was such ease between them after years of distance, and every once in a while, he felt as though he had never been gone. His crew welcomed them all excitedly, cheering as Ian introduced his children. Niall continued asking all kinds of questions, and Louis quickly led the way, guiding them all back to the cavern where the *Chevalier Noir* lay hidden.

The moment his children's eyes fell upon the tall-masted ship, their mouths dropped open. "It's so...big," Niall exclaimed with wide eyes. Then he turned to look up at Ian. "Can we go on board?"

Smiling, Ian nodded and then spent the rest of the morning escorting his children around the ship, telling stories of raging storms and sea battles while Niall and Blair inspected each and every inch of the *Chevalier Noir*. . One after the other, with Ian watching over them, they even climbed up the rigging into the Crow's Nest.

It was a wonderful morning, and once they returned to the clearing and sat down with their friends and family for a hearty meal, Niall and Blair shared everything they had seen that morning. The other children were as riveted as they had been before, and Ian smiled, not ever wanting to forget this moment.

"You look happy," Noèle remarked quietly as she leaned in. "I like seeing you like this."

Ian nodded, meeting her eyes. "I never thought..." There were still mornings when he woke up and for a few seconds believed that everything had simply been a dream. Gut-wrenching sorrow speared through him in these few seconds before his eyes fell on Noèle and Ophélie sleeping beside him, before he remembered what had indeed happened.

"*Oui*, sometimes it can take a while for reality to sink in," Noèle replied, a shadow passing over her face. "For the good and the bad."

Ian knew that she was thinking of her late husband. Of Étienne. And yet he did not feel as though he were her second choice. Something had changed as they had spoken that night upon the cliffs. Something that had changed how he felt. Ian could not name it nor did he wish to. What mattered was that he breathed easily these days. He felt safe in his love for Noèle.

"Let's focus on the good," Ian said, reaching out and taking her hand. "We shall never forget the bad, but perhaps we dunna need to dwell upon it every day."

Noèle turned surprised eyes to him.

Ian chuckled quietly. "I know what ye're thinking," he murmured. "I'm surprising even myself these days."

Noèle leaned against his shoulder. "I like this side of you. I always knew it was there, but seeing it now is simply wonderful."

And although a farewell lingered upon the horizon, they were all determined to see the good in these days they had with one another. There was a lot of laughter and joy. Sharing of stories and adventures, and Ian promised Maggie that they would not be gone for too long. He promised Blair as well, and when the time to say goodbye finally came, his little daughter embraced him and whispered, "I'll see ye in my dreams. Until ye return."

Ian knelt down and looked up into her face. "Thank ye for never giving up on me, little Blair. Ye're truly the wisest one of us all."

She smiled at him, placing her little hands upon his cheeks. "I know," she replied with a smirk. "Only no one will believe me."

Ian chuckled. "Give it time," he told her. "Sometimes we have to be patient. Only because something is taking long, that doesna mean it will never happen."

A thoughtful expression came to Blair's face. "Perhaps I got it from ye, Father." When he frowned at her, she added, "The dreams. When ye're not sad or angry, ye see things very clearly, too."

One last time, Ian embraced his daughter and then stepped back, his eyes meeting Maggie's as they all stood upon the beach. "I will take good care of him."

With tears in her eyes, Maggie nodded. "I know," she said, hugging Niall to her chest. "And while ye're at it, take good care of yerself as well."

Ian nodded, and after a few more hugs and kisses, they stepped away and climbed into the dinghy. Noèle and Ophélie had already said their goodbyes and were awaiting them upon the *Chevalier Noir*. It drifted just offshore, ready to set sail. Niall's gaze remained fixed upon the beach and the family he was leaving behind as Ian rowed them both toward the ship. "Are ye sad to leave?"

His son nodded, his gaze fixed upon the beach. "But I'm also excited." Then he turned and met his father's eyes. "I've dreamed of this, but I never thought it would come true."

Ian smiled at him. "Ye dreamed of sailing the seas?"

Niall shook his head. "No, I dreamed of being with ye."

Touched, Ian held his son's gaze, momentarily too overwhelmed to say anything. Then he nodded, blinked away the tears that gathered in the corners of his eyes and said, "I dreamed of that, too."

And he had.

He had simply never realized how much he wanted that dream to come true.

Chapter Forty

A NEW FAMILY

N oèle loved being back at sea. She had not realized it until the moment she once again felt the wind in her face and breathed in the fresh sea air. With Ophélie in her arms, she walked across the deck, enjoying the bright warm day as the sailors scrambled around her, bringing the ship about and turning it into the wind. Everybody moved with precision, calm expressions on all their faces as they did what they did best.

Standing at the railing, Noèle pointed out a whale in the far distance, whispering to Ophélie of all the wonderful creatures that lived in the world below their feet. The little girl giggled and gasped, wide eyes sweeping over everything. Her little hands reached out, as though she wished to grab hold of the wind.

Turning to look over her shoulder, Noèle spotted Ian and his son on the quarterdeck. The sight of them together always filled her with joy, both their faces betraying how deeply they enjoyed this time they now had together. Niall laughed at something Ian had said, his usually sour expression vanishing, suddenly replaced by something carefree and cheerful. These days, there rarely was a scowl upon his face, and he seemed to utterly enjoy this sudden turn his life had taken. The bond between father and son grew from day to day, and Noèle could see a very similar transformation in Ian.

Now, he resembled the man she thought he had once been. He was no longer distant and always on guard. He spoke freely and sought the company of others, laughing and chatting, telling stories and jokes. Noèle had taken note of the occasional confused frown upon one of the men's faces; yet with time, they had quickly come to accept this change in their captain.

And so, the days passed in blissful tranquility until the French coast once more appeared upon the horizon.

Ian was up on the quarterdeck discussing something with Louis when Niall suddenly came to stand beside Noèle. Although he cast her a tentative smile, he kept his distance, at least one arm's length between them as they stood side by side at the railing. Ophélie, of course, had no such qualms. She delighted in seeing him, instantly reaching out her little hands.

Noèle laughed. "She adores you."

Again, that shy smile played over Niall's face. He appeared a little embarrassed, and yet Noèle thought that he liked the fact that Ophélie was so fond of him. "I adore her, too."

Again, Ophélie stretched out her arms toward him, her little fingers opening and closing, as though somehow she could pull herself closer to him.

"Would you mind holding her for a moment?" Noèle asked, for she wanted nothing more than for them all to become a family, to feel comfortable with one another.

A little apprehensive, Niall nodded. Then he stepped forward and held out his arms, taking Ophélie. Instantly, his whole demeanor changed. An easy smile played over his lips, and he tickled Ophélie and whispered silly words to her.

Noèle watched them, amazed at how the exchange reminded her of Ian. Both father and son knew how to hide their feelings well, and yet they possessed such warmth and kindness that others felt drawn to them.

"Father says," Niall began, glancing up at her, "that we'll reach La

Roche-sur-Mer late this afternoon." It was a mere statement, and yet Noèle could hear a question in his words.

"Oh, you will love it there!" she assured him with all the exuberance that danced beneath her skin. "The Durets are a wonderful family just like the MacDrummonds." A pleased smile flashed across Niall's face. "They are kind and loud and always there when needed." She sighed, aware that Niall was watching her intently out of the corner of his eyes. "When I was all alone, they stood with me, helped me in any way they could." She met his gaze. "They became my family as they became your father's. That is the beauty of it, of life, that sometimes you turn a corner and you find something utterly unexpected."

Niall bowed his head, and Noèle could see a shadow fall over his face. "But Father already had a family."

Noèle nodded. "He did, *oui*. But, at the time, he knew not how to be the man he wanted to be. More than anything, he wanted to be your father, teach you about life, and help you see its beauty. Yet there was pain and sadness in him, and he knew not how to be that man."

Disentangling one of Ophélie's hands from his red hair, Niall met Noèle's gaze, his own thoughtful. "I remember him being sad and angry. A lot. All the time." He sighed deeply. "It was because of Mother. I always knew it was." He paused, his green eyes narrowed as they searched Noèle's face. "He no longer loves her, does he? That's why he feels better now."

Noèle paused, sensing an underlying question beneath the one the boy had voiced. "He still loves her," she assured Niall. "As I still love my first husband. Love never truly goes away, but sometimes it changes." She reached out a hand, and Ophélie grabbed her finger. "One's children, however, are the exception. A parent's love for her child never changes, never wanes, never becomes anything less than absolute."

The tense expression upon Niall's face softened, and the corners of his mouth quirked.

"I love my daughter with all my heart," Noèle told him. "And yet I can see myself loving other children in the future. We can all be a family. We don't have to choose whom to love. There is no quarrel between your mother and me nor is there any between Nathan and your father. We've all found love and happiness, and you, Blair and Ophélie are all our children."

The wolf came padding over in that moment, lifting his nose to sniff Ophélie's leg and then poke Niall in the side, clearly feeling excluded from something important. Ophélie instantly reached out a hand and grasped his fur, yanking hard while giggling with delight.

Niall, in his calm and gentle way, urged her to loosen her hand and then showed her how to gently pat the wolf's head. He kneeled down, then sat with his back against the railing, holding Ophélie in his lap as the wolf moved to lie down beside them.

Noële loved watching them, and yet she felt like an intruder to this peaceful moment. "Will you watch her for a little bit?" she asked Niall, and as he looked up at her, he smiled, nodding his head.

Crossing the deck, Noële then climbed the ladder to the quarter-deck, occasionally casting a look over her shoulder at her children. *Oui*, they were all a family. They all belonged, and nothing would ever change that.

She simply would not let it.

"'Tis wonderful to see them like this, isna it?" Ian murmured as he came to stand beside her, his hand brushing against hers with a feather-light touch.

Noële turned to look at him, a wide smile upon her face. "It is wonderful to see you like this as well," she told him, wishing she could step even closer, embrace him, kiss him. Still, that would have to wait until no eyes were trained on them.

Running a hand through his hair, Ian grinned. "Aye, life is good. It never was quite like this before, but now that I know what I have," he reached out and took her hands into his, "I will hold onto it for the rest of my life."

"Is that a promise?" Noële teased him, her own fingers curling around his.

"Aye, it is." Ian pulled her closer, ignoring a soft chuckle as Louis stepped down from the quarterdeck, an amused glint in his eyes. "We shall reach France soon, and the first thing I'll do is make arrange-ments for our wedding." That teasing grin once more appeared upon his face as he looked down at her. It was an expression Noële could not remember from before. It was new, or perhaps very, very old from when he had still been young and carefree, unburdened by unrequited love.

"The first thing?" Noèle continued to tease him, delighting in the way his eyes sparked with mirth.

Ian chuckled. "Perhaps not the verra first thing," he murmured, then he quickly dipped his head and placed a kiss upon her lips. It was fleeting and far from what she wanted, but it would have to do.

For now.

Chapter Forty-One

UTTERLY WRONG

For the longest time, Ian had thought that a day like today would never come. Not for him. He would have bet everything on it. Even his life. And he had never been so happy to be wrong.

Utterly and completely wrong.

Standing high up on the cliffs overlooking the sea on one side and the Durets' home on the other, only a few steps away, Ian held on tightly to Noèle's hand, overwhelmed by everything today had brought.

His gaze swept over friends and family alike, all the guests who had joined them today, witnessed their wedding, their hope for the future. Henri's grandparents, Hubert and Colette, had once again outdone themselves. The house and garden had been decorated with flowers and ribbons alike. Refreshments, sweet and tart, had been set out on long tables beneath the trees offering shade on the southern side of the garden. A fiddler was playing in one corner of the terrace, the joyful notes drifting through the warm air, mingling with the sound of seagulls screeching overhead.

"Today's truly a perfect day, is it not?" Noèle remarked with a happy sigh as she leaned into him, resting her head against his shoulder.

Ian's arm came around her naturally, as though it had always belonged there, as though she had always belonged in his embrace. "Aye," was all he could say, more words than that lost to him.

Niall was running through the garden with Antoine's four children, enjoying the camaraderie that had quickly grown between them. His French was still heavily accented, and yet he had mastered it in a way Ian knew he, himself, never would. Seeing his son come into his own like this brought him great joy.

"And what now?" Noèle asked, craning her neck a little to look up at him. "Where will we go from here? Will we stay here? In La Roche-sur-Mer? Or go elsewhere? Back to sea?"

Ian shrugged. "I dunna know. Is there a place ye wish to go? A place ye wish to see?"

Noèle smiled at him before her gaze moved and found their children, Niall with his new friends and Ophélie seated beneath a tree patting the wolf the way Niall had shown her. "I like being out at sea, and I like being here. Most of all, though," she reached up a hand and cupped his cheek, her blue eyes finding his, "I love being with you and our family. No matter where we go, I know I will be happy so long as I have you."

Ian placed a kiss upon her temple, holding her close as he intended to do for the rest of his life. "I received a letter from Blair just this morning," he told her, still uncertain how he felt about its contents.

Taking a step back, Noèle met his gaze, her hands resting leisurely upon his chest. "What is it? Is everything all right?"

Ian nodded. "Aye, everything's fine."

Noèle's gaze narrowed.

"'Tis simply that," Ian swallowed, trying to find the right words, "she wrote about a dream of hers, and…I dunna know what to make of it."

Noèle's eyes widened slightly. "A dream? You mean about the future?"

Ian nodded again.

"As she foresaw your return to Scotland?"

"Aye."

"What she sees, does it always come to pass?" Noèle asked, a mixture of eagerness and apprehension upon her face. "What *did* she see?"

Ian shrugged. "I canna say how reliable her dreams are. I canna say I understand why she sees what she sees nor what it means. She told me that Moira helps her make sense of them, and yet the way she speaks I think even Moira sometimes struggles with their meaning."

"I see," Noèle said, a slight tremble in her hands. "What did she see then? The look upon your face suggests nothing good."

Ian exhaled a deep breath, raking a hand through his hair. "I'm not certain if it's good or bad. She wrote that she dreamed of a ship in a foreign harbor, a flag she has never seen before. She saw a red-haired man standing at the helm."

"Niall?" Noèle's wide eyes darted to the boy as he playfully tackled Antoine's son, Vincent, to the ground. "Was it him?"

Ian shrugged. "She wrote she couldna see his face."

"What happened to him?" Her hands tensed upon Ian's.

"Nothing," Ian replied, remembering each and every word Blair had written.

"Nothing?" Noèle frowned. "What do you mean? I thought..."

"Nothing *happened*," Ian stressed. "All she wrote was that she could see a storm gathering upon the horizon."

"A storm? You mean, like a real storm or was it rather meant as a metaphor for something dangerous?"

Scoffing, Ian shrugged. "I have no way of knowing that. She didna say more. I suppose, she doesna know herself."

Again, Noèle's gaze wandered to Niall. "What do we do? Do we tell him?"

"Tell him what?" Ian asked, unable to shake that sense of dread lingering nearby whenever he thought of his daughter's letter. "No, I dunna think we should say anything. After all, we hardly know anything at all."

Noèle nodded. "And whatever it was Blair saw is far in the future, is it not? If it truly was Niall standing at the helm, then whatever happens will not happen until he is a grown man."

"Aye, ye're right." Pulling his wife into his arms, Ian looked at his son. "Whatever we say would only confuse him. Better to let him be happy now." Indeed, Niall was happy. Ian could not recall ever seeing his son laugh this much or be this carefree.

Noèle smiled up at him. "Of course, he is. He has you back in his life."

A part deep down in Ian's soul still cringed away from these words, unable to believe that he meant so much to another. That his being there could affect another's life in such a profound way. It made him proud and fearful at the same time.

However, that was the lot of parents, was it not?

To be fearful, to always worry about one's children, to look at them and wonder what would happen to them down the line. And now, with Blair's words hanging over his head, Ian knew he could not simply stand by and do nothing.

Yet, what *could* he do? He did not even know if there truly was any danger lingering upon the horizon for Niall. Perhaps an entirely different meaning hid behind Blair's dream. Indeed, all Ian could do was prepare his son as best as he could, teach him all he knew, open up the world to him, allow him to make his own experiences, regret his own mistakes and celebrate his own triumphs.

Aye, all he could do was allow Niall to live...and hope that his life would know more happiness than sorrow.

Smiling at his wife, Ian drew her closer. "Would ye like to dance with me?" he asked her, knowing that the greatest mistake one could make in life was wasting it, wasting the time one was granted. He did not know what the future would bring, but he did know how precious the present was.

Noèle's face lit up, a dazzling smile answering his own. "I would love nothing more." And with that, she slid her hand into his and followed him onto the terrace.

Indeed, life was what one made of it, and Ian was determined—now more than ever before—to make the most of it.

To love.
And laugh.
And be happy.
For as long as they possibly could.

Epilogue

Somewhere off the coast
About two decades later

Momentarily stunned speechless, Niall MacDrummond stared down at the letter in his hands. His eyes barely managed to hold on to his sister's faint handwriting as the floor beneath his feet moved and swayed. Tall waves rocked the ship from side to side, constantly testing his balance and threatening to throw him off his feet at any moment.

"Did she say where she had gone?" Victor Duret, eldest son of Alexandra and Antoine Duret, demanded in a harsh tone, his green eyes sparking with anger as he ran a hand through his black hair. "Why would she write a letter if she does not wish to be found?"

Niall shrugged, gritting his teeth as he tried his best to remain calm. "How am I supposed to know?" His hand balled into a fist, crushing the letter into a tight ball, which he then tossed across the cabin with a frustrated growl. "I know as much as ye do!"

Vincent Duret, Victor's younger brother, and Collin Brewer, Niall's step-brother, exchanged an uneasy glance, their eyes going back and forth between Niall and Victor. Then Collin turned away to pick up the crumpled letter in the corner of the cabin, almost losing his balance as the ship tilted sideways before righting itself again.

Niall exhaled a deep breath as he looked from Victor—clearly close to exploding!—to Vincent and Collin. The two Duret brothers had been his closest friends for the past two decades ever since he had come to France with his father. While Niall had only seen Collin every other year after leaving Scotland, his step-brother was still a dear friend, a man who knew him well. It had been he who had come to France with a message from Blair.

Her first letter.

Their first clue.

"We should remain calm," Vincent counseled, a hard glare in his usually kind eyes as he met his older brother's furious gaze. His light blond hair stood in stark contrast to Victor's black locks, revealing for all the world to see that the two brothers resembled one another no more than fire and water. "All of us!"

Victor growled something unintelligible, and almost certainly unflattering under his breath, before he turned away, stalked a few steps across the cabin and then braced his hands against the wall, hanging his head.

Despite his own fears for his sister, Niall watched his friend with concern. "We will find her," he said in what he hoped was a reassuring tone.

Victor turned his head and glared at him. "If we do, I will kill her!" he growled, then stalked back to the table the other three were grouped around. "What now? What do we do?"

Collin smoothed out the crumpled letter—Blair's second—and they all leaned down to examine it again. "There is no mention of a time or place," Collin summed up what they already knew. "She speaks of a land in peril, brother against brother—"

"What is that supposed to mean?" Victor snapped, his green eyes flashing with anger...and fear.

Niall knew that something had happened between his friend and his sister upon her last visit to La Roche-sur-Mer. Yet neither one of them had shared any details with him, and quite frankly, Niall preferred it that way.

"Perhaps it is not the contents of the letter," Vincent remarked thoughtfully, a finger poised at the right corner of his mouth as he was wont to do when considering a puzzling situation. "Perhaps what we should ask ourselves is how it came to find us here."

Niall's gaze narrowed as he recalled the merchant vessel they had encountered by pure chance earlier that day. Only it had not been chance at all, had it?

The sea had been calm that morning, and when the other vessel had hailed them, Victor as captain, had ordered the *Voile Noire* closer. The other vessel's captain had inquired after Niall by name, surprising them all, and then handed him Blair's second letter. Apparently, a young lady had instructed him to deliver her letter at precisely these coordinates at precisely this time of day to a man by the name of Niall MacDrummond upon a ship with black sails.

"How could she have known?" Collin remarked, looking around their circle of friends. He paused, then swallowed, running a hand through his light brown hair. "Her dreams?"

"What else?" Victor snapped, once again stalking around the cabin, unable to remain still.

"Even if we knew what she saw in her dreams," Collin pondered, "it might not tell us anything. She always said they were vague, mere clues."

Vincent nodded in agreement before he held up his right forefinger as he always did when he had something important to say. "What I meant to say was," he paused for emphasis, "that we know which port the ship sailed from." His brows rose meaningfully. "Therefore, we know where—"

"—the captain was handed the letter!" A jolt went through Niall, and for a second, he could not believe he had not made the connection before. Aye, his heart had been in an uproar ever since Collin had arrived with Blair's first letter a fortnight ago. "Boston!"

The other three nodded. "Then we'll head there!" Victor ground out angrily. "She had to have been there at some point, and even if she is no longer, perhaps she left us another clue." Turning upon his heel, he rushed out of the cabin and up on deck, Collin and Vincent following upon his heels.

Niall heaved a deep sigh, wondering what his sister was up to. Always had Blair been secretive about her dreams. Not about her dreams themselves, but about what meaning they held for her. Aye, some were obvious, but others she held close to her heart, pulling strings and setting things in motion to *aid Fate* as she called it.

What had prompted her to leave Scotland in the dead of night? To this day, no one knew where she had gone or by what route. Would she continue leaving them letters, guiding them onward. What was she doing? And why had she left in the first place?

Niall wished he knew. "Blair, please, be safe," he whispered as the storm continued to rage outside. "Whatever ye're doing, little sister, please take care of yerself."

Blair had always been wise beyond her years and cleverer than was good for her. Yet she had also always been daring, almost fearless, trusting Fate to see her to where she needed to be.

Niall hoped with every fiber of his being that Fate would not lead her astray, that it would prove worthy of Blair's trust.

A world without his sister was not one he cared to know!

THE END

Thank you for reading *Wronged & Respected*!

This was the final installment of my *Love's Second Chance Series: Highland Tales*.

Have you yet read all the tales of Clan MacDrummond?

LOVE'S SECOND CHANCE: HIGHLAND TALES

If so, did you know that we first meet Moira in *Abandoned &*
Protected – The Marquis' Tenacious Wife? If you haven't read it yet, grab
your copy now and learn why Moira was banished from her clan.

Check out all the other tales in my *Love's Second Chance Series*. They
are all connected, so you can meet some characters again, before they
got their own story!

Browse all books in the *Tales of Lords & Ladies* as well as the *Tales of*
Damsels & Knights!

LOVE'S SECOND CHANCE: TALES OF LORDS & LADIES

LOVE'S SECOND CHANCE: TALES OF DAMSELS & KNIGHTS

If you are an avid reader and already know all of my Love's Second
Chance Series, you can also jump right over to my brand new Regency
romance *The Whickertons in Love Series*. It is portraying the at times
turbulent ways the six Whickerton siblings search for love.

If you enjoy wicked viscounts, brooding dukes as well as head-
strong ladies, fierce in their affections and daring in their search for
their perfect match, then this new series is perfect for you!

Read a Sneak-Peek

Once Upon a Devilishly Enchanting Kiss
(#1 The Whickertons in Love)

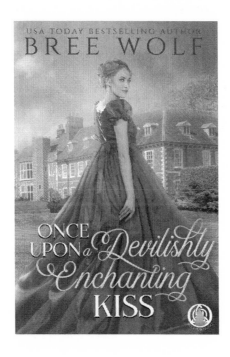

Prologue

London, England 1800 (or a variation thereof)

"Anne, you look as though you're about to faint," Lady Louisa Beaumont, second eldest daughter to the Earl of Whickerton, commented upon seeing her cousin's whitish, pale face and her huge, round eyes staring at the crowded ballroom as though facing a firing squad. "This is your first ball, not your execution." Chuckling, Louisa squeezed Anne's hand reassuringly. "You'll be fine."

Whether or not Anne believed her was unclear as she continued to eye her surroundings with wary caution, her shoulders tense and her steps all but steady.

Turning her head to look at her younger sister—by only one year, mind you—Louisa whispered over her shoulder, "She looks worse than you did, dearest Leo." A sisterly snicker followed.

For a short moment, Leonora all but ignored Louisa's comment. Then she remarked in a mere observational tone, "I comported myself in a perfectly appropriate fashion."

Louisa nodded, unable to keep a grin from stealing onto her face. "Yes, you did, and you looked awfully uncomfortable the entire time."

Leonora sighed and then looked past Louisa at their cousin. "Do not look at all those you do not know," she advised. "Seek out those you are acquainted with and remind yourself that you're not alone." She moved to Anne's other side and took ahold of her hand. "We are here."

For a moment, Anne closed her eyes and inhaled a deep breath. Then she nodded, a hesitant smile coming to her lips as she looked at her two cousins affectionately. "Thank you for being here for me."

"What are cousins for?" Leonora smiled warmly.

"To tease each other mercilessly?" Louisa asked mockingly as she gently patted Anne's hand.

"Not today!" Leonora stated, a warning tone in her voice and a rather authoritative look in her blue eyes.

Louisa nodded. "Very well." She let her gaze sweep the crowded ballroom. "On the lookout for acquaintan—" Louisa flinched when Tobias Hawke all but materialized out of nowhere in front of them, his chocolate-brown eyes fixed on Anne as he held out his hand to her. "Care for a dance?"

Sighing, Anne seemed to relax on the spot, and her hand slipped into his without thought.

When Anne's childhood friend pulled her onto the dance floor, a few whispered words left his lips and that endearing half-smile of his once more curled up the corners of his mouth.

Louisa moved closer to her sister, both watching the two of them stand up for the next dance. "There's a couple in the making," she remarked with absolute certainty. "Mark my words; this is Anne's first and last Season."

"You cannot know that," Leonora objected, a slight frown upon her face as she regarded the young couple. "They've been friends for years and—"

"That is precisely what I mean," Louisa interrupted her sister, wondering how to explain to Leonora the magic that could exist between two people; not that Louisa herself had ever felt it. Since her own debut two years ago, she had frequented balls and picnics, concerts and plays, hoping to find the one man who would melt her heart.

All she had found had been disappointed hopes.

At least so far.

Still, Louisa understood well the smile she often saw on their parents' faces when they caught each other's eye across a crowded room. After over thirty years of marriage and six children born to them, Lord and Lady Whickerton were still as smitten with each other as on the day they had first met, at least according to Grandma Edie. Of course, Louisa and her siblings had not been born at the time so could not speak from experience.

But they all believed Grandma Edie; the woman had never been known to be wrong.

Ever.

Younger than Louisa by no more than a year, Leonora, however, had never been able to grasp the effect love could have upon one's life. She had a very rational way of looking at the world, even when it came to emotions. She was not cold or unfeeling, not at all; she possessed a truly watchful eye—not unlike Grandma Edie's—and knew how to spot the first sparks of love or the pangs of heartbreak. Still, for Leo, it was hard to calculate with something as unreliable as emotions. Yet, she was fascinated by them, perhaps even more so because they could not be added up like two and two.

Louisa, though, was the opposite in every way.

Like fire and water, day and night, the two sisters could not be more different. Where Leonora was rational and calculated, Louisa was passionate and spontaneous. She followed her heart, loved to feel the sun upon her skin and the sensation of twirling in the open air until her head spun. Balls meant delightful company, dancing until dawn and people she cared for sharing in her joy. They also allowed her to mingle with eligible gentlemen, whispering of a match not unlike her parents'.

That had been Louisa's dream ever since...

...ever since she could remember.

A man who would set her world on fire with a single look.

A man who—

"Lord Barrington is looking at you," Leonora remarked with no more than a slight suggestion in her voice; indeed, for her, it was merely an observation. Nothing more, and nothing less. Or was it?

Louisa had to admit that sometimes she was not certain what hid behind Leonora's dark blue eyes.

At her sister's words, Louisa stilled, then carefully glanced in the direction Leonora indicated. Of course, Louisa had taken note of him the second they had stepped into the ballroom.

Of course, she had.

She always did.

Tall, with raven-black hair and devilishly dark eyes, Phineas Hawke, Viscount Barrington, was an imposing man. Often, one could find a bit of a wicked grin upon his face and hear a daringly teasing remark fall from his lips.

Elder brother to Mr. Tobias Hawke, Anne's childhood friend, Louisa had known him for years; however, they had never spent much time in each other's company. Lately, though, she had felt his gaze linger upon her.

As it did now.

Louisa inhaled a slow breath as his dark gaze swept over her face before seeking hers with bold curiosity. Something in her stomach began to flutter, excitedly, teasingly, deliciously.

"Do you welcome his interest?" Leonora asked curiously beside her as she brushed a dark curl behind her ear as though it was obstructing her view, hindering an accurate observation.

Louisa sighed, then forced her gaze from Lord Barrington's. "What interest?" she asked, displeased with her sister's watchful attention. "He's merely looking in our direction."

Leonora's gaze narrowed before she turned to observe the man in question more thoroughly.

Louisa wanted to sink into a hole in the ground. "Do not stare at him!" she hissed at her sister, urging her over to the side where two large refreshment tables were set up.

"Then you *do* care for his attention," Leonora concluded, her blue eyes settling on Louisa before they narrowed once more. "What bothers you? Your interest in him? Or the fact that I observed it?"

Louisa sighed loudly, "Both. Neither." She shook her head. "Would you mind seeing to Grandma Edie for a little bit so Jules can have a chance at dancing? The woman will end up an old maid with our dear grandmother glued to her side."

Leonora nodded and hurried away to where their beloved grandmother sat on the fringes of the ballroom with their eldest sister Juliet —or Jules as their family called her. While Grandma Edie still possessed as sharp a mind as ever, her body was slowly failing her.

While Lord and Lady Whickerton had been blessed with six children, five of them were girls, which was a bit of a curiosity among the *ton*. Indeed, most believed that after welcoming a son, Troy, as their first-born, they had sought to provide a spare after procuring the heir without any difficulties at all. However, five girls had followed and even today Louisa sometimes saw a bit of a pitying glance from an old matron here and there.

Of course—as usual!—people could not be more wrong.

Carefully, Louisa glanced over her shoulder back at Lord Barrington to find him in conversation with another gentleman. A small stab of disappointment settled in her heart that surprised Louisa. Never had she thought of herself as dependent upon a man's attention; nevertheless, the temptingly dark look in Lord Barrington's gaze had never failed to stir her heart. Truth be told, she wished she were better acquainted with him. Perhaps Anne would help her in the matter.

At present, though, Anne was following her childhood friend out of the ballroom, a wide grin upon her face as he whispered something in her ear. Louisa smiled, seeing her prediction all but confirmed. If only she could say with the same certainty how the man's elder brother thought of her.

Gathering her courage, Louisa sidled across the ballroom, doing her utmost to appear inconspicuous. She smiled left and right, exchanged a word with an acquaintance here and there and accepted a glass of punch, her hands grateful to have something to occupy them.

And then, she had reached her destination, her feet coming to stand no more than an arm's length from where Lord Barrington was conversing with a friend. With her back to him and his to her, Louisa hung on every word as she pretended to observe the dancers.

"How is life treating you these days, Barrington?" the other gentleman inquired, the tone in his voice suggesting the answer to his question was not of great interest to him.

"As expected," Lord Barrington replied. "And yourself?"

The man sighed before he shuffled on his feet, turning back toward the dancers.

"Is something wrong, Lockton?" Lord Barrington asked, and Louisa noticed him shift from one foot onto the other out of the corner of her eye. She wished she could turn and look at him more directly; that, however, would reveal her interest, and at present she was not quite ready to do so.

"Are you looking for someone?" Lord Barrington asked his friend, a hint of exasperation in his voice as the man failed to answer.

"A moment ago, she was across the ballroom..."

Lord Barrington chuckled, a teasing, slightly dark sound that snaked its way down Louisa's spine. "It is about a woman then? Who pray tell caught your eye?"

Lord Lockton sighed, "The Lady Louisa."

Louisa stilled. He couldn't possibly be talking about her, could he? Nevertheless, only moments ago, she *had been* across the ballroom...

"Lord Whickerton's daughter?" Lord Barrington asked to clarify.

"The very one," the other man confirmed, warmth in his voice. "She is remarkable, is she not?"

Louisa could barely keep herself from turning to look upon the gentleman's face, who held her in such high esteem. His voice did not sound familiar, and she had only just caught his name. Could she have made such an impression on someone she did not even know?

"Are you acquainted with her?" Lord Lockton inquired then.

Lord Barrington inhaled a slow breath. "A little," he replied, his voice somewhat tense as though he wished to say more but did not dare.

Louisa felt a cold chill sneak down her spine. and her hands tensed upon the glass of punch she had all but forgotten.

The other man seemed to have noticed Lord Barrington's reservations as well, for he asked, "Do you object to the lady?"

Again, Lord Barrington sighed, his shoulders rising and falling in a shrug. "I know you to be a man of many intellectual interests, which is why," he sighed yet again, "I must advise you place your attentions elsewhere, yes."

Louisa's jaw clenched harder and harder until it felt as though it would break clear off.

"Although she is a beautiful woman," Lord Barrington continued, "her mind deserves less adoration." He cleared his throat and leaned toward the other man, his voice dropping to a whisper. "To be frank, she is a pretty head with nothing inside. I wouldn't be surprised if she didn't know how to read."

"I had no idea," the other man exclaimed in astonishment as Louisa felt her insides twist and turn painfully. Tears shot to her eyes, and her jaw felt as though it would splinter at any moment. The delicious flutter in her stomach had turned to a block of ice, and without another thought, Louisa fled the scene.

Her feet carried her out of the ballroom and into a deserted hallway where she sank down in a puddle of misery, the glass of punch still clutched in her hands. Fortunately, no one came upon her there, giving her a much-needed moment to collect herself.

Still, the words she had overheard would forever be burnt into her memory for Lord Barrington had spoken the truth.

As much as it pained her to admit it—even if only to herself—Louisa did not know how to read. She could write her name, but not much more than that. Never had she been able to make sense of letters and words and their meaning.

Still, to this day, no one knew.

No one had ever suspected.

Until now.

Until Lord Barrington.

How had he discovered her secret? Or had it merely been a lucky guess?

Whatever it had been, it had shattered Louisa's delicate, little world. Somehow, she had found a way to stand tall even without the skills that everyone took for granted. She had developed ways to distract others where reading and writing were concerned. Somehow, she had always found a way. She was clever and ingenious and prided herself on her quick wit.

Still, deep down, Louisa had always thought of herself as inferior. In every other regard, she and her siblings were simply different. Different in many ways. Each had their own special talent. Each possessed a unique way of looking at the world. Each used their mind in different ways.

In this one regard, however, Louisa was inferior. She had always known it, and now Lord Barrington's words had confirmed what she had always known to be true.

Never would she forgive him for this off-hand remark.

Never.

Never again would she be able to look at him and not remember this crushing feeling of loss and disappointment.

To be considered wanting.

To not be worthy of another.

To be inferior.

Series Overview

LOVE'S SECOND CHANCE: TALES OF LORDS & LADIES

LOVE'S SECOND CHANCE: TALES OF DAMSELS & KNIGHTS

LOVE'S SECOND CHANCE: HIGHLAND TALES

FORBIDDEN LOVE SERIES

HAPPY EVER REGENCY SERIES

THE WHICKERTONS IN LOVE

For more information visit www.breewolf.com

About Bree

USA Today bestselling and award-winning author, Bree Wolf has always been a language enthusiast (though not a grammarian!) and is rarely found without a book in her hand or her fingers glued to a keyboard. Trying to find her way, she has taught English as a second language, traveled abroad and worked at a translation agency as well as a law firm in Ireland. She also spent loooong years obtaining a BA in English and Education and an MA in Specialized Translation while wishing she could simply be a writer. Although there is nothing simple about being a writer, her dreams have finally come true.

"A big thanks to my fairy godmother!"

Currently, Bree has found her new home in the historical romance genre, writing Regency novels and novellas. Enjoying the mix of fact and fiction, she occasionally feels like a puppet master (or mistress? Although that sounds weird!), forcing her characters into ever-new situations that will put their strength, their beliefs, their love to the test, hoping that in the end they will triumph and get the happily-ever-after we are all looking for.

If you're an avid reader, sign up for Bree's newsletter on **www.breewolf.com** as she has the tendency to simply give books away. Find out about freebies, giveaways as well as occasional advance reader copies and read before the book is even on the shelves!

Connect with Bree and stay up-to-date on new releases:

facebook.com/breewolf.novels

twitter.com/breewolf_author

instagram.com/breewolf_author

amazon.com/Bree-Wolf/e/B00FJX27Z4

bookbub.com/authors/bree-wolf

Made in United States
Orlando, FL
06 February 2023

29620725R00169